UNTRACED MAGIC

CUTTERS COVE WITCHES
1

RACHEL SCOTTE

Copyright © 2024 by Rachel Scotte Publishing

All rights reserved.

UNTRACED MAGIC By Rachel Scotte

No part of this publication may be reproduced, distributed, or transmitted in any form or by any means, including photocopying, recording, or other electronic or mechanical methods, without the prior written permission of the publisher, except for the use of brief quotations in a book review.

The story, all names, characters, and incidents portrayed in this production are fictitious. Any resemblance to actual persons living or dead is entirely coincidental.

No part of of this work may be used to create, feed, or refine artificial intelligence models, for any purpose, without written permission from the author beforehand.

THIS BOOK IS INTENDED FOR MATURE AUDIENCES 18+

Published by: Rachel Scotte Publishing

Cover Design: Okay Creations

Editing: Enchanted Author Co

1st edition – June 15 2024

Epub: ISBN 978-1-7386011-0-3

Paperback: ISBN 978-1-7386011-1-0

Ingram: ISBN 978-1-7386011-3-4

Hardcover: ISBN 978-1-7386011-2-7

Created with Atticus

ALSO BY
Rachel Scotte

The Cutters Cove Witches Series
Untraced Magic

Mani

*For believing I could move mountains
when I was barely treading water.*

Author Note

Untraced Magic is the first book in the Cutters Cove Witches series. It's a paranormal romance novel, and includes profanity, sexual content (*open door*), and mentions themes such as death, and suicide (*off page*).

Listen to the Untraced Magic playlist on Spotify.
https://spoti.fi/3K2t06G

Unknown

"You must take her. Go now," his voice rasped against the still of night, an urgency staining my son's lips.

"Don't ask me to do this," I whispered, cradling the bundle into my arms, wincing as it stirred from the unsettling movement. "Please come with us. We could go to the coven, talk to the elders. Ask for their help."

He shook his head, desperation haunting his features.

"You know I can't. It's the only way to keep her safe." He gestured inside the darkened house our family had called home for generations, his voice lowering to a mere breath. "She's gone mad. And if what I believe is true, she will come for her too. Take the power that is rightfully hers. I can't let that happen. *We* can't let that happen."

Tears slipped from my stinging eyes, and I swiped them from my cheeks, wondering how long he had held this burden within. Hidden behind thick brown hair that looked as if not cut in months was the answer I knew, deeply embedded in irises that had once shone bright yet were now barely a shade of ash. They sunk deep amidst the shadows framing them, a ghastly tale of their own. It pained me to see him like this.

There had to be another way. Another option. But deep in my heart, I knew he was right.

He pulled me into his embrace, and for an agonizing moment I took comfort in arms I knew I may never feel the warmth of again.

His lips pressed delicately against my forehead. "I love you. Now leave."

Every part of me screamed for this not to be, a wretched ache tearing at my heart. But I nodded, taking one last look into the eyes of a love so deeply rooted in my soul it stung.

A sob laced with emotion escaped me. "I love you, too." And by the gods, I always would.

My boots shuffled against gravel as I retreated to the edge of the forest. Raising my fingers to my lips, I kissed the air between us, and the wind whisked it away.

My son blended into the midnight shadows, a silhouette barely visible under the overhanging veranda.

His hand lifted in the air.

A final tear slid down my cheek.

Under a bright crescent moon, the forest wrapped me in darkness.

Then I fled.

Morgan

A *thud* startled me awake as a different world moved past my window, my eyes raising to the towering mountain peaks kissing a somber sky.

I stared at the passing scenery as the bus wound its way down a road encased by a forest so close, daylight found me in dappled moments, until finally grinding to a halt at my destination. Cutters Cove, a fishing village home to 6,521 people.

Swinging my bag over my shoulder, I thanked the driver before stepping outside, a chill in the salted air prickling my skin as relief left me in a long breath. Just what I needed, fresh air and a fresh start, away from the sympathy stares that had followed me since my parents' death.

If I heard 'I'm sorry for your loss' one more time, I would have screamed. So, I left.

My gaze flicked over my immediate surroundings, where antique lanterns evenly lined the narrow street ahead, three perched on each pole. It gave the town a gothic vibe, and I imagined their amber glow would offer the cove an entirely new perspective at night.

Beyond that, aged storefronts led down the road, where paint cracked from them as if creatures shedding their decayed skin.

How hard was it to pick up a damn paintbrush around here?

The familiar grind of coffee beans sounded from a nearby coffee cart, a brunette around my age smiling at me as I approached it.

"Hi." I fumbled through my bag for my wallet. "Could I grab a latte, please?"

A dimple creased her cheek. "Sure thing. From what I've seen, whoever gets off that bus is either in town for a few days or moving here. Which is it?"

I laughed at her observation, leaning against the side of the caravan. "The latter. I'm about to pick up my house keys. Are you from here?" I asked.

She glanced over her shoulder while working her magic on the coffee machine, her eyes a shade of blue-green I hadn't seen before. "Sure am. Welcome. I've been gone a few years but moved back not long ago. I'm usually at Coffee Cove a few blocks down. You should pop in and say hi sometime. I'm Skye."

She leaned out of the cart, and I lifted onto my toes, taking the coffee from her.

"Thanks. I'm Morgan. And I might just do that." With a nod, I waved goodbye.

At that moment the bus pulled away, revealing the waterfront I hadn't seen from where I'd exited moments prior. I mean, nothing ever looks like the photos, but hell, the real estate agent had really oversold this place.

In the previous town I lived in, I'd found myself instantly drawn to a new board listing properties for sale in Cutters Cove. The house prices seemed reasonable, and before I knew it, I'd fallen in love with a cottage from the pictures alone and bought it. The agent had described the town as a quaint seaside village.

I guess that much was true, but quaint?

It was an insane thing to do, move to a town I'd never been to, to buy a house I'd never seen in person. I was never spontaneous, but something about Cutters Cove spoke to me, invitation by instincts you could say. Aside from the small rental house I'd lived in, with a roommate that seemed to think neon was the new black, I'd only ever lived with my parents. But life threw me a giant curve ball.

I learned that when your parents die, a piece of you dies with them. And that piece, the gaping hole in your heart, I don't believe ever mends. It could be stitched, or patched up, like the worn knees on your pants as a child, but never fully mended. Turns out you also get a reasonable inheritance... and an unfathomable urge to just get the hell away from *everything*.

I surveyed the bleak harbor, where trees drained of life stood bare in the ill waters. Others floated on the surface, evidence of storms since past that had claimed their souls.

There seemed to be a channel in the grave of limbs that led beyond the murky scene, and I wondered what lay beyond its blanket of secrecy. Closer to shore, boats scaled with grime bobbed like ghost ships in the thin mist that skimmed the water. Its harbor docks proved uneven and weathered, held together by brazen bolts seeping rust into its hollows.

It was like it had no heart. Like no one cared. I grimaced at the sight.

A brittle gust swept my long, dark hair over my face, and I gathered it in my hands, pulling my wool coat tighter around me.

Walking up the main street, I continued along the pavement where I passed a corner shop, an apothecary, and a large stone complex that appeared to be a town hall. I was halfway across the road when a prickle chilled the nape of my neck.

The kind that told me curious eyes followed my every move.

I was the new girl in town. The outcast. But my parents had moved often for work, so it was something I'd become used to over time and I no longer cared, happy to fade into whatever town they dragged me to next.

People could stare all they wanted with their eyes that assumed who I was in one wild sweep. It was usually backed up by an onslaught of verbal diarrhea among the elderly that had nothing better to do than gossip, like a rite of passage in small towns.

I expected nothing less. Still...

I stole a glance to my side, convinced I was the center of someone's attention.

Turns out I wasn't wrong.

Except the eyes that found mine lacked the usual crinkled corners framed by gray hair I'd become accustomed to.

Fifty feet away, in what I thought was an abandoned gasoline station, charcoal irises found mine with an intensity that made time drag into a *moment*.

Curiosity piqued my senses. So much so that my feet faltered as I greedily searched to uncover the figure attached to the dark coals that had brought me to a sudden halt. Dressed in coveralls, his sleeves were rolled up to his elbows. Oil-smudged hands gripped the side of a car hood.

His thick brown hair matched the morning shadow that edged his jaw, but his eyes...

They were locked onto mine.

An intense heat slid over me. Into every part of me.

The *slam* of the hood shutting made me jump as he turned away, walking deeper into the building.

Who was *that*?

Men rarely grasped my attention.

My feet fell into step once more, and I chanced a glance over my shoulder but didn't see him.

I let out a long breath, trying to calm the beat that thundered in my chest.

Seriously. Get yourself together.

I continued on, approaching a group of strangers standing off to one side of the footpath. All in matching uniforms, they were obviously from a nearby school.

I inwardly smirked at the uneven hem of the girl's skirts, clearly rolled over at the waist to look shorter. Their white long-sleeve shirts matched the guy's ones, complimented with a tie hanging so loose around their necks it was clear they didn't give a shit.

The group stilled as I approached, and I felt their scrutiny on my skin as I passed.

"Hi." I smiled at them casually.

They deadpanned me.

I heard a lone snicker before their chatter returned.

Charming.

That will teach me for being polite.

Rounding a corner, I noted the sign above me. *Cutters Terrace.* Scanning the houses down the street, I found number 17, a white cottage wrapped with a crooked picket fence.

Bent over a garden bed, a well-dressed lady in her 60s plucked out a stray weed, and having heard my footsteps, she whipped around to face me, dusting dirt off her slacks and blouse.

"Hello, dear, you must be Morgan. I'm Betty. Welcome to your new home!" She smiled one of those smiles that reached her eyes, her arms stretched wide in greeting.

"Hi, Betty, thanks for meeting me here," I said, following her as she guided me inside.

She drew back the curtains, and daylight spilled onto the washed-out floorboards covering the kitchen and dining area.

It was cozy, just as I'd imagined, the cottage kitchen light and airy like the only ray of sunshine is this town's uniform of gray. I surveyed the living room filled with furniture and boxes, before Betty insisted on giving me the tour room by room, the subtle scent of jasmine following her.

She finally turned her gaze to mine. "I hope you don't mind, but the moving van beat you to it. I just got them to pop most of it in here."

I offered her a smile. "It's no problem. Thank you for everything."

"You are most welcome," she said on a sigh, staring longingly around the room. "I'm going to miss this place. Up until now, it's the only home I've ever had in Cutters Cove."

I remained silent, watching a sparkle return to her face.

"Mavis and I always had our cup of tea just over here." She pointed to an empty space near the window. "It's not like we get much sun here, but when we do, this is the spot."

A sadness tugged at my chest, watching her recall some of her fondest memories in the house that was now officially mine.

There was something about Betty I easily warmed to; she just had a *way* about her. I moved closer, resting my hand on her forearm briefly. "Thank you for the tip, I will make sure I do the same."

Betty ran a hand over the side of her pant leg before straightening.

"Dear, I don't mean to love and leave you, but I have a few errands I must attend to. If there's anything you need or if you run into a spot of bother, I'll leave my number right here."

She scribbled on a notepad in the kitchen before placing it back on the countertop next to a set of keys.

"Thanks," I replied, looking around at all the boxes. "Hopefully there shouldn't be anything I can't handle myself."

I followed her onto the front porch where she gestured to the flowerbed she had been attending to earlier.

"I planted those last spring. They should bloom again as long as you keep up the water."

The grey clouds above made her request seem ridiculous, like rain could fall at any moment, but I nodded, hiding my amusement. "I'll be sure to take special care of them."

"Thank you, dear." Her blue-gray eyes suddenly filled with mischief. "Also..." she paused before wiggling a bony index finger in my direction. "You watch those lads next door. They can be a bit of a handful, but they really are harmless."

I raised a brow, my gaze sliding over the fence to what looked like an ordinary split-level house. "I'm sure I'll be fine," I said, hiding my amusement.

When she left, I rested against the doorframe of the entrance to my living room, my gaze veering once more to the boxes taking over much of the space. A place of my own, and somewhere I could finally call home. A new beginning and fresh start, where the secret I held close to my chest would remain just that.

The sadness that had taken permanent residence in my heart seemed to dim, a warmth discretely filling its place. I walked over to my phone, syncing it with the speaker I had purposely packed in my bag with me. As the familiar playlist filled the room, my hips moved to the beat.

A smile broke over my face.

These boxes wouldn't unpack themselves.

Tyler

Damp concrete scuffed my boots as I shuffled out from under the Camaro I'd been working on, the permanent lack of warmth in this town sinking into every inch of the already drab workshop I owned.

"Tools down. Let's call it a day!" I yelled, swiping an oily rag off the workbench and running it over my hands.

Wes whooped beside me, steering his gaze to the clock on the wall that read 4 p.m.

"I could get used to this whole knocking off early thing," he chimed with a grin.

"Don't get any ideas. I couldn't work alongside *that* face every day," I joked, giving him a shove as I walked past.

He jutted out his lip in mock-insult, his hand palming the chest of his stain free coveralls I'd thrown at him earlier. It wasn't the norm to have Wes around the workshop, as his hands were better suited to a tattoo gun, but he knew his way around a gear box, and today I needed an extra set of hands.

I flipped over a retired oil drum sitting on top of its base. "You got a hot date or something tonight?" I asked, knowing full-well I'd be lucky to get an honest answer out of the guy, banter being his preferred response to everything.

He flashed me his pearly whites. "Can't keep them off me. You know that."

I shook my head with a knowing smile. His pretty-boy image had never failed him where the ladies were concerned. With dark hair, green eyes, and a jaw that could rival the angles my grinder cut, Wes always had women hanging off him.

I cracked open a beer on the side of the drum and passed it to him, then did the same for myself.

"Who's the lucky lady this time?" my apprentice asked, fishing for details no doubt. I'd only employed Max a couple of weeks ago and already he'd proven worthy of his employment.

Wes tilted his beer in the youngster's direction, leaning lazily against the work bench that ran the length of the building.

"Real men never kiss and tell," he retorted with a smirk.

I chuckled to myself from behind my beer. The cheek of the guy. Wes had game, I'd give him that, but Max was none the wiser. I'd known Wes my entire life, having grown up together in the same coven, all but a few years of friendship cemented from a very young age.

I looked at the new guy sitting quietly, his gaze still fixed on my best mate.

"Don't worry about him," I said to Max while nodding in Wes's direction. "Many a man have tried to figure out why women love a cocky guy. Even the elderly woman who lived next to us took a special liking to him." I paused, raising a brow suggestively. "Said his best *asset* was his eyes."

Wes raised his arms in the air defensively. "Who was I to correct her? She'd flip if she saw the *real* one."

Max threw his hand to his mouth, laughter and swallowing his drink at once not working out so well for him.

A heavy chuckle left my lungs at his innuendo.

"Speaking of..." I looked over to Wes, taking a swig of my beer. "I see Betty sold her house. Any clue who the new kids on the block are?"

He shook his head. "I haven't heard a thing. I'm sure going to miss her pumpkin pie, though. Never did ask her what the spice was she put in it," he mused.

Betty had been our neighbor for years now. We didn't see a lot of her, but she'd made a point of coming over with a fresh batch of pumpkin pie every so often, having always made an extra one for us. She was a kind woman, had always lived on her own, but I knew her and the nosey neighbor from across the road could start up their own column in the local news with the amount of gossip I'd heard from over the fence. It was sad to see her go, but she'd downsized to a more manageable section for her age.

Cutters Cove was not your average small town. Every supernatural being imaginable lived in or around here, but we flew under the radar for the most part. Witches, vampires, werewolves... to name a few. You name it, we had it.

We lived where the veil between here and the Underworld was at its thinnest, and we guarded it with our life. There was an unspoken rule between most of us to remain undetected, to cause no harm to the humans who lived alongside us, oblivious to our kind.

There were a few vampires who conveniently forgot that, with human blood being their preferred main course, but the humans seemed none the wiser.

It was one place you never went out alone. Not without the element of magic in the palm of your hand. The thought reminded me of the stunning brunette I'd seen walk past the garage earlier that day. Dare I say it, she'd sucked the air from my chest and rendered me immobile for longer that I'd like to admit. I'd come so close to costing myself a month's wages in repairs from the distraction under the hood alone.

Not that she was aware, but I'd watched her, hidden in the shadows of my workshop as she continued down the street. She had to be new to town, I hadn't seen her before. And I knew most people.

After locking up the garage, Max headed off in the opposite direction, with Wes and I jumping into the van I'd converted into a mechanic-on-the-road type thing. He slid in beside me, resting his boots up on the dash.

"Get those fucking things off there, would you?" I ordered, slamming the van through the gears out of the drive. It was hard enough keeping the work van tidy without him adding to the mess.

He parked his feet back on the floor and wound down his window, his hand riding a wave in the air. "Ty, you seriously need to get laid."

I flicked him the bird.

He was fucking right. I hadn't touched a woman in years, but I couldn't care less. He knew he'd hit a nerve. And about my history with *her,* the human who I'd let into our world. But that was just how our friendship was.

In some ways, Wes and I knew each other better than we knew ourselves.

The last of the day's light filtered over the town as we made our way down the narrow streets of Cutters Cove. Although we rarely saw it, the sun always set early here. But it also meant trouble came out to party earlier, too.

I pulled the van into our drive and cut the motor, walking up the path towards the house we shared. There was nothing special about it from the outside, just your everyday split-level home. I'd been saving for years to buy it, then converted the lower level into a basement-turned-man-cave as the years went by.

It had quickly become a popular gathering place among our close friends.

Discarding my boots at the door, I headed through the open-plan living area and down the hall to the bathroom, needing to freshen up. Stepping out of my coveralls, I threw my clothing into the laundry basket and turned on the hot water, sliding under the steady stream of heat.

I had a thing about showers.

If it wasn't hot, I wouldn't come out clean.

A dewy mist filled the room as the water carved a pathway over my back, its heat like jagged razors branding my skin. It sent a shiver down my spine, and the hairs on my arms stood on end.

Running my hands through my hair, my eyes closed as I thought of *her*. Ava, and her dark irises that used to look up at me when on her knees. She'd been my girlfriend for over two years, much to the disgruntlement of the supernatural community.

It wasn't the thing to do, fall in love with a human, and I hadn't been popular. I'd sworn her to secrecy when I'd told her *everything*. Of the beings that exist in *our* world.

My fist connected with the shower wall, sending pain through my knuckles in protest. I splayed my palms flat on the tiles as water sprayed over my face, shaking my head as if to clear my mind.

Like it could heal my haunted heart.

Fuck. *She's dead. Get a grip.*

Shutting off the water, I reached for a towel, wrapping it around my waist.

"Come and get a look at this," I heard Wesley say as I shut the bathroom door behind me.

Making my way into the living area, I spotted him looking outside where he nodded towards Betty's old house next door.

Through the window, a woman with long dark hair danced to a muted beat, oblivious to her audience. Her curves swayed with seduction and ease as she danced around what I knew was Betty's old living room.

When she turned to the side, I recognized her as the woman I'd seen outside the workshop earlier. Her jeans had hugged her in all the right places, those same jeans now sending the both of us into a trance of our own, seducing us in silence, every move of her hips commanding our attention.

I tore my gaze from her, turning back to Wes.

I arched a brow. "Human?" I asked.

Brows furrowed and eyes squinting, I knew Wes was trying to get a read off her. He finally said, "Unsure." He slowly cracked the knuckles on his fist. "I think we need to invite our mesmerizing little neighbor over tomorrow to find out."

I didn't object. With his sensor gift, Wes could feel magic near him through intuition or touch, and when new neighbors were concerned, it came in handy knowing who or what had moved into our neighborhood.

I turned on my heel, waving over my head. "Do your thing. I'll invite the guys and give Skye a call. She's just moved back to town."

"Your sister? I haven't seen her since we were kids."

I shook my head. "Yeah, time flies."

Wes walked past me, heading next door to extend the invitation no doubt. He had a natural way with women, and I'd never met one able to refuse his charm.

Good luck to her.

Morgan

Later that evening, a chill had set upon Cutters Cove. Not that there had been an ounce of warmth in the day, but dusk had swallowed daylight, leaving a newfound bitterness in its wake.

A shiver staked its claim over my body, and I was about to seek refuge in the warmth indoors when the padding of footsteps had me glance over my shoulder.

A guy in a black hoodie with eyes a bright tint of green leaned over the crooked fence separating our properties, his lower half hidden from view.

"I thought I'd come over and introduce myself. You must be our new neighbor. I'm Wesley."

He pulled back his hood, revealing a square jaw and thick dark hair that fell loosely over his forehead. I waved awkwardly from my front steps.

"Hi. I'm Morgan," I said, offering him a polite smile.

He looked at me with intrigue, his head cocked to the side, in thought it seemed. When he spoke again, his demeanor changed, and a cheeky grin filled his features.

"We're having a small gathering here tomorrow if you wanted to come and meet a few people in town."

A question that sounded oddly like an order.

His eyes took a dive to my feet then slid back up to meet mine again.

I inwardly groaned.

Flirt.

No wonder Betty was getting all giggly talking about the *boys* next door. Wesley was not a boy. He was all man. I guessed in his late 20s and a good-looking one, too.

Except he knew it.

I knew all too well how these guys worked, thanks to my ex.

I gripped the handle of my broom tighter, sweeping the last of the season's bronze dusting my front porch off the side. The leaves floated over the edge and onto the ground. I wanted a day for myself to get settled in, but I knew I should at least *try* and do the neighborly thing.

"Thanks, I'd like that," I lied. "What can I bring?"

He waved me off. "Don't worry about that. Just come over around five-ish and leave the rest to us." Then he winked before turning back towards his house.

I watched him until he disappeared back inside.

Luckily, flirty guys like him were no longer my type.

***

After waking the next morning, I shoved my feet into my runners, tugging a knitted beanie over my ears. Morning air was the one thing I could count on to help clear my mind, but sea air was intoxicating.

Borderline addictive, even.

There was just something *fresh* about it, like the salt on my lips could cleanse me in some way. Every breath like a brand-new day.

I set off towards the bus stop until I stood before the town map I'd seen yesterday, skimming over the labyrinth of trails I could follow. There seemed to be a track that looped around the perimeter of the town which would take me past the forest, so I opted for that.

As I walked, I couldn't help thinking about Wesley's invitation, or *gathering* as he'd put it, that afternoon. A heaviness settled in the pit of my stomach. There were things about me I kept hidden, things I didn't know how to explain, so I naturally kept people at arm's length.

A party with a bunch of strangers was not part of my plan, and liquid courage would definitely be required to calm the nerves.

The footpath soon turned into a dirt trail that wound its way around the outskirts of town, pockets of darkness peering back at me through dense forest. It trailed off to the right up a grassy bank that spoke of hushed whispers in the breeze, and I rested on a rock for a moment taking in the view overlooking the town.

Cutters Cove was small without being *too* small, and I liked that about it.

Mountains curved their way around the town as if protecting it with their broad expanse, and in the distance, swampland lay littered with willow trees chasing another life. Further to the north, large cliffs boarded the edge of the cove, their baren rockface scarred by the elements that evidently tore through the exposed side of the town.

A raven sounded high above me, its raspy *craw* breaking my attention.

I searched the sky, and beady eyes found mine as it stalked me from its perch on naked limbs. Some people thought ravens were a sign of death or a bad omen. They just gave me the creeps.

With a sigh, I hopped down off the rocky overhang and began following the trail back into town.

Coffee Cove soon came into view, the converted villa a faded timber that had obviously aged over its time. Four women sat at a rustic outdoor table that encroached on the footpath. Wrapped in jackets and deep in conversation, they clutched their coffee mugs, lapping up the morning air.

An older man with a receding hairline leaned against a lamp post. He lifted his gaze at me.

"Good morning." He smiled genuinely, tipping his head and straightening the newspaper in his hand.

"And to you." I waved, turning towards the small villa.

Set back a few feet off the footpath, I followed the three cracked pavers to the entrance where a quirky owl held the door open at its base.

As I walked inside, the familiar scent of coffee hit my senses, and the timber floorboards and rustic interior warmed my insides. I admired the reclaimed whiskey barrels serving as leaners in their second life before my head lifted to the wall of photos, all in mismatching frames and randomly placed on the wall in no particular order. It seemed Coffee Cove was certainly the place for a morning brew, with most tables full of customers of all ages.

A young child's eyes sparkled as they met mine, evidence of hot chocolate around his mouth in a prominent circle. I laughed freely as his mother caught my eye, shaking her head with a smile.

Heading over to the fridge, I plucked a bottle of water from it.

"Morgan?"

I followed the voice to find the girl from the coffee cart clearing a table, a tea towel draped over one shoulder.

"Oh, hey." I smiled at her. "It's Skye, right?"

"The one and only." She returned to the counter. "Lovely morning for a walk. This is my favorite time of the day."

"Mine too," I agreed, handing the water over to her along with my payment.

My gaze shifted to the window where a haze of sea fog still lay over the cove. Its muted tones stood frozen in breathless air, begging for an artist to recreate its dreamy masterpiece.

A palette made for my soul.

The thought spilled from my mind before I could stop it, and I squeezed my eyes shut for a moment to collect myself. I hadn't picked up a brush since the accident; I wasn't ready.

The emotions that were bound to my brushes, still heavy. Too raw.

I wound my attention back to her, swallowing over the lump in my throat.

"Tell me, what does a girl do on the weekends around here?" I asked as I worked to keep my voice level, determined to bury my thoughts.

Skye shrugged. "Depends on what you're into. My brother's having a party at his house this afternoon." She tipped her head to the side. "Actually, to be fair, it's more of a gathering than a party by the sounds of it... but a girl can bring wine and it soon turns to a party, right?" Her irises glistened at the thought.

The word *gathering* caught my attention for the second time in less than twenty-four hours.

Coincidence maybe?

I pulled the lid off the water and took a sip, welcoming the liquid as it slid down my throat. "You don't mean at 19 Cutters Terrace, by chance?"

Skye's brows creased. "Yeah. Have you been invited?"

I nodded. "Yes, by a guy named Wesley... Is he your brother?"

She shook her head. "Wesley's my brother's flat mate. You must be the neighbor he mentioned. This place is *way* too small."

At least I would know *one* person there apart from this Wesley guy.

Skye whipped the tea towel off her shoulder to dry a coffee mug from the rack behind her.

"How about I stop by your place. We could go together? I'm hardly going to know anyone there either. What do you say?" she suggested.

I smiled cautiously as Skye turned to take another customers payment, unsure if making friends was the best idea, but I liked her theory.

I waited until she was free to speak again. "Strength in numbers, you reckon?" It was better than walking into a party full of strangers alone.

Skye laughed. "Yeah, something like that."

I paused momentarily. "I'm at number 17. See you at five?"

She grinned, waving me goodbye. "Sounds like a plan."

I raised my bottle to her on my way out, taking a deep breath to calm my nerves. I only had to make an appearance; I didn't have to stay long.

***

Later that afternoon, I shimmied into my favorite black jeans and slipped a tank and sweater on. I was always the first to feel the chill, and my pale skin was proof of that. Running my hands through my hair, I applied some mascara and a nude shade to my lips before smacking them together.

The heaviness in my stomach had lifted knowing I had Skye to go to this party with, happy to go along with her 'strength in numbers' plan. The possibility of making a new friend in town made me cautiously uneasy, yet another part of me, the part that longed for friendship, tingled with comfort.

Knocking came from the front door, and I hurried to swing it open. Skye stood dressed in black leggings and an oversized denim jacket with a cropped tee peeking out from beneath.

She held up a bottle of bubbles in one hand and did a ridiculous dance "Are you ready?"

I cracked up. "Just let me put my shoes on."

It seemed strange to hear my laughter again. The sound so foreign to me after so many years in a state of permanent mourning.

I ducked inside, glancing in the mirror one last time to smooth my hair. Shoving my feet into my sneakers, I grabbed my ciders before following her outside.

We walked over to the neighboring house where the front door hung wide open, a pair of work boots neatly lined up to the side.

We let ourselves into an open-plan kitchen and living area that had an instant 'boys' pad feel to it. It had no particular color scheme, and men's clothing sat drying on a rack off to one side. When I noticed the older-style couch and couple of armchairs positioned in front of a large TV and oversized speakers, I was certain of it. The dull thumping of a baseline hit our ears, followed by a few hoots of laughter erupting from somewhere below.

My head ducked to the side, following the noise that filtered from downstairs.

Skye turned to me with a raised brow.

I pointed down the dimly lit stairwell. "You first."

The stairs lead to a large room with walls smeared black as if the night sky had spat out its insides in revulsion. Couches and armchairs occupied one area, a makeshift bar set up in the corner and a large door held open, leading outside.

The rest of the room was vacant space, now filled with what looked to be some sort of sparring competition between two guys. One topless, one not. They were both good-looking and well built, but not in an over-the-top way. My eyes widened as I took in their fighting, each blow making me wince.

Skye instantly deserted me, racing over to a guy who was outside with his back to me. She gave him an enormous hug from behind. It had to be her brother.

I stood pinned at the bottom of the stairs beneath the doorway as curious stares landed on me from around the room, piercing my skin. Perks of being the new girl. I was used to it by now.

"Hi, I'm Morgan." I waved to no one in particular, and a curvy girl with dark auburn hair, heavy eyeliner, and a black choker around her neck approached me.

"Hey, I'm Scarlet." She smiled in greeting, her hazel orbs giving me a onceover. "Don't mind them; they're just having some fun." She nodded toward the two guys jostling in some supposedly not-so-serious sparring match, but damn, it looked real to me.

It was like something out of a movie, the guys ripped with all their muscles and—

"And that's Jade," Scarlet continued, pointing at a girl with bright chestnut hair over the other side of the room. She waved in response.

"Hi, it's nice to meet you," I replied, giving Jade a wave as well. My gaze swung around the room, landing on familiar green irises.

Wesley leaned against the back of a couch, beer in hand. He lifted it in the air. "Morgan, glad you could make it."

"You asked so nicely, I couldn't refuse," I countered with a chuckle.

Scarlet moved into my line of vision. "Aaannndd you've obviously met Wesley somewhere along the way?" Her hazel eyes watched me with interest.

"Yeah, I just moved in next door, he invited me over."

Scarlet's lips formed a thin line, her head bobbing in understanding. She moved in closer, her voice lowering. "Between you and I, many a woman has probably had an invitation to *his* house, if you get what I'm trying to say."

I nodded. "Loud and clear."

No surprises there.

A heavy thump sounded from the center of the room, drawing my attention. Of the two guys sparring, the broader one with light hair stood over top of the other, the darker haired one flat on his back. Blondie extended his hand, helping the guy on the ground to his feet.

They slapped each other on the back in good spirits before circling each other again.

"That's Reid and Colton," said Scarlet, motioning to the two guys, but her words misted into the background as my attention gravitated to the guy who I assumed was Skye's brother, still facing away from me.

When he turned to the side, my breath stilled, lungs holding tight, recognizing the familiar brown hair.

It couldn't be. The guy from the gas station?

His feet were bare, and he wore a dark t-shirt and faded black jeans that hugged his thighs in a way that should be dubbed sinful.

I was sure it was him.

Scarlet's voice broke my stupor. "Oh, and last but not least... that's Skye's brother, Tyler." She nodded towards Skye and the stranger from the gas station.

My mouth went dry, falling open slightly. Like I could catch a taste of him.

Skye's *brother*.

Tall, dark, and handsome. As if his mother had checked all the right boxes.

I didn't need the distraction of a male. But against my better judgement, I found myself silently willing him to turn to me.

To find my eyes.

Tyler

Above me, the glow of two amber lanterns lit up the deck as daylight disappeared beneath the horizon. The air was stiff, but on nights like this I still managed to run hot even in a t-shirt. Thermo magic had a way of doing that to me.

"God dammit, Wes, it's the wrong connection size," I muttered just as arms engulfed me from behind. My eyes widened in surprise before a familiar voice met my ears.

"Hey, big brother, thought fixing the grill would be your jam."

I turned to find Skye standing beside me with a knowing look on her face. She hadn't aged a bit in the years she had been away, still looking as young as the day she left. I was sure she had inherited our mother's seemingly ageless genes.

"Hey, sis, long time no see." I grinned back, landing a peck on her cheek. Wrapping my free arm around her, the gas bottle balanced precariously on my thigh. "No more blonde?" I asked, motioning to her hair.

She laughed, tugging at a strand. "Yeah, thought it was time for a change." Her eyes darted to the bottle. "Problem with the grill?"

"Yeah, sorry, just let me get this sorted and I'll be back shortly."

As I turned to head towards the stairs, my feet froze mid-step when I spotted our new neighbor standing at the bottom of the stairwell.

Chocolate-brown orbs connected with mine, and a foreign heat washed over me. Intense. Like an outgoing tide, threatening to pull the sand from under my feet and take me with it. My gaze fell to her full lips, and her tongue slid over them as if parched.

Heat licked at my insides, only intensifying as I walked closer.

We both moved to the side, but in the same direction, causing us to do the whole 'you go that way, I'll go this way thing' but both got nowhere.

Standing face to face, she clutched her drinks in one hand, shoving the other in the pocket of her jeans.

Those jeans.

I chuckled under my breath. "I can't dance with you all day."

She let out a sigh. "Don't worry, I don't intend to."

A smile played on my lips. Witty *and* attractive... damn.

She moved to the side and jutted out a hip, a mask of indifference replacing the heat that had flooded her eyes moments ago.

I swiped my hand over my jeans before stretching it to hers.

"I'm Tyler. You must be our new neighbor."

She paused, and for a moment I didn't know if she would introduce herself.

Finally, she replied, "Hi. I'm Morgan." Her soft palm enclosed mine before quickly pulling away as she eyed the gas bottle still parked on my thigh. "I'll get out of your way," she mumbled, stepping aside.

My reaction to her presence caught me off guard, because ever since Ava's death, I'd not given a single woman my attention.

"Thanks," I said with a nod, moving past her.

I found the connection and ventured back to the man cave, hooking up the gas bottle easily this time. Watching the action inside, I grinned as Reid pulled a roundhouse kick on his sparring partner Colt, sending him hard into the ground with a *thud*.

Cheers erupted around the basement.

"You'd better up your game, Colt," I joked, and he swiftly responded with his middle finger.

From outside, I saw Wes talking to Morgan, catching the way his hand innocently brushed her arm. She would think he was being overly friendly, coming on to her even. She wouldn't know his true intentions.

He caught my eye over her shoulder, subtly nodding his head to the side.

Human. I figured as much.

Reid threw me his classic cheese-dick smile. "Up for a tousle?" he challenged, his arms open wide as he beckoned me forward.

Colt eyed me from where he stood, still catching his breath. "Ty, get out there. Last time I looked, you were getting rusty," he taunted.

I wasn't big on fighting, but when push came to shove, I could hold my own.

"You wish," I bantered back as I moved inside.

Approaching Reid, I didn't think before pulling my top over my head and throwing it to Morgan. She caught it with wide eyes, her stare drilling nine-inch nails into my back as I walked away.

Fuck. I clenched my fists. Real smart move.

I didn't mean for it to happen, to discard my clothing into her hands like that, but there was no going back now.

Reid moved closer, his stark blues stalking mine like a scope to its target, waiting for me to make my move. I had height and muscle on my side, but Reid was lean and fast.

We had one rule when sparring: No gifts allowed. It was fair game that way.

"Make your move, Ty..." he goaded me.

I knew how Reid worked. I'd seen him spar many times, and he was mainly all talk, although his fast reflexes were not to be dismissed.

He gave in first, sending a quick jab to my left that I blocked before quickly connecting two blows to his side. He adjusted to the impact, showing no sign of slowing down, then he came at me.

Launching a high kick to my shoulder, I blocked and took hold of his leg, twisting until my back was to his stomach. It left him on one leg, and wasting no time I grabbed the back of his neck, propelling myself forward and hurling him over my shoulder until his back met the ground with a *thump*.

"Too much talk, not enough game, pretty boy." I smirked, looking down at him.

He made a face. "Whatever, Ty, you won't be so lucky next time."

I pulled him up, and we shook hands laughing.

Colt slapped me on the back. "Not so rusty after all."

I leaned against the wall, my gaze lifting to Morgan who was walking in my direction, my top between her delicate fingers.

"I believe you may be looking for this," she stated matter-of-factly, squaring her shoulders. Her heavy stare lowered to my chest before darting away.

"Thanks." I took it from her and slipped it back on. "Good to see you haven't auctioned it off without an autograph."

She rolled her eyes. "You're pretty sure of yourself, aren't you?"

My brows pitched, surprised at her observation that couldn't be more wrong if she tried. My fire element crackled inside me, itching my palms. Something about her baited me. "Are you always this... friendly?"

She folded her arms across her chest, scowling. "You threw me your clothes."

I held back a smile. She was feisty for a human.

"I threw you the top half," I corrected. Her pale cheeks flared with heat, her irises stirring. "And you caught it," I added.

She huffed out a breath. "You're such a jerk."

I laughed to myself, shaking my head. "And you have me all figured out."

A moment silently stumbled upon us, collecting our breaths. Her eyes were dark brown, so rich, so intense. I felt the way they crawled over me as she studied me, my skin an inferno under her scrutiny.

Caution edged my tone. "I was just messing around... before, I mean."

She shifted her weight between feet, her hand falling to the plain silver chain resting over her collarbone. Her fingers glided over it as if nervous.

I didn't blame her. The poor girl had walked into a basement of brawling, but whatever conclusions she'd jumped to, it was better than the truth.

"Sorry if we freaked you out with the antics here. We can get a little competitive." I shrugged.

Her eyes landed on mine, then moved to the action again. "I'm not complaining…" She gestured to Wes, now topless and about to spar with Reid. "The cold doesn't seem to bother you guys."

I chuckled at her response. I understood; every guy here was ripped and built to hold their own. If only she knew who she was really hanging out with.

As she continued to watch the guys, I studied every curve of her hips.

There was something about her that drew my attention. Demanded it, even. I couldn't put my finger on it.

"How well do you know your way around a grill?" I asked.

She turned her head to mine. "I know my way around a grill."

"If we stuff up the meat, there'll be hell to pay from the guys…"

She folded her arms, raising a perfectly manicured eyebrow at me. "I can handle my meat just fine."

I stifled a laugh. This girl had sass.

"I'll go get it…" she said, turning swiftly on her heel, perhaps regretting her choice of words.

"The garage," I instructed, loud enough so she could still hear me.

From over her shoulder, she turned back to look at me, confusion stamped on her forehead.

"The meat to be *handled,* it's in the fridge in the garage."

I couldn't hide my amusement, a smirk tugging at my lips.

She nodded once, the makings of a smile hinted at the edges of her mouth. Not long after, she returned with a tray of steaks, setting it down on the table beside me.

Morgan whistled. "When you said meat, I didn't think you meant an entire beast." She let out a chuckle. "What do you lot do all day?"

"And she laughs," I mused, prepping the grill.

She shot me a piercing look, and I raised my arms innocently.

"Like I said, hungry men. So, what brings you to Cutters Cove? It's not exactly a thriving metropolis."

She stole a sideways glance at me, a long pause following.

"I just really needed a fresh start, and it seems this is the place I've ended up."

I wasn't sure what to make of the comment but didn't push it.

A loud cheer erupted from Scarlet and Jade as Wes yielded to Reid, who had his elbow wrapped firmly around his neck. It wasn't like Wes to lose, let alone need to yield, but I guess we all had our off days.

My attention turned back to Morgan, who was loading the grill with meat.

There was more to her than the tough exterior she put on; I was certain of it. But that was another rabbit hole I couldn't afford to go down, so I tucked those thoughts into my back pocket and left it with the rest of the dirty images her ass had been torturing me with ever since she'd arrived.

"So, are you a mechanic?" she said, her gaze sweeping over me as if trying to figure me out.

"What gave me away? Is it because I'm exceptionally great with my hands?" I raised a brow, holding up the tongs.

"It's definitely not the hands." She snorted before a more serious expression settled over her face. Her brown eyes locked on mine. Longer this time. The same way they had connected at the gas station.

I tore myself from her heavy stare, breaking the moment. She was human, and I'd vowed never to fall for another human again.

It pained me to think that even after losing Ava, my body reacted to Morgan in ways I couldn't comprehend. I felt like a fraud. They were similar in looks, both with dark hair, only where Ava had been reserved and softly spoken, Morgan was witty with a subtle confidence about herself.

Her lips opened then shut again, like she was deciding if she should speak. When she did, it barely came out a whisper.

"It was you at the gas station...wasn't it?"

I couldn't let her know how much the moment had affected me. How my heart had hammered the side of my ribcage like it was fighting for air.

I needed space. A fresh breath. Air not tainted with her strangely overwhelming scent.

She was human, and I knew first-hand how that scenario played out.

I wouldn't make that mistake again.

My gut twisted into a knot, knowing I had to pull the asshole card.

"I think Skye needs some help inside," I said bluntly, so she got the hint.

I knew I sounded like a jerk, but it was better than the alternative begging for mercy in my pants.

She remained silent, and I shifted my gaze to hers to be sure she'd heard me.

Her lips tightened, and an expression clouded her face I couldn't read.

Finally, she muttered, "Sure," then walked away.

The evening seemed to drag, maybe because I was in the same room as a human who had managed to awaken every cell inside of me. My calm exterior was nothing but a façade, a carefully curated mask of indifference I'd mastered to perfection.

But beyond that, blood scorched its way through my veins, my nerves misfiring it seemed at her mere presence.

Leaning against the back of the couch, Morgan stood deep in conversation with Scarlet, her long hair falling over her shoulders in subtle waves. Every so often, she adjusted herself, capturing my attention, before I had to turn away.

Beside me, Reid sat perched on the edge of a lounge chair, his elbows resting on his knees. "What's the go with the new girl?" he asked, low enough to keep the conversation between us.

"Human," I answered, just as low.

Hearing the word aloud hit me like a punch to my gut.

Reid took a swig of his beer. "Pity, she's hot."

I huffed a laugh, running my palms down my jeans. "Yep," I muttered.

At that moment she caught my eye again, and my insides fucking crumbled. Her curious irises captured mine, holding our connection. This time, I couldn't look away.

She stared at me like I was an artifact to decipher. I stared back pokerfaced, when all I could think about was the taste of her perfect-as-fuck lips.

What was wrong with me?

Our eyes remained anchored in place, like some magnetic form of torment as the corner of her lips lifted into a tight smile. I lifted my beer to my mouth, absorbing her intensity.

Reid let out a quiet whistle. "You're in trouble."

"Fuck off." I grumbled.

He clamped a hand on my shoulder. "Keep that one in the 'look but don't touch box,' Ty."

I dragged a hand down my face. God dammit, I was going straight to hell.

Morgan

In the spare room, dust settled on boxes, and I ran my hand through it, the pads of my trembling fingers collecting its remanence. They cut trails over a large box that held memories I couldn't yet swallow or bring myself to face.

It held my easel and brushes, the smaller boxes full of colors waiting for a new identity on paper.

I had a special love of painting. When I was three, my father set a paintbrush and bucket in front of me. I remembered it so clearly, like it was only yesterday. I never knew I was only painting the fence with water, but the paintbrush stoked my imagination, and I painted in lines, splotches, and swirls until there was no more water in my bucket.

Retracing my steps, I shut the door behind me, resting my head against the timber frame. My eyes lazed shut as I let out a deep breath, trying to lull my aching heart.

Two long years, and I still couldn't bring myself to indulge in the thing I loved most. The one thing my father and I shared a love of.

I needed this door to disappear. Out of sight, out of mind.

My gaze landed on the bookcase down the hall, and I strode towards its towering height that stretched almost to the ceiling.

It would fit perfectly.

Precious tales filled my palms as I emptied the bookcase of epic love stories that allowed me to escape from my world and into their pages.

When it stood empty, I gripped its sides, heaving it down the hall until it filled the door frame. Full of books once more, I could no longer see the door. Memories smothered by books, better than a daily slap in the face.

I sank against the wall until I rested on the floor, long breaths leaving me as I collected myself, my chest rapidly rising and falling.

I badly needed to get out. To go somewhere, do something.

It had been four days since the party, and I had surprisingly enjoyed it. For a bunch of strangers, they'd made me feel very welcome. Well, most of them.

My eyes closed as I thought of Tyler and how freaking hot it was watching him spar with Reid, wearing only a pair of jeans. The way his muscles had moved, carving shapes over his back as they had wrestled, was a piece of art alone. I'd thought he was a total jerk, another guy with a big head.

But another part of me felt like I had been too quick to judge. The part that was still thinking about the 'you have me all figured out' remark.

Call it a hunch, but I had a feeling I had him all wrong and couldn't place my reason for it. Even when he had dismissed me so suddenly after asking if it was him at the gas station, like he wanted to avoid the topic completely. I was certain it was him.

He spent the rest of the night putting as much space between us as possible, but his eyes however, had found mine, again and again.

More times than I could count.

Like an itch I needed to scratch, something about Tyler intrigued me. But despite the unusual way I found myself attracted to him, I was almost happy for his rudeness.

Because I had one rule.

Don't get close to anyone.

And for a good reason.

Getting close to someone meant they got to know you *well*. And that I couldn't afford.

I sighed. Skye had invited me to the opening night of a new bar in town tonight, and I'd told her I would go. Something in the back of my mind willed me to say yes.

One night out with her didn't mean we had to be besties, and it had been so long since I'd let my hair down.

I pulled myself up from the floor, then quickly showered and dressed.

"Where the hell are my shoes?" I muttered, scanning the bedroom floor. How I lost stuff in this house was beyond me.

I finally spotted them poking out from beneath my bed before shoving them on my feet. Skye wanted me to get ready at her place, so I skimmed the clothes in my wardrobe and picked out two outfits, then packed them into my bag. Shrugging on my jacket, I slung my bag over my shoulder, bounding out the front door and down the steps.

Thick clouds coated the sky in its usual spread of gray. It didn't surprise me. I swore this town was cursed, never to see the sun.

Tyler's van turned into his driveway as I walked past, and he swiftly cut the motor, jumping out. I instantly recognized the oil-smudged coveralls, confirming it was definitely him I saw at the gas station.

I didn't understand his need to avoid the conversation the way he had. Why didn't he just say it was him?

There was no avoiding him.

Our eyes locked with an intensity that stole the breath from my lungs, and I willed myself to speak, but nothing came out.

"Hey," he finally said as he locked his van, veins from underneath his pushed-up sleeves straining with the movement.

"Hey," I managed.

My fingers clenched around the strap on my shoulder like it was my lifeline out of this awkward moment, a cool breeze licking the nape of my neck causing me to gather my hoodie under my chin.

I took a deep breath. "Thanks for the invite, and introducing me to your friends. It was... interesting."

Leaning against the van, he adjusted his sleeve.

"About Wes, he can be a little touchy feely sometimes, but he means well."

I folded my arms around myself. "That's okay." I shrugged. "it's nothing I can't handle."

He chuckled, and the way his head tipped in my direction made me think he was enjoying some private joke.

Tyler's gaze traveled over my body, and I felt every inch of it, warmth melting into certain parts of me I chose to ignore.

"You look like you're heading somewhere." he said pointedly.

My fingertips skimmed the length of the chain over my collarbone.

"I am. Skye invited me to the opening night at Jinxed. Are you going?"

I inwardly groaned. Crap. Why did I even ask that?

His stare was heavy, and I felt like the weight of it could sink me to the bottom of the ocean. "Yeah, I might. Reid owns the bar, so I probably should."

I adjusted the strap on my shoulder, keen for any distraction from the way his eyes bore into me. "Well, I might see you there." I motioned further up the street. "I should get going."

Tyler nodded, grazing his palm over the stubble sanding his jaw. "Enjoy your walk."

His features remained impassive as I left.

My brows creased as I walked away. I couldn't figure him out.

Tyler was the walking definition of hot in a rough around the edges type of way. As rude as he had been at the party, I couldn't ignore the way I found myself drawn to him, and it irritated the hell out of me.

Climbing the rise to Skye's house on the far edge of town, wind whipped through my hair, fierce and untamed as it unleashed its fury on the only part of the cove exposed to the elements. Below me, the ocean lashed against the shoreline, carving its name into the rocks, and I stilled for a moment, admiring the raw beauty.

Someone once told me to never turn my back on the ocean, and I never had.

It was wild and unpredictable.

It was everything I was not.

Walking up the drive, the house stood two levels high, framed in aged timber, a large balcony wrapping around its second story. It was a beauty surrounded by trees that yawned toward the property.

With a start, I jumped back as the front door flew open before I could knock. Skye wore a silver sequin dress cut just above the knee, orbs of light reflecting in every direction as she moved.

"Skye, wow, you're sparkling!" I exclaimed in surprise. "You look amazing."

She spun in a circle, the orbs following her. "What, this old thing?"

I grimaced, remembering the clothes I had packed that were plain in comparison. "I'm going to be so underdressed."

Skye tutted, "Don't worry, I've got you covered."

She grabbed my hand, dragging me through the door and upstairs into her bedroom, disappearing into her wardrobe. My gaze floated around her room, neat and tidy, with an armchair perched in the corner.

I walked over to the large sliding door where the ocean melted into the horizon.

"Here try this."

I whipped around to find Skye with a hanger in her hand, holding a dress that looked like it would barely cover my butt.

I flashed her a skeptical look, my lips pursing. "No offence, but I don't do dresses."

She strode over to the bed, laying the garment down, her hands finding a hip each.

"Put it on. I'm not taking no for an answer."

Our eyes met in a standoff.

"Fine." I pointed a finger at her. "But if it doesn't cover all *assets*, I'm not wearing it."

A dimple pinched her cheek as she smiled in victory. "Deal."

I reluctantly took the dress to her bathroom, sliding it up my thighs and over my hips. Zipping it up at the back, I returned to her bedroom, standing in front of her full-length mirror. The dress was black and hugged my curves to just above the knee. I'd never personally seen a dress with long sleeves, but the plunging neckline certainly made up for my arm coverage.

A wolf whistle filled the room and Skye appeared, holding a pair of black stilettos. "Now these," she beamed.

I slipped them on in silence. The perfect fit.

I surveyed the stranger in the mirror with awe, wrestling my hair from its bun until it fell freely down my back and over my shoulders.

Skye leaned against the doorframe. "Damn, girl, you should wear a dress more often. Just saying."

Honestly? I had to agree. The woman in the reflection was freaking hot.

I turned to Skye, smoothing the fabric over my hips with uncertainty.

"Are you sure we aren't... *too* overdressed?"

She fervently shook her head. "Trust me, we look amazing!."

Next, she dug through a makeup bag sitting on a set of drawers. She pulled out lipstick and handed it to me.

I gaped at her. "Red? Skye, this is for women with perfect everything, and I'm not one of them," I protested.

Maybe this night out was a bad idea.

"Don't be silly. Look at you! You're a sultry brunette temptress. Now, put the lipstick on or we stay here and listen to Old Man Cutter."

I arched a brow. "Old Man Cutter?"

"Sorry, I forgot you're new. Old Man Cutter runs the local radio station's graveyard special from 8 p.m. every night. The scary thing is... no one knows who he is, or how every night the radio just clicks over to him."

I frowned. "You can't be serious."

She held her hands in the air, shrugging her shoulders.

"Legend is, there's a town somewhere around here, cursed never to be seen again. No one knows if it's true. Some people believe he's stuck there and doesn't know we can hear him."

"That is just crazy," I scoffed, looking in the mirror again.

"But you have to admit, very cool." She held up her arms in front of me, revealing a length of goosebumps covering both. "Look at my arms!"

I shook my head at her, and she laughed.

"What? Don't give me that look. I love that shit. Now, let's get the hell out of here." She motioned cheekily to the lipstick in my hand.

I smiled at her. "Fine."

Reluctantly, I applied the redder-than-a-freaking-fire-truck lipstick and smacked my lips together.

"I guess it's not that bad," I said, trying to convince myself as I raked my fingers through my hair. I mean, I *did* look pretty damn good.

"Perfect, let's go." She craned her neck into the hall. "Jade, can you give us a ride?"

"Wait, Jade lives here too? Is she not coming with us?"

At that moment Jade walked into the hallway wearing shiny black pants and a cotton tank, her chestnut hair twisted high on her head, held together by what looked like a wooden pencil.

Her blue eyes lit up when she saw me. "Hey, Morgan," she greeted. "Big night out tonight, I hear?"

I chuckled. "Sure seems that way. You're not joining us?"

She shook her head. "Nah, full moon tonight... All the crazies come out to party." She circled her fingers near her head with a stiff laugh.

"Ah, okay." I gave Skye a questionable look as Jade turned towards the door but got nothing in return.

She led us out to a red mini cooper, and I crammed into the backseat, my knees almost hitting my chin. Skye fumbled with the radio knobs.

"Ohhhh, I love this song!" she yelled over the music and started dancing in her seat.

I smiled as the familiar melody filled my ears, and I welcomed its buzz on my skin.

As the chorus hit, Skye's arms flew wide, and I chimed in with her and Jade, singing at the top of our lungs. "I wanna dance away these days!"

I loved how music had a way of taking you back to your past or escaping the present. Suddenly, you could be somewhere else. Be *someone* else. Or take you back to a time that you never wanted to forget. I still remembered the song that was playing when I kissed a guy for the first time, dancing in a boozy bar fueled by far too much liquor.

I'd never forgotten *that* song, and every time I heard it, it was like I was there again, reliving the moment. Music to me was like the passport of memories. Moments stamped in my mind to its own lyrics.

I stared out the car window as it wound through the narrow streets, my eyes gravitating to the streetlamps glowing amber above me as we made our way through town. I was right, they did make the place look spooky, barely bright enough to light up the street.

I bounced off my seat as Jade took a stone bridge over a river at a steady pace. "Ouch!" I cried out as my head hit the roof of the mini.

"Sorry!" she chimed from the front seat. "That one always creeps up on me!"

Skye's hearty laugh erupted from the seat beside her, her head whipping round to find mine. "Nearly there, hold on," she said with amused eyes.

The car finally came to a stop, pulling me from my thoughts.

Jade wound her head to mine in the back seat. "We're here. Stay safe, ladies. I'll meet you in there later."

I nodded as Skye tugged at the front seat so I could get out, crisp air gnawing at my legs as my heels hit the pavement.

I leaned back inside the vehicle.

"Thanks for the ride," I said before shutting the door.

Outside, the streetlight above us flickered on and off on its own terms, our surroundings only otherwise lit by a milky full moon. It cased the area from behind dark clouds, leaving edgy shadows in its wake.

I glanced over at the bar, the stone building's square structure reminding me of an old courthouse. A line of people stood alongside it eagerly waiting entry. A large black door was centered at the front, and my eyes fixed on the metal letters that sat above the doorframe.

JINXED.

"Weird name for a bar," I said as we made our way across the street.

Skye eyed me sideways. "I know, but so good, right?"

The air was charged with something unfamiliar; I couldn't put my finger on it, or maybe it was just my nerves. New town, new venue, new people. Something tugged inside me, nagged at me still.

My gaze found hers. "Are you sure about this place?"

Skye grabbed my wrist, tugging me along. "It'll be fine! Let's go."

She dragged me to the front of the line until we stood beside two stocky security guards that were a few good feet taller than us both. I flashed them an apologetic smile, aware we were jumping the que, but they didn't seem to care.

"Looking good, ladies. Go on in," one said, motioning us inside.

They made no attempt to hide their roaming eyes, causing me to hitch my dress down with my free hand. I frowned once again at how short this thing was.

"Do you know them?" I said under my breath.

Skye glanced back with a smirk. "Not at all."

We walked through the bar's intimate entrance, a mixture of pine, fresh leather, and men's cologne hitting my senses. Like lust in a jar if ever there was a fragrance.

Oil lamps lined the walls, giving the entrance a moody vibe, and a large bar ran the length of the massive room off to one side. At the back were leather-covered booths, each with its own floor-to-ceiling velvet curtain surrounding it. The booths overlooked an area of dated couches positioned into groups, a pool table off to one side, and at the front was a dance floor full of people.

I eyed the original record player perched on top of what must be some sturdy suitcases from the 1920s and smiled. The dull lighting and grungy music had a seductive stupor about it, and I sank into it, absorbing its energy.

This place spoke to my soul. I loved it.

Skye mouthed over the music, "Let's get a drink."

I nodded, letting her zigzag me toward the bar, my eyes scanning the crowd.

We were clearly overdressed.

Damn you, Skye.

She handed me a drink and I tipped my head back, taking a large gulp to take the edge off. I screwed my nose up at the strong taste of liquor easily overpowering whatever was meant to dilute it. My guess was vodka, double shot.

A familiar song came on. "Let's dance!" I yelled at her, unsure whether she could hear me.

Skye nodded, and we wound our way through the crowd to the dance floor.

Raising my glass over my head, the music consumed me, the bass vibrating through my veins as the lyrics corrupted my mind.

Damn, it felt good to be out. This was my kind of bar.

We circled each other, laughing as we moved to the music, the dance floor a continuous wave of bodies all riding the same high. At some point, the music changed, and the vibe of the bar naturally shifted, people coupling up around us.

I looked across to Skye, who was dancing with a guy I didn't recognize, when I felt a presence behind me.

Firm hands took hold of my hips from behind, the faint hint of cedar filling my senses. It'd been a long time since I'd felt the rush of a male's touch, and the mixture of alcohol and lack of sex in my life rifted a need deep within.

The stranger's lips scraped my ear, his hands brushing my hair away to expose my neck.

"You look divine. I bet you taste delicious."

His voice was smooth and held a sly confidence about it. I felt the smile in his tone, like he knew what his body against mine did to me. But taste? This guy was more than confident.

"And your name is?" I said over the music, my back still to him. Hell, I might as well enjoy the rest of the song.

He spun me around to face him, and a smile quirked his mouth as his intense gaze captured my own, his fair complexion taking me by surprise. With hair dark as night and pale skin, his eyes glowered with interest.

He had an aged beauty about him I couldn't grasp. Like centuries had perfected him.

"Jett, and yours?" he said.

I was about to introduce myself to this beautiful stranger when a foreign sensation washed over me. I couldn't shake the feeling that I was being watched.

"Your name, darling?" he repeated, skimming his hand over my forearm.

His words didn't register in my brain, my mind somewhere else. Someone was watching us; I was sure of it.

Without warning, a familiar heat landed on my skin, prickling the hairs on my arms.

I knew that feeling… I'd felt it before.

Tyler.

Tyler

Like a hunter to prey, my eyes followed her from the moment she entered Jinxed, shadows hiding me from where I sat at the back of the bar as I watched them sing and dance among the wrath on the dance floor.

Morgan and Skye looked completely out of place dressed the way they were, but they didn't seem to care. Oblivious to the creatures around her, Morgan's movements seduced animalistic eyes from all corners of the room as she moved to the music. There were other humans in here undoubtedly, but that red lipstick screamed prey.

It would be the end of her.

And possibly me.

What did Skye think she was doing, befriending this innocent woman?

Let alone bringing her to a bar full of *us*.

She had a throw-yourself-into-it-and-think-about-the-consequences-later type of attitude that came from our mother, and it got her into trouble more often than not.

I tensed, tightening my gaze.

A guy had his hands on Morgan, and I shifted in my seat, unable to look elsewhere.

A feeling I wasn't used to crept over me. White-hot jealously. It had been a long while since I'd felt its presence, the green-eyed bite both unexpected and unwelcome.

Unbuttoning the top of my shirt, I adjusted the collar, swiping the nape of my neck. It was normal to run hot being a thermo mage, but this was different, and I mentally zoned into the thermostat of the bar, turning up the air con. Being able to create and control heat certainly had its perks.

I watched as the stranger ran a finger down the length of her neck, furious heat streaking through my veins, flooding my nervous system.

Vampire.

I emptied the rest of my drink.

"Wes, go get that leech off Morgan before she becomes his next Bloody Mary," I ordered, unable to move from my place in the booth from between everyone else.

Wes followed my train of sight, his eyes morphing to a terrifying shade of black.

"Wes." I kicked him under the table. "You good?"

He snapped out of it, jumping down from the booth and storming off towards the dance floor.

Colt stiffened beside me, setting his glass back on the table. "That's not like him to lose control," he said, glowering towards Wes's disappearing form.

Colt was the eldest of the group and sourced his magic from the earth. He was the strong, silent type. A thinker. He seemed to struggle with women more than the rest of us, and I never quite understood why.

Where we all had a mop of brown hair, he was the polar opposite. Blond with blue eyes, you would think he'd have the women hanging off him, but not Colt. He was the responsible one, the one we went to when we were deep in shit, because being an earth mage, his intuition was usually spot on.

"Agreed," I replied, brows furrowing. "What's going on with him?"

Colt thrummed the side of his glass with a shrug. "Unsure."

I watched as Wes fended off a stunning blonde eager for his attention, but he dismissed her, wrenching some guy off Skye who was closest, followed by Morgan.

He returned with them in tow, and fuck if I couldn't predict it would happen, Morgan slid across the leather booth beside me, with Skye and Wes on the other side of her. Her dress hitched high up her creamy thighs as she shuffled closer, trying to make room for everyone in the now overcrowded booth.

"Hey, you made it," she said to me in a breathy gasp.

Nodding stiffly, I retorted, "Yeah, here I am."

I shuffled along, attempting to make extra room, but I was crammed in between her and Colt, with Scarlet who had just arrived on the other side of him. It left Morgan's arm and thigh bolted to mine, spreading heat between us with every movement.

"Letting off some steam out there?" I remarked, attempting to make small talk.

The corners of her lips curled up into a smile, and it lit up every delicate edge of her face. "Definitely. This place is something else..."

A familiar voice came from the head of the table. "Well, this place is mine, so thanks, I'll claim that one."

Morgan's eyes shot over to Reid leaning casually against the end of the booth. He'd bought and revamped the oldest bar in town, and he'd done a killer job.

Reid had the darkest gift of the group. A blood mage with the ability to heal, and with that sort of power came huge sacrifice. I knew his bravado act was just a front hiding a world of pain, but he kept it to himself. His natural charm and rough around the edges look of tattoos and brown hair made him a fan of most women, but he had no plans to settle down anytime soon, even when the four of us guys were pushing thirty.

My attention turned back to the group, where Morgan looked more relaxed now, both giving and taking the banter around the table. Funny how alcohol did that to a person.

Reid eyed me. "Ty, when will you have that Mustang finished?"

I felt Morgan's gaze return to me, and I straightened, causing her skin to brush against mine again. I adjusted in my seat, trying to regain some space, but it was no use.

Clearing my throat, I told him, "Just have to replace the leather, then a lick of paint and it should be done."

Reid grinned. "Sweet, new wheels in town. I swear I get high off a new fit out." He chuckled.

He was right. The hit of a new leather interior was dopamine at its best.

"So, you're not a mechanic," said Morgan, a curiosity wavering into her tone. "You restore cars?" She raised a brow.

I slid my gaze to hers, adjusting my collar. There were barely inches separating us; being this close to her in any other situation would be borderline intimate.

Colt slid a beer in my direction, and I took a drink.

"The workshop was my grandfather's; it was left to me when he passed. I restore classics, and the Mustang was his. He never got to finish it," I explained.

Her face fell the tiniest bit. "Oh. I'm so sorry to hear that. But it's nice you're able to finish it for him."

"It is," I stated simply with a nod. "He was one of a kind, taught me to drive in it."

Her eyes held mine for a passing moment until I had to look away. I tightened my grip on my beer.

"My dad had a classic." My ears pricked at her comment. "An original Ford Escort."

"Yeah?" I took another swig of my drink.

She nodded. "It was his pride and joy. Drove it round town like a hobnob."

I stifled a laugh but couldn't stop the slight smile turning up my mouth. "Was? Did he sell it?"

She shifted in her seat, and the motion grazed the side of her leg over mine once more. Her body seemed to tense, and she fiddled with her necklace again.

Before she could answer, a bell sounded from the bar.

"Who's keen on a dance before last drinks?" said Skye, her voice commanding the table.

Relief washed over me when the girls disappeared to the dance floor, even if it wasn't ideal. The vacant space beside me was now a much-welcomed pocket of solace.

"This place reeks of vamps," said Wes, wrinkling his nose. He emptied the rest of his drink in one smooth gulp. "Let's get out of here."

Colt pushed his empty glass away from him. "Good luck trying to drag that lot out the door." He nodded towards the girls.

Reid smirked. "I've clocked off for the night. Let's get them out of here before this place turns into a meat fest."

All in agreement, we made our way to the dance floor, with Wes leading the way. I shook my head with a laugh as he put himself between Skye and another guy. She stared daggers at him. Brave man.

To my right, Reid and Colt approached Scarlet and Jade, who I hadn't seen arrive. The guys looked like they wanted to get the hell out of there as the two girls bounced between them.

Morgan caught my eye as she lifted her shoulders, her hand extending to me.

Bad idea.

"Can you dance, or will I be sporting bruises on my toes tomorrow?" she asked with an alcohol-fueled smile, her irises glinting with mischief.

Grazing the stubble on my chin, I let out a light laugh.

I should walk away. Get her out of here.

But as much as I didn't need this, her sass fired me up.

"I have a few moves up my sleeve." I countered.

I stepped closer, my palm slipping into hers, the other molding to the curve of her hip until only inches separated us.

Forcing her away, she spun around in a circle, and I tugged her back towards me harder than intended, causing her to land firmly against my chest.

Dick move. There was a line, and I didn't just cross it. I'd hauled my ass commando-style right the fuck through it.

I looked down to her chest where a sinful cleavage pressed against me, and I loosened my hands, giving her the chance to pull away.

She didn't.

Looking up again, I found that her eyes bore into mine, the dark storm thumping between us thick and charged with lust.

Her eyes mirrored a matte black sky until they morphed, and a playfulness joined the party. That sass was back, locked and loaded. It made me wonder what look I'd get if I were between her thighs. A thought I knew I shouldn't have, but my liquor-fueled self-restraint now hung on by mere threads.

I never backed down from a challenge, and I wouldn't bow to her boldness. If anything, it only spurred me on.

I wasn't used to a woman like this and couldn't help myself.

My lips grazed her ear. "Keep looking at me like that, and we're going to have a problem." My gaze met irises that never wavered, like she was turning the pages to my soul one by one.

Her touch traced a line down the nape of my neck, and desire licked my insides.

Raw. Carnal.

Everything my body ached for.

I pulled her hips to mine, molding us together, the sexual tension between us so fucking obvious, I was sure.

We danced like no one was watching. Like it should be fucking illegal.

A voice in the back of my mind willed me to end it, to walk away while I still could, as if my past was haunting me. It was the ultimate torture of wanting what I couldn't have, another human life I couldn't risk.

But as I stared into the eyes of this one, she had me fired on every edge of caution known to man.

One kiss would be all it took for her to become the second biggest mistake in my life, and the lyrics blaring in my ears should've served as a warning, like fate was telling me not to fuck with it.

But I didn't believe in fate.

I watched as Morgan's lips sounded the lyrics, inches from my own. 'When the crazy world turns to hell on earth.'

It was then I should have stopped.

Backed off and committed her to nothing more than my new neighbor.

But as the small of her back drew my hand to it, her body arched against mine, and I could have sworn a moan tortured my ears over the music.

Suddenly, light spilled through the bar to acknowledge closing time, air filling the void between us as she took a step back.

Her hand rested on my forearm. "Thanks for not stepping on my toes," she mused.

I looked down at her heels. "It wasn't *your* toes I was worried about."

I was a tall guy, but she was almost eye level with me wearing those things and damn, they could do some serious damage.

I heard Wes's voice. "Let's go. Nightcap at ours." He motioned toward the exit.

Morgan's warmth slipped from me, a bitter cold replacing her touch.

I followed everyone outside, my gaze travelling up her legs from behind, unable to pry my attention from the subtle crease of her ass under the thin material of her dress. It drew my attention like a neon sign, and it was *not* denied.

Stumbling home, we pulled Wes out of a bush he tried to pick a fight with, or rather it tried to pick a fight with him, so he said.

A grin spread over my face as Colt sorted him out, with Morgan beaming from ear to ear as she watched the scenario unfold.

Filing inside and downstairs, I headed straight for the bar in our man cave. I needed something that would numb me from the inside, or numb me from her rather.

Tequila. That would do it.

Opening the liquor cabinet, I pulled out some shot glasses, lining them up on the bar. Morgan sauntered over, a sway in her step from either her heels or the alcohol—I wasn't sure. Nonetheless, she drank me in with curiosity.

She leaned on the other side of the bar eye level with the glasses, watching as I filled each one.

It took every effort not to look at the perfect curves of her breasts at this angle.

"Nicely done," she purred. "I might have to see how your skills are at pouring cocktails next time."

She had a newfound confidence about her, but I knew it had to be from the booze.

I took the bait, pushing two shots over to her.

"Name it... Are you a Moscow Mule or a Sex on the Beach kind of girl?"

She paused, never breaking eye contact. "I prefer a Harvey Wall Banger."

Then she fucking *winked*.

It was as if she was sent to this earth for one purpose, to test my limits and fuck with my head. A hurricane of sorts, tearing at my self-restraint. My hand clawed at the stubble shadowing my jaw. If I didn't pull it together, I was done for.

Morgan turned on her heels. "Here you go, Wesley." She passed him a shot as I dished the rest out to the others.

Reid handed out the lemon slices and salt before holding his shot in the air.

"Bottoms up!" he yelled.

"Tequila!" we all cried out in unison before licking the salt, knocking back our shots, and sucking on the lemon slices.

Colt shook his head, his lips curling in distaste. "Hell, Ty, I don't know why you love this shit."

I shrugged. "I don't love this shit. No one does."

He eyed me sideways, raising a brow, and I looked away.

The girls started dancing to a song on the coffee table and I laughed, remembering I bought it solid for this exact reason. I sat back watching them when Morgan's eyes found mine.

It was becoming a regular thing, seeking her out in a room full of people, and it sent a fiery heat through me.

Taking a deep breath, I looked away, rubbing the back of my neck.

We were dancing a fine line, and I was grasping at the edge of reason and self-control. I'd let my guard down on the dance floor. I'd come so close to fucking up. *Again*. I needed to drown these thoughts. Numb my body to *her*.

I poured another shot of tequila, knocking it back.

Wes held an empty bottle in the air. "I call for truth or dare," he announced over the music.

"Really, we aren't eighteen anymore," groaned Scarlet from where she was dancing with the other girls.

"Oh gods," I heard Skye murmur, hopping off the coffee table to the ground.

Jade laughed. "Scar, you make us out to be ancient. I'm keen."

I turned to Reid. "This is a bad idea…"

He necked another shot. "I'm down for whatever."

Morgan jumped down from the coffee table, choosing to sit on top of it.

Wes turned down the music, and the rest of the group formed a circle. Spinning the bottle in his hand like a drumstick, his attention pinged around the room as he placed it in the middle.

I cursed. "Are we really doing this?"

"C'mon, Ty, lighten up." Jade teased from the other side of the circle.

"If I do, I'm not touching *you* filthy pricks *or* my sister," I argued.

"Don't worry, I'll take care of that," Wes joked, flashing Skye a cheeky look, and she gave him a stare that could have rivalled the Devil's.

"Like fuck you will," I scoffed.

Wes wouldn't dare touch Skye. None of the guys would.

He rested the bottle in the middle of the circle as a grin spread over his face. "Let's get the party started."

Flicking his wrist, the bottle spun wildly before finally coming to a stop on Colt.

"Truth or dare, big dog?" Wes asked.

Colt sat on the floor against the couch, an arm resting on his raised knee. He pursed his lips for a moment before shrugging. "Dare."

Wes smirked. "I dare you to kiss Morgan."

Fucking hell.

Morgan shifted her weight, her expression tightening.

Colt remained unmoving. "Anywhere specific?"

Wes leaned back, casually placing his hands behind his head. "I'll leave that up to you."

I leaned forward in my chair, my elbows edged on my knees. My foot tapped continuously on its toe as I watched Colt rise from his seat before stopping in front of Morgan.

"Go for the toes!" Jade yelled.

Morgan shot her a dirty look. "Oh my God, gross!"

Colt kneeled to her height, and my breath held firm in my chest.

"If I'm going to kiss a woman, I'm doing it right," he retorted before connecting his lips with hers. My stomach bottomed out at the sight, something unfamiliar and unpleasant stirring beneath my skin.

Morgan's brows shot up, her lids fluttering closed as he took full advantage of the situation. My arms ached to rip him away as jealousy coursed through me.

I averted my gaze.

"Welcome to Cutters Cove, Morgie babe," Wes teased, giving me a sideways glance.

Seeing them together grated a part of me I didn't expect, but I kept my expression carefully blank. Like I didn't care.

Did I care? Taking a deep breath, I let out it slowly.

If it had to be any of the guys, at least it was Colt. He knew the rules and never bent them.

Colt returned to his perch on the floor, swiping a thumb over his bottom lip before taking the bottle in his hand. Whipping it around, it came to a standstill, pointing directly at Morgan once more.

She threw up her hands, scrunching her nose. "Oh c'mon, that's unfair!"

Colt shrugged nonchalantly.

"Rules are rules," said Reid, from the opposite side of the circle. He raised a brow. "Truth or dare?"

She narrowed her hazy gaze at him. "Dare."

"I dare you to give Ty the sexiest lap dance you've got."

Morgan turned her attention to Colt, looking for affirmation.

Colt shook his head with a low chuckle. "You opted for dare." He said simply.

I cursed under my breath. It was bad enough I just had to watch her get mouth-fucked. Now this? *This* would be torture.

Fuuuccckkk.

Morgan arched a brow at him. "Do I get music, or do I have to freestyle this?"

Fuck me. Was this really happening? My head turned to her, locked somewhere between 'hell no' and 'fuck yeah.'

Reid whooped. "Ooh, strap him down, Ty. She's coming for you, big fella."

This.

Here.

Right now.

Was going to be the end of me.

Scarlet turned up the music, and a grungy song filled the basement. Something about chasing a storm.

Morgan sauntered towards me as the music filled the room, her hips swaying as she inched closer with each step. When she was close enough, she dragged a finger up my knee, skimming my thigh as she moved to my side.

My eyes slid shut at the contact, sending stars to the void of my eyelids.

I felt her touch slide up my shirt until her hands caressed my shoulders behind me, and I willed myself to open my eyes as the pad of her finger carved a trail between my shoulder blades and down the other side of my torso. Then she stood before me again, staring back at me in that goddamn tight dress and those sinful-as-fuck red lips.

This woman was my kryptonite. My weakness.

The thunder caving my chest.

The lightening splitting my bones.

She was my fucking hurricane.

Her curves moved with a seductive roll, and my hands itched to claim her sides. To feel the curl of her hips in the palms of my hands. Instead, I sat motionless as she climbed onto my lap, a leg landing on either side of my thighs, sending her dress dangerously high up hers.

Her hips tortured mine, while silent words soaked with lust spilled between us.

Our own delicious storm.

I didn't dare look down, knowing full well the view between her thighs would cut the last bindings of my self-restraint currently keeping my hands clawed to the armrest.

When the song ended, the room erupted with wolf whistles and howls.

Morgan leaned into my ear; her voice filled with liquored confidence. "*Now* we've got a problem."

Then she was off me. And that lack of warmth made my body practically beg for her return.

The group continued to play the rest of the game, but I couldn't ignore the heat-filled glances connecting with mine from across the room.

I adjusted my pants, aware I was worked up like a bull that hadn't fucked in six months.

Had life not tested me enough?

But here I was, lost in a world where all there seemed to be was *her*. Grinding her way under my skin.

As the game ended, the mood in the room mellowed.

Reid walked over to the far wall and grabbed his guitar from its case. He perched on the end of the couch, started to strum some chords. The guy was a maniac for music.

Morgan stifled a yawn. "I think I'm about ready to head home."

"I can walk you over." The words tumbled from me before I could stop them.

Fuuucckkk.

Morgan stilled. "Ah sure, thanks," she said before turning on her heel and heading for the door.

I followed her outside, where shadows stained the sky and the moon watched us from its disconcerting corner of the world. The night was eerily quiet, the crunch of gravel as we made our way down my drive and over to her place seemingly magnified.

Our feet soon scraped against Morgan's front porch, and she turned to face me, swaying slightly on her feet from the aftereffects of the evening's alcohol.

"Tonight's been… fun," she said, looking up at me now her heels were in her hands.

I leaned against the beam holding up her porch. "Yeah, you seemed to fit right in," I lied.

It couldn't be further from the truth.

She was the beauty.

We were the beasts.

I held her gaze longer than intended, not daring to look at her full red lips. To look down would be considered an invitation, causing a follow-on chain of events that included my lips on hers and more.

She grinned, her words slurring slightly. "Thanks for walking me home. You really didn't have to."

"Yeah, I did." *Before those leeches scent your blood and come back for more,* I thought to myself. "No one should be out alone at this time of night."

She straightened, folding her hands over her chest. "I can hold my own, you know."

I chuckled to myself. "Yeah, I bet."

She frowned. "You don't sound convinced."

"You're drunk," I reminded her.

Morgan raised a brow. "And you're not?"

I held my hands in the air. "I never said I wasn't."

She wrapped her arms around her waist, and it plumped her chest. I looked away, shoving my hands in my pockets.

She must be freezing. It was well past midnight, and the bite in the air was deathly cold.

I nodded towards her door. "You should go inside. It's cold out here."

My hands fisted the denim in my pockets as if it would keep them from escaping. From landing on her waist and walking her backwards until she connected with the door. From every bad idea her wicked eyes asked of me and more.

I held onto the material as if my life depended on it, my palms burning, and I knew it was only a matter of time before the denim would singe under my heated palms.

She tipped her head to the side, like it would help read my mind.

Finally, she murmured, "Goodnight, Tyler."

"Night."

She turned towards her door, glancing over her shoulder at me.

I walked away, fearing that to stay a moment longer would be my undoing.

Barreling back into our house, I eyed Wes now sitting in our upstairs lounge, an arm draped over the back of the couch. I pointed a finger in his direction. "Don't even say it."

I made the distance to my bedroom in seconds, slamming the door behind me.

This had to stop. This couldn't happen again.

Except it was.

Thoughts of her consumed every part of my goddamn mind as I ripped off my clothes, attempting to ease the heat-filled tension crawling under my skin.

Who was I kidding? I saw the way she looked at me.

It was the same way I looked at her.

Tomorrow, I had to put an end to whatever this was before it was too late to stop this trainwreck. Before the ache in my pants got another human killed.

Morgan

Air scraped the back of my throat as I hurled in a breath, bolting upright in my bed. My chest rapidly rose and fell, and I swallowed as I took in the view of my room, reminding myself that it was just a nightmare. It wasn't real.

They came to me once a week now, always the same vision of the dark-haired woman with those intensely sharp eyes. She called out to me on the nights she found me in my dreams, like a tether I couldn't break.

I pulled my bedcover high over my head, away from the light spilling through my window. What the hell was I thinking, not shutting my curtains?

Then memories of last night flooded the peaceful space between my sheets. Holy crap.

Tyler.

Tequila.

The *lap* dance.

I groaned. *Idiot.*

Dancing with Tyler felt like a sin. A giant, mouthwatering sin. I couldn't get the guy out of my mind. He had a confidence about him without being cocky, but his eyes gave nothing away. Dark and guarded.

Banging came from the front door, breaking me from my thoughts.

"Morgan, are you awake? Open up, it's me, Skye."

I threw back my covers before padding to the front door, swinging it open. Skye still had on her sequin dress from the night before, her heels dangling in her hands. Shadows hung under her eyes, and she massaged her temple, the tell-tale sign of a wicked hangover.

I laughed. "You look ridiculous."

"I feel like a bag of arseholes. I haven't had a night like that in ages," she replied with a groan.

"You and me both," I agreed.

Following me inside, she helped herself to a glass of water and flopped down on the couch. "So, what's going on with you and my brother?" She eyed me curiously. "You guys looked pretty cozy on the dance floor last night."

She was right. We *were* cozy on the dancefloor. Really freaking cozy.

Crap.

"Well, he can dance. I thought he'd have two left feet," I said matter of factly.

A laugh erupted from Skye.

"Tyler never dances. Seems you convinced him otherwise."

I cringed, leaning against the kitchen counter. "What's his deal anyway? He's so…" I struggled to find the right words.

"Ty's been through a lot over the past few years." She hesitated as if unsure about something, almost as if it wasn't her information to share. She finally squared her shoulders, her voice lowering. "He lost someone close to him. If he wants to talk about it, he will, but he's a private guy, so don't bet on it."

"Oh, that's horrible," I said softly. My heart pained to hear what he had been through. He hid it so well. Too well.

"Please don't tell him I said anything," she pleaded, her tired gaze meeting mine earnestly.

I shook my head. "I would never."

I had no plans to talk to Tyler. In fact, I needed to put as much space between us as humanly possible. Secrets were better *kept* sober, and in one's own company.

"Thank you." She smiled with relief. "The last thing I need is another male with his sack in a twist," she mumbled.

A laugh forced from me. There was quite obviously someone *else* with their junk out of joint in her life.

I arched a brow. "Do I detect man trouble?" I joked.

She stilled momentarily, drawing her eyes to mine before waving a hand through the air.

She shook her head. "No, *No*," she said, as if convincing herself. "It's really nothing. Honestly. Not even worth a mention." She stood, clearly stating her boundaries.

Got it. It wasn't like we were close friends anyway.

"So, what's the plan for today?" Skye asked, sipping the last of her water, then placing her empty glass in the dishwasher.

"You mean besides getting rid of this god-awful smell of liquor off me?" I screwed up my nose and sighed. "I need to find a job."

"Maybe try Jinxed; Reid was looking for extra staff. If I hear of anything else, I'll let you know."

I smiled. "Thanks, I'd appreciate that."

She gave me a quick hug before heading towards the door, heels in hand.

***

That afternoon, the unmistakable sound of the front door creaking open turned my head to the hall. The familiar voice of Betty made me smile.

"Yoohoo, anyone home? Morgan, it's me, Betty."

She appeared in my living room, having already let herself inside.

She gave me a sheepish look. "Sorry, dear, I hope I didn't frighten you. The door was unlocked, so I just let myself in."

"Oh, hey Betty." I motioned her over, hiding my smile at the lilac pantsuit she wore. "Am I going to have to change the locks?" I joked with a knowing look on my face, half serious.

She flushed. "Sorry, dear, old habits die hard, I guess. I will knock next time, promise."

"Thank you."

I smiled at the elderly woman who always seemed to be 'made up.' Not an inch of her gray hair was out of place, and she wore matching makeup to suit her choice of color for the day.

She came closer, sitting on one of the wooden barstools perched on the opposite side of my kitchen counter. Smoothing down her pantsuit, her eyes met mine again. "I thought I'd check if there was any mail for me to collect? I haven't had the chance to change my postal address just yet."

"Sure thing," I said, passing over the small pile of envelopes I had collected. I mustered an apologetic look. "Here you go. Sorry, they look like bills."

Betty kindly waved me off. "Don't be sorry. There's no way to avoid them." She scanned the room. "Looks like you're all settled in. The place looks cozy."

I nodded with a grin. "Thanks. I like it here. I met a few of the neighbors last week, too. They seem friendly enough."

I laughed inwardly at my own words. Friendly was an understatement. Smoking hot would be a better term as I recalled the way Tyler's hands had curled around my waist on the dance floor.

Betty beamed. "Oh, well, I'm glad you're settling in okay. It's always hard when you move to a new town and don't know anyone."

She paused for a moment, lines rippling her forehead.

"Dear, where did you get this?" she asked.

I followed her gaze to a gold necklace with a large heart shape locket hanging off it. I'd placed it in a small bowl on the kitchen counter with a few other odd bits and pieces I hadn't sorted through yet. "Oh, that? It's a family heirloom of mine." I could recall when mother gave it to me on my twenty-first birthday. She said she knew little about its history, but that it dated back many years.

Her gray-blue irises clouded with interest. "It appears rather antique. Do you mind if I take a closer look?"

I shrugged. "Sure. I'm not really sure of its history, but it must date back a few years."

She picked up the necklace, turning it over in her hand. "Well, it must be very special indeed." She stood suddenly, placing it back in the bowl. "I must go now. Thank you for the mail."

She gave a quick smile that didn't quite reach her eyes, and a moment later, she was out the door and gone.

Strange.

I picked up the necklace, turning the locket over in my palm, my fingers tracing the intricate details of its exterior.

Its licks of golden bronze hinted its age, possibly antique like Betty said, the symbol on the back unfamiliar, but etched into both my mind and my dreams.

I placed it back in the bowl; it was something I would never wear. Too big, and *bold*. It just wasn't me. I ventured outside, hoping some fresh air would kick my hangover.

Turning down a track that snaked its way along the waterfront, my shoes made footprints into the silt behind me as I walked aimlessly to nowhere in particular. In the distance, a willow tree with naked limbs hung low to the ground, weeping for its spirit to return, and I found myself underneath it on an aged wooden seat.

A stillness had settled over the cove. Its murky waters looked like death floating on a blanket of midnight, always surrounded in that mist that felt like it was a living thing. Like it watched us all.

I was sure it breathed the same oxygen but survived on our exhales, the decrepit part of us its fuel.

Its calm demeanor drew me in, although to what I wasn't entirely sure.

But whatever it was, it was working.

I felt it.

Cutters Cove had hummed its melody, and its beat had embedded itself deep within me.

My fingertips tiptoed over the natural knots woven into the seat's timber, and closing my eyes, I leaned back, allowing nature to breathe its life back into me.

"You look like you're enjoying yourself."

My hand clamped my chest at the voice coming from behind me.

"Tyler, you scared me, don't do that!"

He surveyed me with caution. "Sorry. Mind if I sit?"

Dressed in sweatpants and a hoodie, it was a Tyler I hadn't seen before, and I was definitely onboard with it.

"Sure." I gestured to the space beside me on the wooden bench.

He sat down, resting his elbows on his thighs, and I noticed his knee popping up and down on the spot. Was he... anxious?

"I used to come down here with Wes as a kid," he admitted. A distance filled his voice as he looked out over the water. "It hasn't changed much over the years."

Comfortable silence filled the space between us, but his mere presence had every cell in my body on edge. I didn't trust myself to speak, too unsure where the conversation was going. Maybe the lap dance was too much. I should have refused the dare and taken the shot instead.

"About last night..." he began but seemed to stall as if trying to find the right words. His thumbs circled themselves, and I remembered how those hands felt on my hips. "Morgan, there are things about me I can't tell you."

I ran my hands over my necklace, my insides somersaulting at the butterflies that had awoken in my stomach.

I wondered what he meant by that. What *things* he considered not worthy of my trust. Compared to mine, I bet his were miniscule. I wanted to tell him he could trust me, have him know anything he told me would stay between us. Because I knew how important one's word was to another.

He looked as nervous as I felt.

Finally, Tyler blurted, "You need to stay away from me."

Okay... I was *not* expecting that.

A nervous laugh escaped my lips. "Was my dancing *that* bad?"

For the first time since Tyler sat down, his heavy stare held mine. Shit, he was serious. "Things are just complicated," he continued.

I couldn't read him, his voice hollow and void of emotion.

"It was just a dance. Don't make this into something it's not," I said carefully, trying to defuse the awkwardness between us.

He remained silent, which only served to frustrate me further.

"Honestly, it's not like we kissed. It was nothing," I added.

But that was a lie. I'd slipped my fingers between my thighs at the thought of him last night when he'd left. Not that he needed to know that.

No, to him, all this needed to be was simple, a casual flirt.

His irises stirred as if sensing the falsehoods on my tongue. As if he knew every way my body reacted to his presence. Heat stroked my spine as his eyes dropped to my lips and for a moment, I thought he might actually kiss me, before they swerved away.

Tyler ran his hands through his disheveled hair, then without warning stood up.

He rubbed the side of his neck in what looked like frustration. Clearing his throat, he said gruffly, "I should go."

His jaw set tight as he turned away from me, running in the opposite direction.

I pulled myself to my feet, unable to comprehend the conversation.

Did that seriously just happen?

I'd never let a man get under my skin before. Not like this. But Tyler had somehow squashed that theory and slapped giant red tape right on it.

I needed to get my shit together.

***

That evening, I made my way up the street towards Jinxed on Skye's recommendation, reaching the bar just as a drizzle of rain started to fall. A line snaked its way around the entrance to the bar and into the parking lot, where scantily-clad women braved the elements as they awaited entry.

I approached the front of the line, where the same security guard stood at the entrance.

"Hey, I'm hoping to speak with Reid about a job."

The guard gave me a once over, my clothing obviously not here for a night out.

"The name's Eaden," he said, shaking my hand and nodding toward the door. "Go on in. Reid's on the bar."

The moment my foot pressed onto the familiar carpet, my heart stammered. There was a strange buzz about the place tonight. Behind the bar, Reid took drink orders as fast as he could pour them, with the line around the bar already a few people deep—all of which looking more impatient by the second. He caught my eye, lifting his chin.

"Do you need a hand?" I called over, leaning around the edge of the bar.

He eyed my standard black jeans and jacket.

I laughed inwardly as he stared at me, weighing up his options. I folded my arms. Reid was in the shit, and we both knew it.

As he poured a beer, I noted the tattoos covering his lower arm under his long-sleeve black tee.

He raised a brow. "You done this before?"

"I need a job and you need help. And yes, I've done this before."

He mulled it over for a moment. "One night," he said with a nod. "If you impress me, you *may* get a job."

I smiled and swung around the side of the bar, dumping my bag and jacket into a vacant space.

He watched me with interest as I took in my surroundings. Glasses, cash register, fridge, top shelf. Typical digs.

I nodded. "Don't worry," I said confidently. "I've got this."

***

As the clock neared 8 p.m., most people retreated to their groups to mingle and dance, allowing us room to breathe for the time being.

Reid eyed me as he dried a glass. "You turned up at the right time. I was getting slammed."

I laughed, leaning against the bar to observe those on the dance floor. "You think?"

He grinned the signature Reid smile I had become used to seeing. I bet he got all the women on that merit alone.

"Usually when we hit a lull, I like to get someone taking orders from the booths. Get to know the locals if you can."

I nodded in understanding before Reid's gaze hardened, focused on someone approaching the bar.

"We meet again. You never did tell me your name?"

I turned towards the voice that sounded vaguely familiar, wondering if the words were directed at Reid or myself.

To my surprise, against the other side of the bar leaned the guy I'd been dancing with on opening night. His dark features emphasized by the black jacket he donned this evening.

I tried to recall his name. "Jett, right?"

His eyes gleamed with that same intensity I remembered as he swirled the ice in his empty glass.

"That's correct. And you are?"

He cocked his head to the side, curiosity twisting his gaze. "I'm Morgan," I replied, leaning over the bar to shake his hand.

He captured my palm in his, holding it to his lips, his touch cool like he'd just come from outside.

His irises sparkled, even in the dimly lit bar. "It's nice to officially meet you. I haven't seen you around before, aside from the other evening... Are you new to town?"

"You ask a lot of questions, don't you?" I countered, unease curling my stomach.

His lips turned upwards at my comment, shifting in closer.

"Only to the women that intrigue me." His eyes fell to my lips, then traveled back up to meet my eyes. "Now, are you going to take my order or not?"

Two could play this game.

"You never said please," I bantered with a shrug.

He shook his head with visible amusement.

"Could you be so kind as to pour me another whiskey *please*? I like it on the rocks."

He had a seductive allure to him that put me on edge, and I was acutely aware of his roaming eyes as he watched me pour his drink. I handed it over to him, and they never left mine as he brought it to his crimson lips, taking a slow drink.

He set the glass back on the bar. "Thank you."

"You're welcome. So, how long have you lived in Cutters Cove?" I asked.

"Lived?" A light laugh left him. "You ask a lot of questions, don't you?"

I should have seen that one coming.

I used his own line on him. "Only to the ones that intrigue me."

He tipped his head back with subtle laughter, his gaze snatching mine once more. A dizziness fogged my thoughts, and I grabbed at the side of the bar.

"Morgan?" came Jett's voice from further than I remembered him sitting.

The room suddenly drifted as in slow motion. A blur. I blinked, clearing the haze.

I shook my head. "Yeah, sorry, I'm good."

What was up with this bar tonight?

Tyler

Music thumped the walls of the staircase, crashing into my ears as I entered the basement. Dropping my shoulder against the wall, I watched as Wes beat the shit out of a boxing bag, never once stopping for breath.

What had *his* balls in a knot?

I turned down the music, just enough to let me hear my own thoughts and get his attention. It earned me a foul look before he slid back into his rhythm again.

Wes ignored me, continuing to pound the bag relentlessly as it swung wildly from an overhead beam. I took hold of it, and he pounded it against my shoulder, assaulting it with an onslaught of jabs before finally finishing with a roundhouse kick that sent it hard into my chest with a *thud*.

His bare chest heaved in air. You'd think for a guy who earned a living tattooing others, he'd be covered in ink himself, but not Wes. He had an artful hand but preferred his own skin unmarked.

I raised a brow at him. "You good?"

Backing off, he remained silent, drawing his forearm across his glistening hairline.

"You're killing this thing," I pushed.

He cracked his knuckles, turning away from me. "It's nothing."

I scoffed, steadying the bag. "It doesn't look like nothing."

He glared at me. "You don't let up, do you?"

I narrowed my eyes at his sharp tone.

He slumped against the wall, tipping his head back, his chest gathering air. Moments passed as he stared at the ceiling before turning his gaze in my direction. "Something's not right. My senses are off."

He splayed out his fingers before the popping of his knuckles returned.

I eyed him curiously. "Off as in... how?"

"It's hard to describe." He paused, considering his next words. "I'm on edge but can't sense why."

He pushed off the wall to pace the room, raking his hands through his hair until they rested on the back of his neck.

He turned to face me. "It started when Morgan moved in."

His intense gaze connected with mine, and my chest tightened uncomfortably. I knew the basics but was unsure of the intimate workings of Wes's gift.

Pulling myself together, I shoved my hands in my pockets.

"Look, I don't really get how this whole sensor thing works, but she seems genuinely human to me."

Wes never doubted his gift, and it never let him down. If I was honest, his admission was really fucking unsettling.

"I know that. I'm just saying be careful," he cautioned.

Wes held the bag against his own shoulder, and I set upon it, unleashing a fury of my own pent-up frustration. The bag heaved violently against his chest with each blow I fired at it, leaving my knuckles aching and raw.

Was Morgan really a wolf in sheep's clothing? It wouldn't be the first time someone had tried to pull the wool over our eyes, and it wouldn't be the last.

He had to be wrong. Every inch of me told me he was wrong. Screamed at me, tearing at my eardrums.

Instinct was a venomous thing.

Deliberate and ruthless.

It held no grudges, made no assumptions.

A naked thing inside that stripped you of any connection or bias.

But Wes had never been wrong where his gift was concerned.

He stepped away from the bag, lines pressed into his forehead. "Are we good?"

I shrugged my shoulders. "It is what it is." I hated that line with a passion, but it fitted the moment. "I don't want to believe it, but you've never been wrong about this stuff before."

He wiped at his hairline again. "You know I can't help the vibes I get. It just happens."

An awkward silence lazed between us.

"Let's get out of here and head out tonight. It's still early," I said, hoping to break the mood.

He smirked, and I knew he was up for it. "Beers and boobs for the win, you reckon?"

I stood up and clamped a hand onto his shoulder on the way past. "As you wish."

We ventured upstairs, and I quickly showered, walking back down the hall with a towel wrapped around my waist.

Colt caught my eye from the kitchen where he leaned casually against the wall. "You rang?" He said with a smirk.

"Yeah." I made my way into the room, flipped my thumb towards Wes. "He needs a night out."

Wes hoisted himself until he was sitting on the counter, a half grin on his face. "And Ty's blue balls need some attention."

I laid a fist into his stomach on my way to the fridge and cracked open a beer.

"My blue balls are none of your business."

Colt chuckled under his breath, eyeing me sideways. "Might find yourself a lady tonight, Ty," he mused.

I threw him a beer, and he snapped the lid off with the opener. I hadn't played around since losing Ava, but the digs were starting to come thick and fast.

Colt never gave me shit about women. He knew when to speak up and when to shut his mouth, so I knew he was being genuine. I veered my gaze to him with a shrug, his gaze following me across the room.

My hand clutched the frame of my bedroom door, and I turned to him. "Blue balls or not, I don't do one-night stands." I grimaced at the thought of getting laid with some drunk woman who I'd have to see around town again. That and the fact it meant *nothing* was enough to keep my dick in my pants. I just couldn't do casual.

"Who said anything about a one-night stand?" He tipped up his beer, still holding my gaze until his attention finally moved to something outside.

I ducked under my door frame to change into some jeans and a shirt.

There was no sarcasm or judgement behind Colt's comment, and I knew he meant well. It was his way of telling me it was okay to move on, to start thinking of a life with someone else.

I eyed the photo of Ava sitting on my set of drawers, her sparkling orbs staring back at me, full of life. Until recently, I hadn't indulged in thoughts of another woman since Ava's death, and to consider going to a bar in search of *someone else* felt really fucking wrong. And a problem I didn't need the morning after just to get my dick wet.

But in the back of my mind, I knew I already had a problem. In the form of a human that kept me up until the early hours of the morning, with thoughts I couldn't rid myself of.

I shook my head, clearing them.

Chasing women wasn't my style, but a night out with the guys I could do with. Good banter, no bullshit, and no drama was what I needed.

I heard Wes yell from the kitchen, "Ty, can we take the van? It's pissing down outside!"

"Yeah, just a minute!" I called back.

Grabbing my jacket, I followed the guys out of the house, sliding the door of the van open for Colt, who jumped in the back. I pulled out of the driveway with a grin on my face, listening to the banter between the two, happy for the distraction.

"Easy, dude, you've got a lot of shit back here!" I heard Colt yell from the back.

I adjusted the rearview mirror to find him and laughed at his sturdy frame balancing on a toolbox among the rest of my shit. His middle finger appeared in the rearview mirror, and I cheekily pumped the brakes just for his benefit.

"You could've walked, asshole," I fired back with a grin.

Swinging the van into the parking lot, I cut the motor, throwing the side door open. Colt jumped out, rubbing his ass.

I slapped him on the back. "Toughen up. No one likes a pussy."

"Speak for yourself." Wes smirked, and I gave him a shove as we escaped from the rain inside.

Jinxed had a wicked vibe about it tonight, and I knew even I was not immune to the magic someone had charged the bar with this evening. It spilled its glamour everywhere, mostly in the way the patrons looked at each other, high on whatever emotion came up trumps for the evening.

Whether it be desire, love, or loathing, it filtered through the bar and our skin eagerly soaked it up.

It streaked through my veins and thumped into my lungs, scorching my nerves. My body willingly succumbed to it in an instant, ready for one hell of a ride.

"Suck that in," said Colt above the music, feeling it too.

I eyed Wes at my side. These nights could be a bit much for him with his gift, a bar full of magic and emotions on steroids.

I gave his shoulder a nudge. "You good?"

He shrugged my arm off. "Yep. Go get us a seat. I've got the first round."

I followed Colt to a vacant booth, and we spread ourselves around, with Wes returning moments later with a handful of drinks.

"Looks like our neighbor got a job here," he remarked, nodding to the other side of the room full of partygoers.

I followed his line of sight, instantly finding Morgan.

Behind the bar, dressed in a black tank, her bottom half was hidden from sight, and I'd bet money she was wearing *those* jeans again. From across the room, she held my stare, and the corner of her lips turned up into a subtle smile as she poured some guy with his back to us a drink.

I pulled my eyes from hers.

I'd told her she needed to stay away from me. But there she was, *again*. Appearing wherever I seemed to be these days. Not that it was hard in a small town, but fuck if I couldn't catch a break from her.

Wes's sarcasm stilled the table. "I think Morgie babe is keen to become the new blood donor in town." He wrinkled his nose.

I ignored him, noting as he turned to the side the same guy at the bar she'd been dancing with the other night.

I couldn't rip my eyes from them, a possessive claw itching my skin as she laughed at something he said.

Colt shifted in his seat. "How well do we know this Morgan woman?" he asked. His attention swerved from me, to Wes, and back again.

I gripped my glass tighter. "Wes thinks she's not who she says she is," I said evenly.

Colt's eyes hardened to mine. "And what do you think?"

"I thought she was legit. But now I'm uncertain."

Colt slowly spun his glass in circles on the table. "Well, whatever she is or isn't, there's a vampire on her tail, and we need to make a call here."

Wes spoke first. "I bet she knows he's a vampire. Some women dig that shit."

My fist clenched tighter. "And what if she doesn't? What if this whole vibe you're getting is all wrong?" I challenged.

Colt's drink landed on the table with a dull thud, earning our attention.

"Everyone's high on magic right now." His ice-blue gaze swept between us. "Ride it with caution." He circled his glass in his hand again. "Either way, it needs to be handled delicately. If she doesn't know, we can't make a scene. If she does..." His voice trailed off, and I knew what he was getting at.

It was none of our business.

I didn't know what to believe, but I couldn't ignore the overwhelming need to protect her. If I was going to do this, I would look like the guy who didn't want her but wanted no one else to have her either.

It was a lose-lose situation. And she'd probably hate me.

Colt straightened in his seat. "Remember, Ty, subtle."

I nodded before downing the rest of my glass and lifting from the booth.

Approaching the bar through the swarm of people, a wash of unease nestled in my stomach. Morgan had her back towards me, and as I got closer, I eyed those same black jeans that no matter how much jerking off I did, still tortured my mind every evening.

I extended to my full height as I stepped toward the guy, stopping short of him a few paces. The vampire turned, sensing my presence, rising from his bar stool.

The weighted stares of Wes and Colt hit hard on my back as the stranger turned to me.

We stood face to face glaring at each other. All Morgan was to this vamp was prey. If he got his way, she'd end up beside a dumpster with two neat holes in her neck and lifeless eyes staring blankly into the distance.

I couldn't let it happen.

I shoved my hands in my pockets. "Fuck off if you know what's good for you," I warned. He held my gaze, motionless save for the deadly narrowing of his eyes.

I was oblivious to the crowd, wild for the grungy beat resounding through the bar as they danced under the dull light flicking over the dance floor.

The ground beneath us tremored as if a train was passing close by, but I knew better. His glare broke from mine, shifting over to where the guys sat back in the booth. Colt's magic vibrated off him, enough to serve as a warning but still remain discreet, the two of them locked in a standoff from afar.

Eventually the guy returned his attention back to me, taking a step closer in my direction until we stood chest to chest. I held my ground, and his head tilted to the side with a smirk. He grabbed his drink from the bar before disappearing into the crowd. I had a sinking feeling that he'd be back.

Seconds later, Morgan turned around, confusion blanketing her features. No doubt wondering where the leech had gone.

Leave it to me to burst her bubble.

"You need to stay away from that guy. He's bad news."

She grabbed at the edge of the bar, her arms spread wide. "Excuse me?" she scoffed in disbelief. A bitterness drenched her tone, as if she knew I was the reason the parasite had fucked off.

"You need to stay clear of him," I repeated.

She folded her arms across her chest. "And why is that, exactly?" Morgan demanded.

I wished I could give her an explanation, but what could I say? The guy's a vampire and wants to drain your body of blood? Good luck with *that* one.

My lips thinned. "I can't explain. I just need you to trust me."

"So you keep saying." She rolled her eyes.

"Please, Morgan," I pleaded over the thumping music of the bar, needing her to listen. Begging her.

"Are you serious right now?" She took my silence as confirmation, shaking her head. "You are, aren't you?"

I hated how every second of this was playing out, but there was no alternative. I couldn't just tell her about our *kinds*. Reid chose that moment to appear from the kitchen, and he stopped short under the door frame, spotting our hostility.

Morgan continued. "How dare you have the audacity to demand who I can and cannot talk to. I can't believe you!"

"Morgan..." I started, but she turned her back on me, storming off to the opposite side of the bar, every movement sharp, agitated.

I didn't know what to expect, but it wasn't this. The venom on her tongue cut deep, like my own self-inflicted poison. If only she knew my true intentions. I only wanted to protect her. People like us, the supernatural in this town? Most were dangerous.

Especially that bloodsucking vamp.

Look at me, I willed her. *See it in my eyes*.

But she didn't, huffing her way through her next few rounds of drinks like she was about to blow her lid.

Reid caught my eye, stifling an amused look.

Fair enough. If I was being honest with myself, I'd probably react the same way. Rage pumped through my veins, having to play the bad guy, but I couldn't let her get killed. The least I could do was make sure that creep didn't come near her for the rest of the night.

I didn't leave my seat at the bar and found her blatant ignorance of my company irritating. I was just trying to fucking help.

Then *everything* changed.

Everything I thought I knew flipped on its axis and threw me a giant *told you so*.

Morgan went to pick up an empty glass off the bar, but before her hands connected with it, it flew off the counter, shattering as it hit the ground.

A wave of magic slammed into the room, knocking me off my stool to the floor. I quickly rose to my feet, noting couches upturned and people scarpering in every direction, unsure what had happened.

Holy. Fuck.

My attention moved back to Morgan, who stood anchored in place as if her life depended on it, her mouth agape. Time stood still as I tried to comprehend what I'd just seen.

My heart thumped in my chest as if clawing its way from within me to find her. Speechless, I stood paralyzed in the moment. Morgan took a step back, fear exploding from her irises as they landed on mine, speaking a thousand words without sounding a single one.

I attempted to say something, but my voice cracked in my throat. Then she ran.

"Morgan!" I finally yelled, but she was already gone.

Those tight black jeans fleeing out the back door of the bar at a pace worthy of a goddamn Olympic medal.

Instinct hit me, and I sprinted around the side of the bar, pushing past the chef, a crash of plates echoing behind me. Barreling through the back door, crisp air whipped my neck as sheets of rain pelted my face.

Then I saw her.

In the middle of the alley behind Jinxed, her silhouette was hunched over, her hands clutching her knees.

"Hey!" I yelled again.

Blind rage streaked through my veins as I strode up behind her, my hand clamping down hard on her shoulder.

She inhaled a deep breath as I spun her towards me.

"What the hell was that?" I yelled as the rain soaked our hair, dripping down our faces.

Wrenching my arm off her, she cried out, "Leave me alone! I don't know what you're talking about." Her trembling form retreated to a nearby doorstep, hardly a shelter against the elements.

Was Wes right all along? If he couldn't sense her, what the fuck *was* she?

When I paced over, she saw me following and inched back against the door like a deer stuck in headlights.

Like a little fucking doe caught where it shouldn't be.

I closed the space between us until only inches separated our dampened frames, strategically placing my arms against the wall on either side of her shoulders.

I couldn't underestimate this woman.

Was Morgan even her real name?

My eyes moved within inches of hers, two dark storms colliding. Dueling.

My voice dipped so low, I barely recognized it. "Who are you, and why can't we sense you?" I seethed.

She glared at me, the bite in her stare fierce. "I don't know what you're talking about. Back off, would you!"

She slammed her hands into my chest, but I wasn't moving an inch. Not until I figured this thing out. Namely, what the fuck just happened.

She was a mess. A sexy-as-all-hell mess. Even when her hair clung to her cheeks in matted strands under the rain.

My finger lifted her chin until she stared directly up at me, and I felt the moment her breath hiked, when an undeniable heat fell between us. Our lips tasted the same air. Our breath found the same rhythm. It took every ounce of my being not to punish her lips with mine.

I lowered my voice further, needing her to know how deadly serious I was. "You know *exactly* what I'm talking about, little doe."

Her dark orbs went wide, igniting at the new pet name.

"I saw *everything*. The glass... I know it was you who did it." I paused, lowering my voice even further. "So let me make this very clear. If you're here to stir shit in Cutters Cove, you've picked the wrong town to fuck with."

Her doe eyes widened at my accusation, but she couldn't deny what happened.

She considered her next sentence carefully, lowering her voice to match mine. "I'm not here to cause trouble. I just don't know what's going on with me and how this is happening, so mind your own business."

And that one sentence broke me.

Morgan

A nerve pushed from Tyler's jaw as he searched mine for answers I couldn't provide.

He towered over me by at least a foot, and backed into the wall, I had no way to escape. His eyes burned into mine, unwilling to give an inch, my efforts to push him away utterly useless against his strength.

He knew I was different; knew the secret I'd been keeping for years. So why was he not running a mile in the other direction?

Our eyes locked in a duel, our breaths becoming one, swirling between us in smoke-like clouds, shards of rain slicing them open like a fresh wound. Every second I counted another breath. Another twitch. Another blink.

Air scattered in my lungs, and it released shakily, like he'd ruptured my façade, the only thing keeping me sane over the last few years.

"I said I'm not here to cause trouble," I evened with him.

Charcoal irises nailed me in place. "Swear it."

How could I make him believe it? That the last thing I wanted to do was cause any trouble.

He splayed his palm against the wall beside my ear, then bunched it into a fist, his dominance both scaring and turning me on at once. I wasn't used to guys taking control like this, completely invading my personal space.

His voice dipped low, his fist slamming into the wall behind me. "Swear to me you're here for the right reasons, dammit."

Given the chance, I would run, but my strength would be no match against his.

My voice came out barely above a whisper. "I swear on my life. I promise I'm not here to cause trouble."

I counted more breaths, and silence favored the space between us.

His gaze softened. Pooling to a liquid silver, they held me in place as if releasing mine would sink me to the ground.

Staring down at me, he seemed to accept my words as my promise and gazed at me as if for the first time. Like Tyler got me, and I couldn't understand it. His nostrils flared, and he lifted his fist from the wall, unclenched it, then ran his thumb along my jaw.

His touch threatened to split any reason I had for this not to happen into a million pieces, and it scared me. A lot.

I'd never craved the touch of a man more in my life.

I wanted this. I wanted him.

He shook his head, cursing. "Morgan, I've been..." His eyes clung to mine for what felt like an eternity.

And then his mouth crashed into mine, devouring my lips with his.

So confident. So sure.

A sigh escaped from somewhere within me, and my hand grazed the stubble on his jaw, a hint of sandalwood wrapping itself around my senses.

His lips eased over mine with passion, teasing my tongue with a hunger that ignited a current deep within me, and when he closed the space between us, my heart pounded in my ears to the beat of a thousand drums. So loud, I was certain he could hear it.

My hands found his hair, then fisted his shirt, skimming underneath to where naked skin warmed my palms. He jarred his hips to mine, his arousal firm against my stomach as he kissed me fiercely, like a man maddened by lust. Two beating hearts tasting each other's souls for the first time, a moment we would never get back.

He pulled away, resting his forehead against mine.

"This thing between us..." Tyler shook his head, his voice trailing off, his eyes falling to my lips once more before returning to find mine. He cupped my cheeks in his hands, staring at me from underneath thick lashes.

He looked at me like I wasn't real. Like this could only ever be a dream to be woken from.

Finally, he whispered, "It's been driving me insane."

"I... I don't understand," I stammered, ripping my eyes from his, instead plastering them to the wall at my side. How could he look at me this way? I was a freak. He'd just witnessed it himself. How did I let this happen?

His index finger turned my chin to him, his thumb grazing my bottom lip.

A blanket of goosebumps stamped my skin, a tenderness in his fingertips as they grazed my cheek.

He moved his lips over mine again, coaxing my mouth open until our tongues met in a torturously slow dance of their own. Only, there was no orchestra playing a beautiful waltz here, and this dance held a string of information he should never have been exposed to.

I needed to stop this.

With one hand on the wall behind me, his other traveled up my side until he cupped my breast, and I inhaled a sharp breath as his thumb delicately circled a peaked nipple through the soft fabric.

"Tyler..." I breathed.

A groan rumbled through him, and my self-control ripped to pieces, a thousand tiny threads floating on a breeze.

I kissed him with everything I had, with every inch of my soul, and he returned the kiss with a passion spreading warmth over my body, nestling right between my thighs.

Tyler kissed me like he'd waited his entire life for this moment and would not dare waste it.

"Ahem." Somewhere nearby, a voice registered, but lost in our own world, I couldn't think straight.

Tyler's arms wrapped around my hips, pulling me hard against him, his mouth taking mine like I was his drug of choice, his secret addiction.

"Ahem," the voice sounded again, and our lips hesitantly separated.

"Leave," Tyler growled. "Go somewhere else." He rested his forehead against mine, two dark coals melting holes into my soul.

"She likes that. Her heart is racing."

Tyler stiffened, his demeanor changing from lust to loathing in a manner on moments.

He grabbed my wrist. "He thinks you're not of our kind. Stay behind me and don't move," he ordered.

Our kind? What the hell...?

Tyler turned toward the voice in the alley, where a figure stood hidden within the shadows. Under a black hooded coat, his cheekbones cut sharp angles into his features, his face unknown to me.

"You," the word dripped off Tyler's lips like bile.

"Did you not learn your lesson, young Tyler?" the man cautioned. He clasped his hands in front of him in a weirdly traditional way.

Lesson? Who the hell was this guy?

Tyler stiffened. "You know the rules, leave her alone. Besides, she *is* of our kind. I've seen it." Tyler growled.

The stranger pondered this for a moment, daring to take a few steps closer. "I'm intrigued. You say she is not human, yet I cannot sense her?"

Tyler extended to his full height in front of me, and I had to crane my neck to see past him.

Out of the darkness sauntered another guy, this one taller but not by much, shadows hiding half his face. He wore black jeans and a leather jacket. I sucked in a breath, noting the same jet-black hair I recognized from earlier, only now, droplets of rain sat like diamonds on each strand.

I stepped out from behind Tyler. "Jett?" I exclaimed, as a gust of wind whipped a sheet of rain at us.

Tyler's grip tightened on my wrist, holding me in place.

Jett's eyes darted between Tyler and me. "I thought you were saving the last drink of the night for me, young Morgan?"

What's with this *young* shit? We were all grown adults. They obviously knew each other, but I didn't recall seeing them together in the bar.

The stranger's attention slid between us and Jett. "You know her?"

Jett's gaze never left mine, a prickle crawling over my skin as if giving a warning. "I believe we have met, yes."

Danger licked the air, his ice blues glistening. He cocked his head to the side, a sly smile twisting his lips.

"Tyler, let's go," I said, squeezing his shoulder.

His hand inched me backwards until I stood directly behind him again. "Don't move," he ordered, his stare locked in front of him. "If you know what's good for you, you'll leave," Tyler cautioned.

Jett's irises flickered with amusement.

Tyler's voice came louder this time, in a way I could only describe as a growl. "Now," he warned. He released his grip on me, his hands bunching into fists on either side of him.

Jett moved to join the curious stranger, grazing his lips with his thumb. "As much as I *love* this chat, I'm done with the pleasantries, and the lovely Morgan here looks absolutely delicious,"

My blood ran cold, chilling my bones.

Jett made out a fake yawn, then sprung toward us. So fast I questioned what I saw.

Suddenly, an inferno of fire sent him flying in the air, back to where his friend stood, shaking his head. My legs gave way, connecting me with the ground, my hands covering my head, my knees, clawing at air.

Somewhere in the distance, I heard screaming. I couldn't think, couldn't move. Pinned to the doorstep, the cold seeped through my pants, water leaking from my hair, dripping down my back.

Tyler's voice came from somewhere. "Next time, it won't just be your pretty little jacket that melts."

I squeezed my eyes shut, fearing for my life. This was all too much. My thoughts were lost somewhere between the reality I knew and what I'd just seen.

Strong arms hoisted me to my feet, tucking underneath my shoulders. Tyler's face appeared in my vision, his hands grabbing my chin, as if waking me from a deep slumber. Forcing reality back on me.

"We need to go *now*," he urged.

I didn't feel my legs move, but the back entrance to Jinxed came closer with each second that passed, the bar becoming a blur before Reid appeared at my side, hoisting me into a van.

I glanced at my hands, finding them shaking.

Reid leaned over, buckling my seatbelt for me. "You're okay. Everything's okay," he assured me, his hands landing on my shoulders.

I nodded, unable to speak, my words paralyzed by both shock and fear.

Tyler jumped into the driver's side, and the two of them exchanged a look I couldn't decipher. Nothing made sense anymore.

Reid nodded. "Get her out of here."

I barely recognized his voice, his usual carefree demeanor now a deeper tone. Controlled and laced with urgency.

Tyler hurriedly turned the key to the ignition, and the engine came to life. He floored it out of the parking lot and down the road.

"What's going on? I... I don't understand?" I stammered, my teeth chattering as sodden clothes hung from my limbs.

Tyler's attention focused on the road ahead. "Let's just get you home." Reaching behind him, he passed me a jacket. "Here, put this on. You're cold."

I accepted it, slipping it on and tucking my knees to my chest.

A silence hung between us as we made the quick trip home through the downpour, coming to a stop in Tyler's driveway. He cut the motor, gripping the steering wheel so tight his knuckles turned white.

I didn't have words, didn't know where to start. If someone had told me how tonight would play out, I would never in a million years have believed them.

Cutting the silence, he finally spoke, his hands pushing into his thighs. "I don't think you should be on your own tonight. You can stay at our place and have my bed. I'll sleep on the couch."

Our eyes collided, unspoken words pressing his lips tight.

I nodded, unsure of what to say.

"Let's get you inside. You need to warm up."

He appeared at my passenger door moments later, opening it for me with an outstretched hand. Jumping down, gravel crunched under our shoes, and I felt pressure at the small of my back, guiding us to his front door.

My mind spun as it replayed the evening's events.

I *think* I'd just witnessed Tyler turn into a total pyro to save my life. But worse... now he knew about my freakshow of a secret.

I sure as hell couldn't handle any more surprises tonight.

Tyler

Walking through the front door with Morgan in tow was *not* how I imagined tonight would go down. Far from it, in fact.

The night had quickly become a shitstorm on steroids, and I had no idea where Morgan's head was at. A thick silence gripped gnarly fingers around us, its hold choking the usual banter that seemed to come naturally between us.

Tonight had revealed a lot. Secrets. Desires. Enemies, even.

Morgan had witnessed the dark side of Cutters Cove. The bloodthirsty vampires who roamed this town, treating it like their own personal playpen. But I couldn't be sure which part of tonight had her most on edge.

I'd witnessed her gift. But in protecting her, I'd needed to expose my own, and to say I wasn't worried about her knowing my truth would be a lie. She *must* be a supernatural. She had to be, in *some* way.

I opened the front door, my hand guiding her inside before me.

Wes had somehow made it home first and sat upright from the couch. "Morgan...?"

I sent him a dark look, enough to shut his mouth.

Sodden hair clung to Morgan's top, and black streaks smudged her eyes, sketching lines down her cheekbones. The rain had done a number on her.

"You need to warm up. The bathroom's this way," I said, motioning for her to follow. Gathering a fresh towel, a t-shirt, and some sweats of mine, I handed them to her. "Here, you can change into these."

Her fingers grazed mine at the exchange.

"Are you okay?" I asked, my brow furrowing in concern.

She looked down to my hand on her forearm, but she didn't pull away, an uncertainty claiming her usually confident stare. "I just really don't know what to think right now."

I hated seeing her like this. Untrusting and guarded.

"Don't be afraid. You're safe here," I insisted.

She nodded, taking the pile of clothing from me before making her way to the bathroom and lightly shutting the door behind her.

Peeling off my soaked top, I grabbed a fresh one slipping it on and headed back to the living room. I slumped into the well-used armchair opposite Wes, grazing my hand over my stubble.

Wes's glare glued me to the seat, a bemused look on his face. "There had better be a damn good reason she's in *our* bathroom and not hers next door."

He must have left early, before all hell had broken loose, so I quickly gave him a rundown of the night's events, conveniently leaving a few private details out. Namely, the kiss of all motherfucking kisses. I didn't need my private life open for judgement.

He stared at me cautiously. "I don't know, man; I'm not buying it. I mean, I can't sense her, Ty. If she's a witch, I should sense her magic easily," he insisted.

I leaned forward, my elbows edged on my knees. "I know what I saw. I wouldn't use my gift if I didn't believe she was like us in some way."

Wes grazed his knuckles together. "I know. I'm just saying I don't have a good feeling about this." He rose to his feet with a shrug. "It's late, let's deal with it tomorrow."

I nodded as he began walking down the hall to his bedroom.

"And Ty?" he said.

I looked up, not expecting him to speak again. "Yeah?"

"Don't do anything stupid."

"Roger that," I mumbled.

Wes stalked off to his bedroom, and I sank back into the armchair, leaning my head against the rest. Morgan promised me. She swore on her life, she was legit.

The creak of the bathroom door pulled me from my thoughts, and a freshly showered Morgan walked out. She somehow made my old tee and sweats look attractive as hell on her, and then my attention dove to her chest. There was clearly nothing between her skin and my tee.

She folded her arms, covering herself, and I cursed under my breath. Real fucking subtle, Ty. Fuck me.

"Are you sure it's fine if I stay here tonight? It's no trouble to go home."

I needed to tread with caution, needed her to know it wasn't safe but not scare her off either. "No, please stay. We need to talk about what happened tonight."

She walked cautiously into the lounge before settling down on the couch opposite me.

Fair enough. Morgan was probably wondering what the hell had just gone down. But truth be told, I was almost as afraid of her as she was of me right now as we sat sizing each other up. I didn't know what she was or how powerful she could be, and if I was honest, it scared the shit out of me as much as it excited me.

Moving closer to her, I opted to sit on the opposite end of the couch from her. There was no subtle way to have the conversation we needed to have.

I came right out with it. "Morgan, are you a witch?"

Her forehead rippled with confusion.

"You really need to be honest here."

When she didn't reply, I pushed a little further, unsure how far was within her realm of okay.

"Morgan, there's a lot at stake," I urged.

More than she realized. Exposing my gift to her was one thing, but if she wasn't a witch, if she was... something else.

Could my fucking heart handle being torn apart *again?*

That kiss was off-the-scale intense. If she was something dangerous...

I shoved the thought aside.

We needed to know what we were dealing with.

She sat silently for a moment until her lips finally parted, exhaling a long breath.

Her head tilted to the ceiling, her eyes closing momentarily before connecting with mine again. "When I said I didn't know, I meant it," she whispered.

My head cocked to the side. "I don't understand. What do you mean you don't know?"

It didn't make sense for her to not know her heritage. Magic usually manifested in our younger years, and for her not to know this was insane. I couldn't comprehend it.

Her eyes challenged mine. Steel connecting with chestnut from each end of the couch.

"It's like my emotions take over and things just... explode." She threw her hands up in front of her. "It's only happened one other time, and I don't know how, okay?"

What the fuck? I scrunched up my face in confusion.

"Someone threw a hex on the bar tonight."

She frowned. "And that is...?"

I sighed. Wow, she really had *no* idea. "The easiest way to explain what was going on in Jinxed tonight, is that everyone's emotions were on steroids, magnified by magic. And that's possibly why your magic emerged."

"My magic..."

She genuinely looked baffled, like she had no idea what I was talking about.

"What about your parents? They must have answers for you. Magic is always in the bloodline."

She stared at me blankly.

I shrugged. "I'm just trying to help here," I reminded her.

Her hands ran along the delicate chain she wore around her neck before knotting together in front of her. "I'm adopted. I never knew who my birth parents were; I never met them. And I have no clue how whatever this is works, or what I'm supposed to do with it."

The words tumbled out of her like she'd been holding onto them her entire life, my mouth falling open at the statement.

I got the feeling I was the first person she'd ever shared this information with.

I gathered a long breath as her eyes held onto mine, like I was her get-out-of-jail-free card. Maybe I was…

"We'll figure this out. I'll help you find out the answers you need," I assured her.

I meant every word, for both her and the rest of us.

A wall of tears threatened to spill from her, and I moved closer. Cautiously, I rested my palm on her knee, grazing my thumb in numb circles; the contact alone sent heat coursing through me.

"Would you like to ask me anything about tonight?" I asked. Surely, she had questions of her own.

She sighed. "Honestly, I don't even know what to say, let alone ask."

"How about we leave it for the morning?" I suggested with a reassuring smile.

"Thanks, I'm just a little overwhelmed with… well, everything, right now."

The warning from Wes still played in the back of my mind. I hadn't decided how much I wanted to tell her, knowing something didn't add up. Wes could sense magic, but he couldn't sense *her*.

"I'll crash on the couch. You can have my bed. It's this way." I stood, motioning down the hall.

She waved me off. "Really, it's okay, I'm happy on the couch."

"No, please, I insist."

I led her down the hall, opening my bedroom door, and for more reasons than one, I wished the neat freak in me hadn't made the bed look so inviting this morning. I held the door open for her, noting her hesitancy as she walked inside, taking in the new surroundings. My *personal* surroundings. Damn, this was a bad idea.

Her gaze swung around the room, to the photo of my grandfather standing in front of his mustang. Her fingers traced the silver frame I'd found in his garage after he had passed. It seemed fitting to sit the photo in it.

Then she found *her*. The photo of Ava.

Fuck.

Words failed me, or abandoned me rather.

I waited for her to say something. Should I tell her?

Morgan's gaze flitted back to mine. Soft, and with no judgement. Like somehow, she understood.

"Sorry, I... wasn't expecting you in my bedroom," I admitted.

I moved passed her, placing the photo of Ava in my top drawer.

"You didn't need to do that..." she murmured, following my movements. *Studying* me.

I walked back over to the doorway, my hands gripping the doorframe. "It was probably time I did." I shrugged.

"Oh, okay," she said, her tone quiet.

Her eyes searched for mine. I could feel it.

Drawing mine to hers again, I felt naked, like she'd just stripped me bare. Seen the parts of me no one else had. It was strangely comforting to have her bear witness to the act, but to me... placing that photo in the drawer was *intimate*.

I'd been avoiding it for years.

Like a riptide pulling me away, I felt it setting me free, a wave of relief replacing the agony that had haunted me for years. If only she knew the gravity of the situation that had just unfolded in front of her.

I didn't know what to do. What to say.

Morgan stood in my bedroom only feet from my bed. I felt the pull to her, the pull I'd resisted until tonight.

"See you in the morning," I said, tugging the door closed before I did something stupid.

***

Two hours later, sleep had evaded me as I tossed and turned, unable to get her out of my mind. It didn't help that the couch was the most uncomfortable fucking thing I'd ever slept on in my life, and I'd slept in some interesting places.

I was restless as hell thinking of Morgan sleeping in my top next door, wrapped in sheets I had only pulled myself from this morning.

The thought of our encounter in the alley played over my mind as I lay staring at the ceiling. Soft moans had fallen from her lips under only my slightest touch. They echoed in my mind. Every. Single. One. On repeat.

I'd got a taste of what I thought I couldn't have, but now things had changed.

I couldn't deny I wanted more.

Gods, I wanted more.

Although Wes had his doubts, I knew she had a gift. I just needed to figure out the missing piece of the puzzle.

I threw aside the bedcover I'd draped over me, shuffling with heavy eyelids into the kitchen. Plucking a carton of milk from the fridge, I tipped it up, and the cold liquid slid down my throat.

A shiver crawled over my skin as the night air wrapped around me. I was only in boxers.

"Hey, night owl."

My hand slammed to my mouth, gulping down the remaining milk faster than intended with a cough as I swung the fridge door closed.

I cursed when I found Morgan leaning against the kitchen counter. "You're lucky you didn't wear that," I retorted sharply, holding up the milk in my hand.

A smile curled up her lips, turning into a light laugh.

It was then I noticed she wore only my top, which while large on her, was *very* short, exposing her shapely thighs. No sweatpants. Fuck.

She raised a brow with a shy smile. "Like something you see?"

Damn, not so subtle.

"Yeah, the top looks good on you. You scared the shit out of me."

She rubbed her weary eyes. "I couldn't sleep."

I didn't miss the way they snaked their way over my bare chest, and I held in my own smile. "Want some?" I asked, extending the milk to her.

"Thanks." Morgan took it, having a sip from it before handing it back to me. "I've decided it's not fair," she said, folding her arms across her chest.

I raised a brow with intrigue.

"I think we need to even the score," she continued.

Curiosity slid into my tone. "Even the score?"

"A lot happened tonight, and I'm not sure what I saw." She paused for a moment. "I showed you mine…"

The way she said it wasn't provocative by any means. But she made it clear that if she was to trust me, it had to be a two-way street.

The warning from Wes was still fresh in my mind, but the way she looked at me made me want to ignore it completely.

Cautious eyes studied me as she fumbled with her necklace again.

She seemed to have gained her confidence back, or at least was putting on a brave face for now. She'd laid down a challenge. Like she was testing the water, dipping me into a pool of trust to see if I would sink or float.

Challenge accepted.

I zoned into the temperature of the room with my mind, sucking every inch of warmth out of it until goosebumps flared their way over our skin.

The almost freezing temperature of the room made her nipples poke out into perfect peaks, and I pulled my attention from them before her effect on me became obvious; there was no hiding in boxers.

Her eyes went wide as she brushed her arms in an attempt to keep warm. "How did you do that?" she exclaimed.

A deep laugh came from within me. "I'm a thermo mage. I create or control heat."

Her forehead creased. "A mage?"

"A male witch," I corrected, using the term I preferred to avoid.

With a flick of my fingers, the temperature in the room returned to normal, a small flame rising from my palm. Its golden glow cast shadows on every wall, stalking us from every corner of the room.

"Wow," she whispered in awe.

Moving towards me, she took my hand in hers, her touch sending a rush of heat to the point of contact. She ran her finger through the flame, fast enough so she didn't burn herself, but slow enough to know what she saw was real.

"That's incredible," she whispered, her doe eyes wide as they stared up at me.

Something about her affected me in ways I couldn't get my head around. It was unexpected, exciting, and it made me really fucking nervous.

It dawned on me in that moment that she wasn't a fragile thing. Something that couldn't easily be broken or discarded. I knew there was a strength in her, somewhere she hadn't yet found, and god dammit I would help her find it.

I felt the moment the air between us changed. It grew thick and charged with lust so heavy, it was impossible to look away. The walls compressed, inching their way closer until it was just us, like nothing else in the world existed. Her mouth lowered to my hand, blowing out the flame, her thumb caressing the area it had just been.

In the sliver of light peeking through the nearby window, dark irises collided with mine. Silently, they commanded what her body desired, a mirror of what my own ached for.

I closed the space between us until her back hit the kitchen counter, my hands landing on either side of her. Her innocent eyes looked up at me as I towered over her, a heat slowly filling them at my proximity.

"You know, little doe," I said, sliding closer until only mere breaths separated us, "you shouldn't play with fire."

This time, she knew the truth. Knew I could be both dangerous but fair. I held back, letting her make the next move, willing to let this play out however she wished. But would her knowledge of me being a mage scare her away?

"I wasn't playing. I blew it out, remember?" she bit back, not hiding the fever in her eyes.

There she goes. That's the Morgan I remember.

I could have easily kept that flame alight, but the sight of her lips had been too much for me, and I'd let her have her moment.

I chuckled at the comment, remembering just how powerful she could be. If Morgan could move shit without touching it, there was no doubt she could do all sorts with air. She just didn't know it yet.

I couldn't deny my attraction to her anymore. I *needed* to have this woman with every fiber of my being, and it scared the living shit out of me.

I grabbed a fist of her hair, caressing it between my fingers as she raked her hands down my arms, a breath shuddering through me at her touch.

"You barely know me," I warned. "I live in one fucked-up world. You haven't seen the things I have…"

She didn't answer but also didn't pull away.

I raked my thumb over her bottom lip, and it slipped between them, her tongue circling it slowly. I cursed, a groan rumbling from me.

Our lips brushed achingly close, but I needed to know for sure. Hear her say those words.

I summoned a deep breath. "Tell me this is real. That it's not some nightmare I'm going to regret tomorrow. Convince me this is worth the risk."

I was hopeless to fight it, to fight her. *Us*.

My free hand traced the curve of her collarbone down to her perfectly rounded breast, her body arching into my touch. The control I had over her body consumed me entirely, a feeling I wasn't used to. What was she doing to me? I never spoke like this.

Her voice scraped my ear. "It's no mistake, Ty."

When my name dropped from her lips, my restraint snapped and I fell *hard*, spinning wildly into something so unknown to me that I couldn't possibly turn back. The need to have her engulfed me like the heat that pulsed within me daily, and I was powerless to stop it.

I covered her mouth with mine, and she moaned as I tasted her, muffled desire filling my ears and fueling my fire.

Scooping my hands underneath her, I raised her onto the counter, and she gasped in surprise before wrapping her legs around my waist, my t-shirt riding high up her legs. Her hands explored my arms, my back, sliding into my hair until they fell to the nape of my neck. Her touch spoke words she didn't need to, the subtle edge in the way she grazed her hands over my skin, bordering on a plea.

I caressed her creamy thighs, until I skimmed the barely-there cotton barrier of her underwear, the only thing separating the pads of my fingers and the most sensitive parts of her. I was instantly rewarded with a light whimper.

She ground against the fabric separating our flesh, and I couldn't help the smile in my kiss, knowing she wanted this as much as I did.

I moaned. "I can feel how wet you are." I tilted her chin to look up at me, her dark orbs drenched with desire staring up at me.

"Please, I need more," she breathed against my mouth as I pressed against the fabric. Her hands dragged down my front, nails digging into my sides as she pulled me closer, chasing the friction she needed.

A door shut somewhere in the house, and I stiffened, hearing shuffling coming from somewhere behind me. I slid my hand from her just as Morgan's eyes widened, connecting with something over my shoulder.

"For fuck's sake, Ty, you know I like to watch, but in my own kitchen and with no invitation…"

Whipping my head behind me, I found Wes leaned casually against the wall in boxers, green eyes glaring daggers as they collided with mine.

"Fuck off," I growled, not turning around, aware I was at full fucking mast.

Morgan lowered herself from the kitchen counter, pulling at my top to cover herself.

Wes threw an arm in the air. "You don't even know who the fuck she is."

Wes never swore. *Especially* around woman.

Words spat from my mouth as I turned towards him. "I suggest you keep your opinions to yourself."

His tone lowered to a serious one I rarely heard. "You know how the last one turned out."

"Enough!" I barked at him, the blood in my veins rising to a new level of heat.

Morgan inched away from me. "I think I should go," she stammered.

I grabbed her hand. "No, stay. You don't have to go."

Her tortured eyes pleaded with me, and I let her pull her hand from my grasp. She grabbed her phone off the counter, and I closed the space between us.

I lowered my voice. "Give me your phone," I said, ignoring the heavy glare slamming into my back.

She paused, looking to Wes before meeting mine again. I took advantage of the moment, quickly taking it from her and dialing my number.

I handed it back to her, resting my hands on her shoulders. "Let me know when you're home safe."

She nodded, heading quickly for the door.

When it clicked shut behind her, I turned to Wes, my hands balled into fists at my sides and dick no longer happy. "What the hell was that?" I demanded.

He glared at me. "I could ask you the same question."

We stood, neither of us moving until he finally stalked off towards his room again. For the second time tonight, he turned to me.

"Yeah, what is it this time?" I questioned with venom.

He shook his head. "I just saved your ass. You'll thank me in the morning." With that, he disappeared to his room.

My pulse pounded in my ears as rage coursed through me. He was wrong. Every inch of me now believed Morgan was an innocent party in whatever this fucked-up situation was.

I felt it in my bones.

Retreating to my bedroom, I slid between the sheets, still warm from Morgan's body heat. Her scent still lingered on my pillow, a hint of vanilla invading my senses.

My phone vibrated.

> Hey, sorry I had to get out of there.

> I get it. Sorry about Wes. Are you okay?

> Yes, thanks for everything tonight.

> I'm just glad you're safe. Can I come over in the morning?

> Sure, I'll see you then. Goodnight.

> Goodnight. Call if you need me.

> Lock your door.

> Will do. :)

I draped an arm over my forehead as the evening played over on repeat. Every word, every touch, etched in my mind and making my dick throb again. I rolled over ignoring it, attempting to name every make of car I could, until sleep finally took hold of me.

Morgan

A heaviness settled in my stomach, like boulders in their final resting place after a wild storm.

Last night had been a disaster of epic proportions, and everything I ever knew to be real had tipped on an axis, leaving me desperately clutching the edge of reality.

How I lost my shit, exposed my *magic* as Tyler called it, and fell for my next-door neighbor who may or may not be a total pyromaniac was beyond me.

The one thing I'd guarded with my life had been exposed.

And worse, Tyler had witnessed the entire thing.

I'd known I was different from a young age. Call it intuition maybe. But witches? And magic?

Last night, everything had changed between Tyler and I, and it felt right. Tyler had secrets of his own, and more it seemed. Could I trust him? I had to. Because right now, he was the only thing I knew to be real.

Popping a pod into the coffee machine, I hit the *on* button, a rich aroma filling the kitchen. Scuffing at the front door followed by a light knock interrupted my thoughts.

"Morgan, it's me. Can I come in?"

My stomach flipped with nerves at hearing Tyler voice. Taking a deep breath, I padded to the front door, opening it wide.

My heart short-circuited at the sight of him leaning against the door frame. He wore a crisp white tee and those same faded black jeans, his hands shoved into his pockets.

A cautious smile creased his cheeks, and I couldn't hold back a smile in return.

"Hey, come in," I said, waving him inside.

Tyler slipped off his boots, and I followed him to the lounge, my gaze devouring the ripple of muscle that tightened across his shoulders with every movement. An awkward silence lingered between us, and my gaze dipped to the floorboards.

"Mind if I sit?" he asked.

I inwardly groaned at my rudeness. "Sorry. Of course."

He lowered to the couch, his elbows settling on his knees, and I sat beside him. The combination of the intensity of his stare and his closeness melted my insides, turning me into a nervous wreck.

"I just wanted to see how you were… after last night."

"Am I going to keep your secret, you mean?" I raised a brow.

His voice lowered. "That's not what I meant."

Tyler inched closer to me, his hand moving to my knee, my breath hitching at his touch. I watched as his thumb skated a line back and forth. The sensation set my nerves on fire, causing thousands of prickles to etch into my skin.

"Sorry," I whispered, lifting my gaze to his.

A smile twitched the corner of his mouth, his steel grays turning over my insides, like he knew exactly what his touch did to me.

I inhaled a deep breath, releasing it slowly. "I'm okay. It was a bit of a blur, to be honest."

"It's alright. I get it. Sorry about Wes; he was out of line."

My voice dropped to a whisper. "I don't think I'll *ever* be able to look him again." I grimaced.

Tyler let out a deep chuckle. "Yeah, Wes has…" he paused, seemingly choosing his words carefully. "*Interests* I can't even begin to understand."

As he said the words, Skye and Wesley entered the living room, and if my cheeks weren't hot enough, they were surely on fire now.

Oh. My. God. Kill. Me. Now.

I covered my face with my hands. "I can't believe you're standing here right now," I groaned.

Wesley spoke, his voice completely void of emotion. "Nothing I haven't seen before."

I lifted my head as Skye smacked him in the side.

"Fine." He lifted his hands in the air. "I'll never speak of it again. Now, tell us about these magical hands of yours." His eyes pierced mine as if he were trying to catch me in a lie.

The whole scenario was so uncomfortable I wanted to be anywhere but here. In my own home, nonetheless.

I held his heavy stare. "So, this little reunion is about me? What is this, an intervention?" This so-called neighborhood watch thing could just leave as far as I was concerned.

Tyler's voice came from beside me. "Morgan, we're here to help. Please let us."

My attention remained locked on Wesley until I felt Tyler's hand tighten on my knee. I turned away to find Tyler pleading silently with me. He was the first person I'd opened up to about my secret, but not by choice. Hell, I didn't even understand it myself, let alone want to share it with others.

Four sets of eyes penetrated the lie I'd sold for years now. The tough exterior I'd guarded my secret with. Their weighted stares withered away the remaining strength I had, and at this point, I knew they were my only hope of finding answers.

"Fine," I sighed, tipping my head back. My eyes slid shut, breath gathering in my lungs in a controlled rhythm, unable to believe I was about to tell them the absolute truth. I forced myself to look at Tyler. "I wasn't quite honest with you."

My breath scattered under the intensity of the moment.

I stood, and started pacing the room. "My *magic* killed my adoptive parents. We were having an argument." I purposely left out the part about my stupid ex who my parents had disliked, who happened to be the subject of the argument. "Something inside me just snapped. I don't know how it happened. But the next thing I knew, I'd blasted a hole in the side of the house, lighting it on fire."

The room stilled, falling into an awkward silence.

I sank my forehead into my hands. "The blast killed them. I'm sorry I didn't tell you earlier," I whispered, turning back to Tyler again.

"I'm sorry to hear that," he said, moving behind me until his hand lay in the small of my back.

Skye shifted towards me and slung a hand over my shoulder, pulling me close. "That's really tragic. That must have been awful."

Saying it out loud brought back visions of the horrifying night.

Ones I had boxed up and placed neatly into the back of my memory, hoping they would someday disappear.

I paused, collecting myself. "That was the first time it happened. The second time was yesterday, when Tyler saw me." I lifted my head again, finding his gaze fixed on me. I couldn't look away.

Something flickered in his irises, emotion spilling between us in a soundless exchange that I knew only two people having lost someone could understand.

Wesley shifted in place, pulling my attention to him. "I'm sorry to hear about your parents. But why didn't they tell you about your gift?"

"I'm figuring my adoptive parents were not... magical, and I never knew my birth parents. I was found on the doorstep of an orphanage when I was six months old, with nothing but a locket in my clothing."

Skye screwed up her face. "A locket? Why would someone leave you with a locket?"

I shrugged. "Your guess is as good as mine. My mother gave it to me on my twenty-first birthday. Take a look for yourself." I walked over to the counter, picking up the necklace with the large locket hanging from it, returning to hand it to her. "I know nothing about it. There's no engraving, only a symbol on the back."

Skye turned the heart-shaped locket over in her hands, her fingers tracing its delicate etchings.

"This symbol is like nothing I've seen before."

Wes stepped up beside her, hovering over her shoulder. "Do you mind?"

He motioned to the locket, and I nodded as he took it in his hands. Without warning, his eyes turned a deathly shade of ink that flooded his irises completely. Only two black holes remained, indented in his skull.

My eyes flew wide, the chill that spread through me devouring my nervous system. I scurried backwards, falling against the hard wall of Tyler's chest. He lowered us to the couch until I balanced on his lap, the pads of my fingers pressed into his thigh. His voice scraped my ear. "Be still, it's okay."

Fear bolted me to his chest. "What the fuck is going on?" I whispered, gripping his leg tighter.

He chuckled, his voice low in my ear. "That's *his* gift. Stay still."

Just as suddenly, the green orbs of Wesley's eyes returned. I blinked repeatedly. Was I the only one freaking out here?

Silence stifled the group, eagerly feasting on our uncertainty. Wesley's eyes swung wildly around the room until landing on Tyler. One word fell from his lips. "Darkness."

I glared at him. "Well, I sure as hell saw that."

Skye pinned her hands to her hips, her glare fixed on him. "You need to give us more than that."

Wesley's stare turned cold as he focused on me. "Dark magic."

At his words, three sets of eyes pinned me in place.

"Can someone *please* tell me what the hell is going on here?" I demanded, unable to hide the shudder in my voice.

A thick tension filled the room.

Tyler edged me off him until I sat at his side. He raised a brow at Wes, then looked to Skye, who nodded back.

Turning towards me, Tyler dragged his hands through his stubble. "Morgan, every supernatural being you've ever heard about is real."

"Supernatural…" I said, the word sliding off my lips like a landslide in slow motion.

There was no hesitation in his voice this time. "As in *everything*. Every being, in every book, in every movie."

My brows furrowed. "You mean…"

"Everything," he finished for me. "As in witches, werewolves, vampires… demons. Just to name a few."

I opened my mouth, as if I had something decent to say but couldn't gather words. Moments passed, and they just *stared* at me. All three of them, silent.

"So, at Jinxed last night…" I couldn't comprehend what I was even saying and turned to Tyler.

He rubbed his knuckles against each other. "Vampires."

"I don't get it…" I started, trying to make sense of all this.

"They were trying to kill you, Morgan, drain you of your blood."

I realized then the seriousness of last night. Tyler had saved my life, and in doing so, he'd exposed his own secret. I found myself staring openmouthed around the room, unable to grasp my newfound reality for what it was.

"So where does that leave me?" I asked quietly.

Wes shifted in his seat, everyone turning their attention to him.

"I'm going to take a stab in the dark here and say you're a witch, and you have a spell bound to you that's somehow suppressing your magic."

Tyler nodded beside me. "That would explain why you can't sense her."

Confusion crinkled my nose. "A spell? That's insane. How did you possibly come up with *that* theory?" I questioned with a disbelieving scoff.

Wes remained unfazed by my skepticism, his arms folded across his chest. "Because I'm a sensory mage."

I stared blankly at him.

He rushed out a frustrated breath. "My senses are heightened. Meaning I can sense magic through mind or touch, among other things." He stilled, his attention fixed solely on me. "The thing is, I tried to sense if you had a gift at the party and couldn't feel your magic. I thought you were human. That's never happened before."

I passed my gaze around the group. "Why would someone cast a spell on me?"

Wes, who had been standing, sank to the floor. "*That* is the question. But what I do know... is that dark magic has touched this locket."

I threw my hands in the air. "Great! I find out I'm a witch, and already I'm downgraded to the bad kind. This is madness. I would never hurt anyone," I insisted, exasperation filling my tone.

Tyler spoke from beside me, "Let's not jump to conclusions. We just need to figure out what this locket has to do with everything. It was obviously left with you for a reason."

Skye moved closer, her palm extending to the middle of the circle. "This symbol must have something to do with a coven, or a specific bloodline of witches. Maybe I can take it to the library and see if I can find anything about it. Just let me get a photo."

I nodded, happy to have any help at this point.

She pulled out her phone and took a snap before stuffing it back in her pocket. "I'll let you know if I find anything. Please don't freak out. We'll try to help any way we can."

I smiled back at her. "Thanks. I appreciate it."

She turned to Wesley. "I'm going to need your help."

Without a word, the pair left. But my mind was reeling, two words repeating over and over.

Dark magic.

It didn't make any sense.

Tyler's hand drew my chin to face him until his familiar irises locked on mine.

"Hey," he said, caressing my cheek as tears stung my eyes. "I know it's a lot to take in. Don't freak out on me." His lips curled up in a comforting smile.

A long breath shuddered in my chest, and I stilled under his touch, my eyelids flicking shut.

"I just don't see how I fit into all of this," I whispered, staring back up at him.

The warmth in his gaze imploded a storm of emotions inside me, and tears fell freely, ghosting wet trails down my cheeks.

"I mean, I'm just me. Plain, boring me. I've had a normal upbringing, with totally normal parents. I've never done a bad thing in my life. I would never hurt anyone." My fingers covered his, pulling them from my face, and he laced his fingers through mine until they settled in my lap.

"Trust me when I say you're not boring. In fact, you're quickly becoming the most interesting person I've ever met."

Through blurred vision, I stared at him as if I he was delusional. He looked back at me as if I was a wonderous gift.

With his free hand, he swiped another tear from my cheek.

I sniffled. "I need coffee."

A grin broke over his face. "Now that I can arrange." He pulled me to my feet. "It's about time you introduced me to your coffee machine."

A light laugh left my lips as I pushed away tears, motioning toward the kitchen. I raised myself until I sat on top of the kitchen counter, studying the *male witch* who was currently going about his way in my kitchen.

Who knew *they* were even a thing? When I pictured witches in my mind, I saw broomsticks and crooked noses, not ordinary people living what appeared to be ordinary lives.

I watched as corded veins ran the length of his arms, straining as Tyler's fingers fumbled over the buttons on my coffee machine. I stifled a giggle. He couldn't work a coffee machine, but I was certain he knew how to use those hands on a woman.

He looked sideways at me, a brow raised at my subtle laughter.

I couldn't help myself. "Can't you just click your finger, and a coffee will appear for us?"

Tyler shook his head. "We can't just use magic whenever we please. It takes time to replenish, so we use it sparingly."

I grinned, a boldness suddenly finding me. "As in… when you have a young lady wearing nothing but your shirt in the middle of the night?" I teased.

He pointed a knowing finger in my direction. "*That* was an exception. There are rules you should know."

I leaned back, my palms resting on the kitchen counter. "Rules?"

"Our magic is governed by our covens; they have rules around the use of magic."

I knew little about covens, remembering them only vaguely being mentioned in movies. "Covens…" I repeated, deep in thought. "Will I have one?"

Tyler gripped the counter, turning his head to mine. "Yes, assuming you're a witch, you will. Our coven is named after one of the founding families of this town. The Cutters. Our coven is called Cutters Coven.

How original.

I chewed my lip. To think somewhere I could have my own coven, that I was a part of something bigger than just me.

"Will I have the same coven as you?" I asked.

His knuckles turned white as his grip tightened. He grimaced. "Unsure."

I couldn't be certain, but he seemed to be avoiding looking at me, and an uncomfortable feeling churned in the pit of my stomach.

I sat up straight, my own hands gripping the side of the counter. "Is that a problem?"

He held my gaze, pausing as if questioning his next sentence. "It really depends on which one you belong to, if I'm honest."

"Why is that?" I said, my eyes narrowing with interest.

He looked to be choosing his words carefully, and maybe he was, for my sake.

Tyler focused back on putting together the coffee. "You're expected to live with the coven you were born into."

I started to speak before suddenly realizing what that could mean for me. For us. That Cutters Coven would most likely not be *my* coven.

I fidgeted uneasily with my necklace. "Where is the next closest coven from here?"

Tyler finally swung his gaze to mine, in a way that reminded me of the time he had backed me into the wall outside of Jinxed. His irises mirrored equal parts angst and... was that dread?

"That would be the coven at Port Fallere, Sacred Souls, but we try to keep a healthy distance between us."

The feeling of unease churned my stomach further. I wondered what had happened in the past for them to feel this way about another coven.

"Why is that?" I asked out of pure curiosity.

Tyler's jaw went rigid. "Sacred Souls are known for their misuse of magic."

I paused, waiting for him to elaborate, but he didn't. I made a mental note to ask him about it later. For Tyler to make a statement like that, it had to be *bad*. He didn't seem the type of guy to make judgement without evidence.

"Okay, so what are *your* rules?" I asked.

He lifted the mugs of coffee closer to me, placing them on the counter beside where I sat.

"The main one is you must only use magic for good."

I nodded. "Got it. So, I can't conjure up all the money I like then."

The joke fell flat, and to be fair, I knew it would be a hard push. I was only trying to take both our minds off the elephant in the room: that living in Cutters Cove could only be a temporary stop for me.

I didn't want to think that something so entirely out of my control could change everything. *Again.*

My attraction to Tyler was magnetic, the pull to him like some external force drawing us together. Physics in its purest form, you could say. I knew he felt it too, and I could tell by the way his jaw had tensed again that he was thinking about what that could mean for us also.

When he finally spoke, I knew I was right. His voice was lower, more serious than usual. "No, you can't. That's why we all have jobs." He pulled in a deep breath before releasing it slowly. "Morgan, there's so much to tell you, I don't even know where to begin. But for now, do you like sugar in your coffee, or are you sweet enough already?"

He was changing the subject; that much was obvious, and to be fair, I was on board with it. I needed to push the what ifs to the back of my mind or else I'd go mad.

I stared up at him from my perch on the counter, his pupils dilated, causing a newfound intensity to claim them.

"I may need a little more sugar," I admitted, biting my bottom lip.

Tyler shifted towards me, his hands separating my legs until he stood between them. He bolted his eyes to mine and grabbed my thighs, tugging me closer to him until I was barely on the counter anymore.

His voice came out a low husk. "Do you now?"

A shudder drove through me at both the movement and his words, my insides humming in response. His lips found mine, and a groan rumbled from him as he kissed me painfully slow, until I needed air.

We broke away, and he rested his forehead on mine, his thumb languidly sliding over my bottom lip and sending shivers down my spine.

"Morgan, what you do to me is..." His voice trailed off, and he brought his hands up to cup my face, his head dipping for a moment. "Sorry, I'm not very good at this."

Honesty filled his features, and I stilled as his thumb caressed my cheek.

He took a deep breath. "You walked into Cutters Cove in those goddamn jeans like you were always meant to be here. You must be part of our coven. You *have* to be."

Tyler's gaze hardened, and steel gray turned to thunderous clouds that crashed into mine. My lips moved, then closed again, unable to voice words. Unable to think. His intensity stole my words and consumed my mind until I finally managed a whisper.

"You don't even know me. What if I turn out to be some sort of evil thing?" I said, tucking a stray hair behind my ear.

His hands drifted down to my thighs, mindlessly skimming over my jeans.

"Unless you're the Queen of the Underworld or the Devil himself, I'm sure we can deal with whatever you have going on here." He swirled his fingers in the air until his pointer finger landed between my breasts. "I know Wes has his doubts, but I don't. I want you to know that."

The weight of his words hit me, his stare becoming lazy and hooded. A grin spread over his face before he kissed me again. Slower this time, pulling me into his arms until I was dizzy from the exquisite taste of him.

When he pulled away, his hands eased my hips off the counter until my feet hit the ground.

He handed me a mug of coffee before we moved outside to my back deck, settling on the step, our legs seemingly gravitating toward each other.

"Any plans for the vegetable garden?" said Tyler.

I followed his line of sight to the boxed planters nearing the end of my section, filled with greenery of all sorts.

"To be honest, I've never been that great at keeping plants alive," I muttered, thinking about the basil I had tried to grow in a pot on more than one occasion. I liked to think it would complement a pizza, but it only ever died.

A low laugh rumbled from Tyler. "To be fair, if you get *anything* to grow here, you're doing well. We don't get a lot of sun."

I didn't doubt him.

We sat in comfortable silence, watching as the wind weaved through the trees in swift movements over the mountain face in the distance.

My lips drew into a circle as I released a breath to cool the steaming coffee in my mug. "I can't believe this is happening to me. I mean, why me? I just don't get it."

Tyler shrugged. "Nor me. It's got me beat for sure."

"Tell me everything. Who is what around here that I don't know of? What about Skye?"

I noted the pause before he spoke again.

"Skye was also born with the element of fire, being from the same family, but she can also see and communicate with spirits."

"Spirits?... Wow." I blew out a long breath before taking a sip of my drink, my mind whirling. I couldn't imagine dealing with the walking dead following me around daily; that must be so distracting.

How did Skye deal with such a thing? I would never have guessed; she hid it well.

He nodded. "Yeah. She had a hard time with it growing up."

"You really weren't kidding when you mentioned things from the movies. So much for the sleepy town of Cutters Cove. It couldn't be further from the truth." I mused.

Tyler set his drink down on his lap, as if he had something serious to say. "Morgan, I was only trying to protect you at Jinxed, I don't think you realize how close you came to being killed."

My throat went dry, and I gulped desperately, trying to salivate it again.

A shiver ran through me at the memory, realization hitting me of how badly that could have ended if he had not been there.

I suddenly felt terrible. "And I was so rude to you. I thought you were just jealous, sorry."

He chuckled. "Maybe I was... a little jealous, I mean." He tilted his head to face mine. "You were effectively off limits, but I couldn't just ignore the situation." He took a sip of his coffee, peering at me over the rim of his mug.

"Off limits." I laughed lightly at the label he'd just given me. "And what about now?"

Our eyes met in a heated exchange, neither backing down from the moment that had silently crept up on us.

A smile tugged the corner of his mouth from behind his mug.

"All bets are off."

Tyler

I pretended not to notice two things. One, the cute little smile hidden behind her coffee mug. And two, the way her thighs clenched together at my last comment.

But it was true. All bets were off.

Since Morgan's arrival, I'd been living an internal battle trying to keep her at a healthy distance, tucked away in the 'you can look but can't touch' box.

Morgan being a supernatural meant what I thought I couldn't have, had been flipped on its ass and tossed sideways. Where did that leave me? Somewhere between I wanted this woman so badly it kept me up at night, and she could still be the fucking Devil in disguise. Surely not.

My gut told me otherwise, my instincts certain I could trust her. But until I found out everything, I had to keep my dick in my pants, and that alone had been a feat the last twenty-four hours.

Morgan shifted in her seat and her knee grazed mine, the contact lighting my nerves on fire. The reaction of such a touch was so unknown to me, and I couldn't grasp any reasoning for it. Ava had been my first girlfriend, and we had shared so much together. But in comparison, our connection was nothing compared to the intensity between Morgan and me.

The dark-haired beauty sitting beside me had no idea that from the moment I'd met her, she had set my nerves on fire and my heart in a knot. At times Morgan had almost rendered me speechless, left my limbs in chains, and I'd never imagined a woman could make me feel those things.

We chatted for what seemed like hours with no awkwardness. I found out she liked lattes because of the extra milk, that she's allergic to cats, and she had moved towns a lot growing up.

Skye's voice sounded from behind us. "Morgan, are you still here?"

Morgan looked over her shoulder. "Yeah, we're out the back!"

Wes and Skye came through the glass doors on the porch, and she looked at them expectantly.

"Did you find anything?" she asked.

Skye held what appeared to be a book in the air. Bound in dark leather and pressed with aged creases, it looked centuries old.

She nodded. "I think so. It took a while, but we found this." She lowered to the deck, and we gathered closer.

"What exactly is this?" asked Morgan, tracing her hand over the etchings on its front.

"It's a history of witch bloodlines," Skye replied with reverence.

Her forehead creased. "And that's just available for public knowledge?"

Wes moved closer. "There's a part of the library that to everyday humans doesn't exist."

Morgan shrugged. "Right. So did you find anything that can help me?" She gestured to the book.

Skye flipped through until her hand landed on a withered page with the same symbol on Morgan's locket displayed.

Morgan pointed, nearly knocking over her empty coffee mug in excitement. "Look! The symbol, it's the same"

Skye's lips pursed into a line. "Yeah. Only, there's a problem."

I fired a look at Skye. "A problem?"

A breeze fluttered through the pages, and she splayed her arm across the book to hold them steady. With her other hand, she ran her finger down the middle seam.

I looked closer, my heart sinking. I hadn't seen it before, but there was a page missing that looked as if it had been ripped out.

Confusion rippled Morgan's forehead. "There's a page missing."

Humble silence settled in the air between us.

Air deflated from Morgan's lungs, her shoulders sagging in defeat. "Meaning I'm no closer to finding out anything about me than I was five minutes ago." She huffed.

"There must be a reason for it," I offered, catching Skye's attention, but her shoulders just raised discretely. No luck there.

After a moment, Wes spoke, "Morgan, do you mind if I try something on you... with my gift, I mean?"

My ears pricked at his comment, every hair on my skin suddenly spiking.

What the fuck was he on about?

"What do you mean by *try* something?" I snapped, the tone of my voice drawing the attention of the group.

Morgan's hand landed on my thigh. "Tyler," Morgan murmured beside me.

Wes turned back to Morgan. "I mean that something's not right with your gift. What if we sat down and held the locket together, almost as a tether? It might help me get past whatever this is and find out what's going on."

"No way," I argued. "It's not happening. You're not using her as your guinea pig."

Skye shot me a hard look. "Ty, we keep coming up blank here. Wes is only trying to help."

"And it's a bad idea," I challenged.

Morgan's hand gripped my thigh tighter. "Wesley, have you done this before?" she asked.

He popped his knuckles. "Not exactly. I mean, I usually brush people as they walk past or get a sense from a distance. What I did with the locket before, I don't usually do on people. I'm not sure how this would work. But I'm willing to try it if you'll let me."

Wes refused to look at me. Like fuck I was going to let her be his crash test dummy. I didn't know how this whole sensor thing worked, but Wes dabbled in ways I didn't understand.

"There is no fucking way I'm letting this happen," I said, rising to my feet and putting myself between them.

"Tyler," Morgan cried out, but I didn't move. "Please sit down. Let's just hear him out." She moved out from behind me, her eyes burning into the side of my face.

I didn't take mine off Wes. He couldn't seriously be considering it, could he?

"If you fucking hurt her..." I warned.

"STOP!" Morgan's hands fell between us. "I want to give this a go."

A stiff gust of air swept between us, causing her hair to fall across her face. Like the elements were sounding a warning. She swiped it away without breaking eye contact.

I held her gaze for what felt like an eternity. A week ago, she'd been a stranger to me. Today, I didn't understand the feeling that urged me to protect her so fiercely.

I lowered my voice, my hand capturing her forearm. "You don't have to do this."

She stared up at me, a silent plea. "I know. But I want to try."

"He could kill you," I reminded her, stating the obvious, uncertain she knew what she was getting herself into.

"Please, let me try this."

I forced my hands through my hair in frustration as she turned to Wes with folded arms.

"What do I need to do?" she asked.

Wes held my stare, a nerve grinding his jaw. "Let's go inside."

Morgan cautiously stepped away, and we now stood chest to chest. If looks could kill, he'd be six feet under, and I'd happily dig the hole myself.

Skye shoved my shoulder. "Okay, enough with the dick swinging contest. Let's go."

I tore my eyes from Wes, reluctantly following them inside as I muttered under my breath.

In the living room, Wes moved the coffee table to the side until there was an empty space in the middle of the room. He motioned at Skye, refusing to look at me. "If you could both sit to the side."

A thumping shunted my bones to the marrow, my heart storming blood through my veins.

I controlled every aspect of my life but was powerless to make them see how dangerous this was. If Morgan wanted to do this, I couldn't stop her.

Morgan and Wes sat crossed legged facing each other, the locket in her hand. Her eyes met mine as if wanting my blessing, but I couldn't grant it. Not when her life was at stake.

She drew in a breath, slowly letting it out again. "Are you sure about this?" she said, suddenly looking not so confident.

Wes rolled his shoulders, straightening. "Like I said, I haven't done this before. Not like this. You're just going to have to trust me."

Uncertainty rolled off them in waves.

Skye looked as uncomfortable as I felt, twisting her ring around her thumb.

Jacked full of adrenaline, it coursed through me, my jaw holding tight. I shot Skye a look, but she only shrugged her shoulders in response. Fuck. This was happening whether I liked it or not.

Wes moved closer to Morgan until their knees touched. "I'm going to place my hand over yours, so the locket is between our palms, then our free hands cover them."

She nodded.

"Now, close your eyes."

I watched as she followed his instruction and shook my head, unable to believe she was even considering this. My gaze fell to her hands now encased by another man's, and a predatory storm brewed inside of me, pushing through my veins in a jealous wash.

Wes rolled his head forward. I figured he was trying not to freak everyone out with his black-as-all-hell eyes when he did this shit. The guy was a freak of nature.

To be fair, we all were in our own way, but Wes was something else.

His hand gripped hers tightly, a line of sweat sliding down the nape of his neck. Moments passed and nothing happened. Then without warning, Morgan's head shot back.

A tremor ripped through her body, her eyes wide and saturated a milky white, fixed on the ceiling above. It was as if the moon had fallen from the sky and taken residence inside of her, or maybe it was something else. Or someone, rather...

"Wes!" I yelled, rushing to her side. "What the fuck?"

I didn't dare touch her, her breath matching the faint rise and fall of her chest.

Her pupils suddenly returned to normal, a gasp of air filling her lungs before she fell limp into my arms.

"What the hell just happened?" I demanded.

Skye ran to Wes's side, his lungs violently heaving air, droplets of moisture coating his forehead. "Holy shit, Wesley, are you okay?" Her voice pitched as her hands landed on his arms to shake him.

His pupils dilated, casting swiftly around the room as he tried to focus his disoriented gaze.

"Morgan, can you hear me?" I urged. She mumbled incoherently in my arms, and I patted her cheek. "Open your eyes." I pleaded as terror gripped me in a chokehold, pressing its hands around my throat.

"Are… they okay?" Skye stammered in shock, her blue-green irises flitting back and forth between Morgan and Wes.

Wes shakily pressed his hand to his forehead. "I'm good. Morgan?" he rasped.

My voice dipped, not bothering to hide my distaste. "I don't know."

Morgan stirred in my arms, and relief flooded through me. Thank fuck.

I stared down at her. "Hey, are you okay?"

She attempted to sit upright but lacked the strength, falling back into my arms. "I think so," she mumbled.

I brushed hair from her face. "You had me worried there."

Morgan narrowed her eyes at Wes. "What the hell were you doing in there? It felt like you were clawing at my brain." She winced.

Wes rubbed at his temples, giving her an apologetic look. "Yeah, sorry, that was all new to me."

Skye surveyed his face, moving his head with her hands to inspect him. "Did you find anything that could help?" she asked.

It was a loaded question, one only Wes knew the answer to.

Whatever Wes just did was not the usual shit. That much was fucking clear.

He lay spread on his back, knees bent with an arm draped over his forehead.

"Yeah. We need to find Betty." He stated.

"Betty?" we all said at once.

He nodded. "I could smell that hideous perfume she wears and heard her voice chanting a spell. Find Betty and you have your answers."

Morgan

The world spun wildly, my eyes pained to the point where I pinned them shut again. Whatever that was, I would never let him repeat it. I'd *felt* him. His presence, his power, deep within me, entering my subconscious and clawing at every nerve ending beyond my skull.

A shudder coursed through my body at the memory. I couldn't be sure, but judging by Tyler's reaction, I'd say Wesley had been seriously downplaying his sensor gift.

The tips of my fingers settled on my eyelids. "Betty? As in Betty who owned this house?" I mumbled.

"Yeah, her," Wesley said from where he still lay peeled out on the floor.

Tyler straightened behind me. "Surely not," he scoffed. "We've lived next to her for years. She couldn't possibly be linked to Morgan."

Skye helped Wesley sit upright, his weighted stare swiftly finding Tyler's. He nodded in my direction. "Ask her, not me."

Wesley wouldn't look at me, and I wondered if he felt he'd overstepped the boundaries between us.

Tyler's breath warmed my neck as he pressed his hand into my shoulder. "Do you know how to contact Betty?" he asked, turning to face me.

I sucked in a breath. Only inches from mine, his steel irises were exquisite. A dark charcoal around the edges, blending into a faint blue-gray as they neared his pupils. His proximity took my breath away.

I fumbled with my words. "It's... on the fridge." I faintly gestured in that direction.

My skin tingled in response to his closeness, each hair coming alive as if it were pleading for mercy. Why did he make me so nervous? No man had ever gotten under my skin like this.

Skye broke my thoughts, handing me the note from the fridge with Betty's familiar scrawls on it. The paper stared back at me, and I exhaled a long breath as I skimmed over her phone number.

I looked around the group. "I don't know, guys, is this a good idea?"

Skye moved closer. "Morgan, we need to speak to her. If *she* cast the spell, maybe she can break it, too."

Tyler clutched his hands behind his head. "I very much doubt Betty cast the spell; we would know if she was a witch." He turned pointedly to Wes. "You would have sensed her."

Wes sat with a bent knee, an arm resting on it. "Don't shoot the messenger," he said with a slight raise of his hand.

My stomach flipped with uncertainty; I knew Skye was right. "She may know who my birth parents are," I whispered.

I found it hard to believe this was all some huge coincidence. Had she known who my birth parents were all along? I didn't know how to feel about that if it were to be true. A flare of anger streaked through me as I studied the numbers on the note again, unsure how to proceed from here.

I adjusted my top, moving a stray hair from my face. This could go one of two ways. The small set of numbers could hold the answers to my entire life or become my worst nightmare.

Pulling my phone from my back pocket, the paper trembled in my hand. When the call connected, nerves scattered my breath.

Betty's voice hit my ears soon after, and it took all my effort to keep my voice steady.

"Hi, Betty, it's Morgan. I have some more mail here if you would like to come and collect it sometime."

"Hi, Morgan darling. More bills, I imagine. I'm going to head downtown shortly. I can stop by on my way past if that works?" she chimed from the other end of the line.

"Okay, that sounds great. I'll see you soon." With that, I disconnected the call.

A silence lingered in the room, weighing heavily between the group.

"So, how are we going to let this play out?" said Skye, glancing around the room.

I fumbled with the chain around my neck, unsure how to proceed from here. Unsure how to feel, about everything. Was it a complete coincidence I had ended up living in her old house? Or as Wesley suspected, had she something to do with this whole scenario in some weird witchy way.

Tyler ran an uneasy hand through his hair. "I think we just need to be straight up with her."

Skye's fingers turned over the ring she wore on her thumb. "Worst-case scenario, you're in a room with three witches." She shrugged.

Her words didn't convince me. But it was my only lead. My only option.

A silence filled the room, tension simmering below the surface like an undercurrent.

Ten minutes later, the doorbell thrummed in our ears, and I rose to my feet.

Tyler moved beside me. "I'll get it." He walked over to the door and opened it. "Hey, Betty, long time no see," he greeted, letting her inside and giving her a polite hug.

She beamed. "Tyler, so nice to see you again, young man." Betty made her way into the living area, dressed smartly in a matching plum pantsuit.

Skye suppressed a cough, and I met her gaze with a mixture of amusement and nerves. Instinctively, I wrapped my arms around myself, wishing I could sink into the many seams sewn into the fake leather on my shoes. Could this *be* any more awkward?

Lines formed on Betty's forehead. "I hope this isn't a bad time..."

"Betty, are you a witch?"

My brows practically hit the roof. Hell, Wesley came straight out with it.

Bettys perfectly set hair sat tight on her head, a crease appearing between her eyes. "A witch? What on earth would make you ask a question like that?"

At first glance, I could be mistaken to think the question hadn't rattled her, until her eyes met mine. In that moment, a flicker deep within her aged orbs told me everything I needed to know.

"Does this locket look familiar to you?" said Skye, holding it in her hand.

Betty didn't answer, instead looking directly at me, asking a question of her own.

"You mentioned this locket was a family heirloom?"

I paused, holding Betty's gaze, her blue-gray eyes full of questions.

I considered my words carefully, unsure how much information to share. "My adoptive mother gave it to me on my twenty-first birthday." It was the truth... just not the entire story. "Why is that?"

"Your adoptive parents," she repeated, more to herself than the room. "Morgan, how old are you?"

An exasperated breath left me. "What difference does that make?"

"Morgan," Tyler warned, his voice low, fingers wrapping around my arm.

I didn't mean for it to sound rude, but patience was never a strength of mine.

I shrugged off Tyler's arm, words spilling from me so fast I could barely gather a breath. "I'm twenty-four. The symbol on this locket matches the symbol in this book. Do you know my parents somehow? *Please,* just tell us what you know."

The room turned silent, everyone turning to Betty.

"What makes you think I would know your parents, dear?" she said carefully, her words smooth. Level, as if she kept them carefully measured.

Wesley lifted to his feet, his arms folded across his chest. "Betty, I know it was you who cast the spell on Morgan. I heard your voice chanting it," he accused.

Her head dipped to the side. "You heard my voice?"

Tyler stepped in, holding his arm in the air. "Betty, can you help us or not?"

Her gaze swept the room before landing on mine.

"Morgan, dear," she said with caution, her voice lowering further. Her gaze swept the room once more before she sighed. "I think you may be my granddaughter."

All the air was sucked from my lungs, my legs wilting beneath me. A warmth circled my waist as Tyler broke my fall, steering me to the couch where I sank into it. The words choked the breath from me, my mind frozen.

Words. They flooded my mind. My mouth moved, but I couldn't produce a single sound. I looked at Tyler in desperation, and he seemed to read my mind, his hand grasping my knee.

His voice came strong and confident. "Betty, what makes you think you could be Morgan's grandmother?"

Her eyes nestled on mine, and I found a comfort in them I hadn't noticed before. "Morgan, were you left at an orphanage as a baby?" she asked softly.

My breath stilled as realization there could be some truth to this. That she could in fact be my grandmother.

"Yes," I breathed, barely loud enough to hear myself. "Yes, I was. How...? How do you know this?" I stammered, a lone tear escaping my lashes.

Betty sighed. "Because, dear, I left you there."

Shock pinned me in place, before words purged from me with force. "I don't understand. Why would you leave me there? How could you leave a helpless baby with no one to look after it?"

Streams of heat coated my cheeks as I rose to my feet with Tyler's help.

Skye's voice came from beside me. "Morgan, I think we need to let Betty speak."

Betty took a step in my direction, and I threw my hands defensively in front of me.

"Morgan, *please,* hear me out. You need to believe me when I say I never wanted to leave you there. I had no other choice. It was the only way to keep you safe."

This wasn't real; it couldn't be. I shook my head.

"Keep her safe from what exactly?" asked Wesley.

Betty frowned. "Morgan, can I ask if you've noticed anything strange happening? Anything you can't quite explain?"

"We wouldn't be asking if we didn't have reason to," Tyler said flatly.

Betty stilled, her finger tapping her forearm. Her shoulders rolled back, chin rising as if a wave of confidence had rolled over her. "Dear, your father made me take you away to keep you from harm."

"From what?" I demanded.

Her expression turned wistful then. "Your father was a great man. He adored you and only wanted the best for you my dear. Your parents are both witches, but your mother became very unstable. She was not of sound mind and started to dabble in dark magic. Your father felt you had a gift so rare he couldn't chance her knowing about it. Couldn't chance your safety."

"And what gift is that?" questioned Wesley.

"Your father believed you had access to the most sought-after magic known to witches. Like I said, it is very rare, and only a handful of witches possess it. Even fewer can handle it. It's obsidian magic, a magic like no other. The ability to call on light or dark magic, and any element that you please, as easy as taking a breath."

Holy crap.

"It skips generations in the same bloodline. Your father's great grandmother possessed this power, and he was certain you would embody it next. He worried your mother would take advantage of your gift if it were to be true, and it had never skipped so many generations before, so he was certain it was to come to you next. He asked me to take you somewhere far away, but I felt I was being tracked, so I had to leave you at the orphanage."

Betty's eyes glazed over, her voice wavering slightly.

"I cast a spell to suppress both our magic, then left you on the doorstep of the orphanage. I had no choice... I couldn't look after you myself with no home, no job. It was my only option. I knew you would be looked after by two loving parents. Fed and watered. Kept safe."

She drew in a long breath.

"Your magic was to return to you when you turned twenty-five, when I knew you would be old enough to fend for yourself. Not even I could sense you or your magic once I left. I never knew where you were. But I would have found you... hired a sensor." She paused, looking at Wesley. "I would have gone to the ends of the earth to find you again, Morgan. I planned to teach you everything, but it seems you found me."

Tears fell freely down my cheeks with the knowledge my father loved me enough to give me up. To keep me from harm.

"That explains why Wesley couldn't sense your magic," Tyler mused, staring pointedly at Wesley, who chose to ignore him.

Betty continued, "As far as I know, your parents are alive. I can tell you everything, but yes, you are a witch. And quite possibly a powerful one, too. Your birthday is soon, if I'm correct?"

I swallowed a large gulp of air, unease prickling my skin. "Yes, on Friday," I said, my voice barely audible.

Skye turned to me, words I couldn't read scattered across her features.

Tyler's voice came from beside me. "So, am I correct in saying that on Friday, the spell is broken?"

Betty nodded. "Yes."

I wasn't one for swearing. Not f-bombs anyway, but *this?* This was worthy of every fucking f-bomb ever invented.

Tyler shifted beside me. "Okay, so we have less than a week to get Morgan as ready as possible for twenty-five years of suppressed magic to come at her in a day."

"And for whatever else may come for her," added Skye grimly.
The room fell into a deafening silence.
I needed to throw up.

Tyler

My feet moved before my brain could register, bolting out the front door after Morgan, but she was fast and had a head start, already halfway down the street.

Her frame disappeared as she rounded the corner ahead of me, and I pushed harder to close the gap between us. Rounding the same corner, my feet faltered, and I whipped on my heel, throwing my head in every direction to find her. The track was straight from here, but she was nowhere in sight.

I slowed to a stop, searching my surroundings when movement caught my eye, spotting her as she ducked behind a large rock on a rise I knew well.

Veering off the road, I followed the narrow trail that became barely visible, long grass brushing my knees as the wind whipped a path through it. The trail soon turned to rocks, and I placed one foot after the other, carefully judging my next steps.

As I got closer, my body froze, feet nailed in place. Air sucked from my lungs, my chest tightening as I stared at the place that held some of my darkest memories.

Morgan stood at the top of an overhang, a gust of wind trailing her dark hair in billows behind her. She was close to the edge. Too close.

"Morgan!" I yelled, and her neck craned to the side, spilling her hair wildly over her face.

Through wisps of hair, even from a distance, I saw the stains of red in her eyes. A life of lies and unanswered questions pooling beneath thick lashes, slowly cascading down her cheeks.

She lowered to the ground, tucking her knees into her chest, staring off into the distance. I needed to get to her.

Letting go of a long breath, my feet clambered up the track as if I were in a dream watching from above, my body lagging like an afterthought. I climbed my way up, settling beside her in silence, a torrent of my own memories rushing at me like a storm's rogue wave, unexpected and forcefully strong.

Visions of Ava's funeral forced their way into my thoughts, remembering how the rain had muddied the ground beneath my boots as I'd stood alongside her casket sheltered underneath a black umbrella.

Fuck. I clenched my hands into fists, the urge to paint the sky with fire so strong, it took every inch of my control to contain it.

"Morgan, talk to me," I choked out, trying to stall my own demons pushing to the surface.

When she spoke, it was to the mountains in the distance, a whisper.

"I just... I just needed to breathe." Her voice was broken. "It's just, too much. I killed my parents, Ty, and now this? Suddenly I'm a witch… and I have a grandmother. And somewhere out there are my *birth* parents. I was barely holding it together, each day molding into the next. But this?… I never thought I would find my *real* family."

I let her soak up the information, breathe it into her lungs. Her new life, that in one week would change, whether she liked it or not.

I focused my breathing. The panic attacks that usually hit in the night, now taking control of me in the worst possible moment. Tear-stained eyes found mine, and I threw my gaze into the distance before they spoke of the storm brewing inside, threatening to break me.

Another vision of Ava's pale face flashed before me, blood matting her hair from the two puncture holes in her neck. She didn't deserve to leave this world in such brutality.

"Tyler…?" Morgan said softly, drawing closer.

I slammed my eyes shut.

"Tyler, what is it? What's wrong?"

One. Breathe in. Two. Breathe out. Three. Breathe in. Four. Breathe out.

No. Not here. Not now. Not like this.

Five. Breathe in. Six. Breathe out.

A guttural noise came from somewhere within me, and I hung my head between my knees, my fists balled tight, too afraid to release them. Too afraid of what magic might explode from this torrent of emotion clawing from my chest.

"Tyler?" The heat of her palm warmed my shoulder blade, and a calm fell over me.

She turned my face to hers, her kind eyes colliding with mine. They felt like home. Like the only sunshine in this shithole town of stone.

"She died," I choked out, shaking my head as if it would rid the words from me. "Because of me."

The last words came as a whisper as I drowned in the guilt suffocating my heart. Words I'd never had the balls to say before.

"I'm so sorry," I sputtered. "This place, it's..." An agonizing sound left me as I fought between wanting to comfort Morgan and fighting the panic building inside me.

"What? Tyler, talk to me. Is this the woman... in the photo?" Morgan grabbed my hand, squeezing it tight.

Another breath.

I nodded. "Ava... she was human."

Morgan's hand fell to my thigh. "Tell me about her." Her voice was tender, conveying no judgment.

My eyes pulled to hers once more. How could this woman be so selfless, to care about me right now when her entire world was in chaos? My palm released, and I ran my free hand through my hair until it rested on the back of my neck.

Morgan turned her body to mine, her brown eyes absorbing my words with an intensity I hadn't seen before.

A shaky breath tore through my lungs. "I fell in love with her. Made a bad call, introduced her to our world." I paused, not wanting to part with the words. "A vampire killed her."

"I'm so sorry," she whispered.

"I used to come here after it happened," I continued, rubbing my knuckles together. "Some of my darkest moments were sitting right here, on this rock. I haven't been back, I couldn't." My eyes found hers. "I'm sorry. I didn't mean for this to happen."

Morgan smiled softly beside me. "Thank you for sharing such a personal thing with me. I'm sorry you had to go through that."

"Don't be sorry," I said with a shrug. "Life is cruel. I'd been meaning to come here but couldn't bring myself to do it."

She didn't speak, her thumb instead drawing thoughtful circles on my thigh. The wind scoured through the trees as it whipped over the cove, my eyes closing under Morgan's touch.

It was like nothing I'd felt before, each caress staining me with her own imprint. Could it be real? The bond talked about among the supernatural that I'd never believed in? A bond I'd scoffed at. I guess not having felt it myself, it was hard to believe such a thing existed.

I couldn't be sure, but this was so different from anything I'd ever experienced. Even with Ava.

I drew my eyes to hers. "I'm sorry this happened. Of all times, now. I can't control these... moments. I've never told anyone about them." The panic attacks. It was nice having someone here.

"Tyler, it's okay, really. I'm glad you did," she reassured me.

I couldn't help but smile, relieved to have her support. "How are you feeling?" I asked, keen to change the subject.

Morgan looked out over the cove, at the lapping waves in the distance. "I'm alright. Just overwhelmed." Her expression held the weight of so many thoughts I knew were going through her head.

I knew the feeling. "That's understandable." I squeezed her hand, and her warmth spread into every part of me. "You may have a grandmother back home wanting to get to know her granddaughter."

She nodded. "I was just thinking that. This whole thing is so surreal."

"We are all here for you and will help in any way we can."

It was a promise, and one I intended to keep.

I looked to the sky where dark clouds loomed overhead, drops of rain starting to fall.

"Thanks." She warmed me with her smile again. "I think I'm going to need it. I feel bad for running out on Betty. You're right; she's probably waiting for me."

We made our way down the rise, where I paused at the bottom, steering my gaze to the side. A vine of periwinkle covered the ground, its violet flowers scattered throughout. What was it even doing flowering in winter?

I turned to face Morgan behind me. "Do you mind waiting here for a moment?" I grazed her hand with my thumb. "There's something I need to do."

Her head dipped to the side. "Sure."

Morgan rested on a rock as I strode over to the periwinkle, plucking off a lone flower, then made my way over to a small cemetery that lay within sight of the track. I hadn't been back since Ava's funeral, the scattering of dirt as it landed on her casket still fresh in my mind, as if it were only yesterday that we'd laid her to rest.

A layer of thick moss clung to the narrow footpath leading up to the grave site, shadows dampening the air from loosely scattered branches above, clinging to winter. A wrought iron fence surrounded the modest cemetery of gravestones, pushing from the ground in all shapes and sizes. Many stood crooked, others cracked.

The iron gate groaned in protest as I pushed it open, clanging shut behind me as I passed through, one foot in front of the other, making my way to Ava's grave.

Her headstone appeared to have barely aged, only muted in color over time with dust nestling in the intricately carved scripture, buried into the stone. Not a day had passed since her death that I hadn't wished my life had been taken in place of hers.

I hated myself for being so selfish. For thinking I could protect a human in my world.

But most of all, I hated the vampires. I didn't know if hate even covered it. A word so brashly used, it had lost its sharp edges.

The overgrown grass pressed into the ground beneath my knee, and I rolled the periwinkle stem between my thumb and pointer finger, spinning it slowly.

One by one I plucked off a violet petal, letting them fall to her grave. One. Two. Three. Four. Five. In my palm lay the remaining stem, and I stripped it back until the fairy toothbrush, as Ava had called it, remained. I remember laughing when she first showed me the tiny stem that indeed resembled a fairy's toothbrush. I'd shaken my head in disbelief.

Placing it in my palm, my breath forced it into the air, where it landed with the petals. My palm landed on the grass beside the dissected flower, and I stilled, shutting my eyes. A raspy *craw* from a raven scraped the silence.

A tightness bobbed in my throat as my knees left the ground again, turning on my heel.

Returning to Morgan, she held out her hand, and I let her warmth press into my palm.

Caring eyes found mine. "Was that her grave?" she asked, her free hand breezing up my forearm.

I offered a tight smile. "Yeah, I haven't been back since the funeral. I hope you don't mind."

Her palm squeezed mine, that same calm spreading through me again. "I don't mind at all," she said without hesitation, locking her gaze to mine.

We walked in comfortable silence, back along the dirt track until we hit the footpath. Rain dampened the ground creating *that* smell I had loved since I was a kid.

I sucked in a deep breath. "I love that smell... When rain first hits the ground, I mean."

"I think you either love it or hate it." Morgan shrugged beside me.

I gave her a sidelong look. "And your verdict is?"

She crinkled her nose. "Not a fan," she said with a laugh.

I playfully scoffed, kicking aside some leaves in our path. "Oh, come on, how could you not? It's nature, something that could never be replicated if you tried."

"Very true," she mused, giving me a nudge. "Still not a fan."

I laughed, loving how honest she was, not afraid to voice her own opinion.

"What do you think I should call her?" She turned her head to mine. "Betty? Gran? Maybe it's too soon."

I shrugged, a smile on my face. "Call her whatever you feel comfortable with, I guess. I can't imagine she would be displeased with Gran, though."

"Hmmm," she agreed, seeming lost in thought.

When we entered the house, there was a silence I didn't expect. Morgan moved to the kitchen counter where a note lay and she picked it up, walking over to the couch. She unfolded it and read aloud.

"Dearest Morgan. This is a lot for you to take in, so I've left for the evening. Catch up soon. Betty." Her shoulders dropped, a sadness spoiling her irises.

I could tell she was disappointed, and I longed to see her smile again. Sitting beside her, I turned my body to hers, giving her my full attention.

"Maybe a night's rest to take everything in might not be a bad thing," I offered.

She sighed. "Yeah, I guess you're right. It's been an emotional day for both of us." She covered my hand with hers.

I glanced down to where our skin made contact, gathering a breath. "I'm really sorry about before. I never wanted you to see me like that."

Until now, when it came to talking about Ava's death, I'd been a closed book. No one had managed to crack me at the spine. But here was Morgan, sitting in front of me, having witnessed parts of me no one else had. She had become my strength in ways she would never know.

She angled her body towards me, her eyes searching mine with a vulnerability that scared me, stripping me bare. "Tyler, it's okay. We all have our moments. Hell, I've had plenty." Her thumb stroked a soft line over the top of my hand.

I steadied a full breath. "I just mean I would have told you in my own time."

Morgan nodded. "I understand. Really, I do. You've been through so much. We both have. Don't be sorry. Whatever this is..." Her free hand motioned between us. "If it's not feeling right," she faltered, "or you need more time..."

There was a vulnerability to her words, my heart pulsing proudly to see her so unguarded, so trusting of me.

Haunted by Ava's death for years now, I hadn't let myself get this close to anyone, but I knew it was time I opened my heart to someone else, and I was certain if souls did go somewhere after death that Ava would want me to be happy.

I was done with stolen glances and guilty kisses.

Locking my eyes to hers, my fire element simmered beneath my skin.

"I don't need more time," I said finally.

Her doe eyes filled with embers as they held mine, and moving closer, my palm caressed her jaw, her eyelids flicking shut.

When I covered her mouth with mine, desire burned through me, searing my insides as it swept a path through every fiber, every nerve within. A mewl escaped her lips as I drew her mouth apart, cautious as her hand stiffened on my thigh.

Morgan's hesitancy bristled my skin for only a moment before her fingers dug into me, like she was afraid to let go. It felt so right, a knowing deep inside that would no longer be buried or ignored.

I pulled away, our foreheads resting together. Steel gray chasing chocolate brown, our breathing synching.

"Come here," I ordered, pulling her into my lap and kissing her once more. No holding back.

I slid my tongue between her lips, commanding her to open up for me, and we met in a delicate tease, slipping our mark on the other. She rocked her hips into mine, deepening our kiss, and my hands fisted her ass, drawing her closer until she pressed firm against me.

Her hands clawed at the nape of my neck, sweeping through my hair, and I matched her urgency, kissing her with a passion we had denied ourselves for too long.

I smiled against her lips. "You're borderline addictive, you know that?"

A sound came from her, a giggle on a smile as she teased my bottom lip, nipping it.

A feeling so unknown to me pulsed within. To feel this way about a woman was a possessive, frightening thing.

Silky curves swallowed my palms as they glided beneath her top, her back curling against me, forcing her closer. Her reaction to my slightest touch hardened my dick against my zipper, the ache for her touch turning desire into desperate need as I kissed her again.

My name fell from her lips with a shudder. "Ty," she whispered against my mouth, eyes locked on mine.

I chuckled and feathered her hair through my fingers, breathing into her ear. "Where's your room?" I murmured.

She motioned down the hallway. "That way."

Before I got the chance to stand, her hand palmed the front of my jeans, my dick throbbing under her touch as it pushed against denim. She hungrily undid my fly, and a groan ripped from me as her hand worked over me through the material of my tight boxers.

I inhaled a quick breath at her touch. "What are you doing to me?" I murmured between kisses, sinking back into the couch in utter bliss.

Her touch sent my skin on fire, our hushed breaths filling the air.

"You like that?" she breathed against my cheek.

"Gods damn, yes." I hissed, not wanting her to stop.

Her hands moved over me through the fabric, and I drank in her scent, burying my face into her neck. Vanilla and musk stained her skin, my senses drinking in every drop of her. Thoughts of my naked flesh in her hands consumed my mind, my dick throbbing as she wound me further, a coil close to its breaking point.

I lifted her from beneath and she gasped in surprise, her hands wrapping around my neck, legs circling my waist as I took us down the hall in search of her bedroom. My mouth never left hers as we stumbled into a wall, a giggle sliding from her lips into mine.

"This one?" I raised an eyebrow at her, backing her into the wall.

She laughed again. "Yes," she said, staring at me with playful eyes.

Twisting the handle, I nudged it open with my knee, loosening my hold on her until she slid down my front to the floor. I walked her backwards, further into the room, and cupped her face in my hands, kissing her again, deeply, as if I could get lost in her.

Pulling away, my thumbs caressed her cheeks. "Do you have any idea how long I've wanted this? To be with you and not feel like I shouldn't?"

I ran my thumb over her bottom lip.

"To kiss you."

I cupped her breast, her eyes flicking shut.

"To touch you?"

I trailed my finger down her midriff.

"To taste you?"

Her eyes flew wide, cheeks flushed, and I dragged my mouth over hers again. She drew in a quick breath at my dick digging into her stomach and pulling away, she stared up at me. I drank in her lust-filled eyes, heavy lids, and dark lashes.

She was so damn beautiful. And she was *mine*.

"I've wanted this from the moment I saw you," I admitted, the truth hammering into me unexpectedly.

Morgan nipped at my neck, her fingers skimming the nape of my hairline. "I've wanted this too," she breathed.

My eyes drowned in hers. Two dark storms, begging for release.

My heart ached.

My dick throbbed.

Morgan had consumed me entirely.

Right then, those doe eyes stole my heart. Something inside me clawed to get to her.

Our mouths crashed together, and everything but her faded to black. We could have been anywhere; I didn't care. I kissed her like there was no tomorrow, like this would be our first and last, giving her all of me.

I edged her back until her legs hit the foot of the bed and she fell back onto it without breaking eye contact.

"Look at you..." I praised, admiring her from above as I moved over her.

Her gaze flooded with desire, commanding what she needed without speaking a damn syllable. I slid my arm beneath her back, hoisting her further up the bed as her hands clawed at my top, finding naked skin underneath.

Her touch sent me into a wildfire, and I slid my tongue into her mouth, heat exploding inside me. Gods, the way we molded together.

Pressing my body into hers, I ground against her, and she moaned lightly beneath me. My hand slid underneath her top, up silky skin, and she helped me pull it over her head, exposing white cotton etched with a trim of lace covering her breasts.

I groaned with approval. So fresh and unexpected. Like my naughty little secret. I'd expected black, only because it seemed to be her color of choice.

The fabric danced over my fingertips until I unclasped it beneath her, my eyes taking in her beauty from above. I lowered my mouth, lapping at a pert nipple with my tongue. Morgan hummed her appreciation beneath me, her hips mindlessly rising and falling against mine.

"Kiss me," she whispered, tugging at my shoulders, and our mouths connected once more. Our tongues danced, teasing and tasting what we thought we never could.

I spread kisses over her collarbone. "You're going to be the absolute end of me," I murmured, moving back to her mouth.

She smiled against my lips, palming my dick through my pants. "You're welcome."

I unbuttoned her jeans, sliding them off her, my breath shuddering at the sight of the matching white thong covering her.

"This," I said, my eyes moving to the lacy thong as my hand traveled the length of her leg, "is a pleasant surprise."

Morgan smirked. "You like them?"

My hand teased the edge of the fabric, my brows rising.

"Do I like them?" I kissed her mouth again, dragging my teeth over her bottom lip. "I fucking love them."

I skirted a finger beneath the barely-there fabric of her thong, causing her to whimper.

"Please," she pleaded in a breathy gasp.

A smile tugged on the corner of my mouth. "Please what, little doe?"

She moved against my hand, but I wouldn't let her have it.

"Please, I need more. Touch me."

I dragged her thong to the side, sliding a finger through her center, and cursed. "So wet for me," I praised, slipping a finger into her soaked pussy and her warmth swallowed me.

A rush of breath filled her lungs as she held my gaze. "Hhm-mmmm," she moaned, pulling my mouth down to hers.

She felt like fucking paradise on a balmy day against my hand, and I admired her writhing against my touch. When I added another, her hips bucked in response as I curled them against her in a tortuous rhythm.

"Open your eyes," I commanded, and she obeyed.

Wide, hazy eyes stared back at me as I dragged her closer to release, one hand on her cheek, one in her pussy, our eyes colliding, unblinking.

"I want to see you fall apart," I said, my face inches from hers. "I want this memory etched in your mind, knowing it was me who made you come undone, without even taking these pretty little panties off you."

I stared down at her, admiring the way her chest rode waves as her breath became uneven.

Burning desire pinched the space between us, and when my thumb found her clit, her hips hiked, her hands clenching white linen as she climbed her peak.

"Don't stop. Please..." she begged.

When her orgasm claimed her, pleasure spilled from her in quick breaths, her core shuddering against my hand. It was the most beautiful thing I'd ever seen. But I wasn't finished.

I pulled my top over my head, and she stared at my naked chest, scouring every inch of me like I could expect marks to appear in the morning.

I slid Morgan's thong down her creamy thighs, kicking off the bottom half of my clothing until our eyes devoured each other, drinking in the other bare. She peered up at me, eyes still hazy as she took in my nakedness.

I felt every slide of her gaze as it traveled over my frame, inch by inch, as if she were marking out her own map on my skin. The prickle of her stare traced down to my dick, and she sucked in a breath as she took in my length.

I palmed it, heavy in my hand, and a smile curved her lips.

I chuckled. "Like what you see?"

She grew bolder in that moment. "Yeah, I do," she said, replacing my hand with hers.

Morgan worked me over, flesh on flesh, and I slammed my eyes shut, taking in the moment.

The first time someone touched you was always a good time. But this? This was like an explosion in my blood, forcing its way through me. I desperately held on, never having had to will myself to keep it together this way before, lost in the caress of her hands.

As if Morgan knew, she eased off, her thumb running lazy circles around the head instead.

I couldn't take it any longer and sat up on my knees.

Moving over her again until her back hit the bed, my hand ran the length of her body, admiring her.

I bolted my eyes to hers, my hand drawing circles on her knee. "I want to see you. All of you."

A blush rushed to her cheeks, but she held my eyes with that same boldness.

"Please," I added, and this time she didn't shy away. Her knees fell apart, and I drank in the most addictive part of her.

My eyes heated. "God dammit," I groaned.

"Like what you see?" she said coyly, and I chuckled at the line that was now becoming an in-house joke between us.

I gave an appreciative nod. "You know I do."

When I claimed her mouth with mine again, our bodies glided together. Skin on skin, hands exploring and tongues tasting.

My dick was dangerously close to her sex, and she motioned to her bedside drawer. I swiftly found what I needed, rolling the condom over me, certain she didn't know about the monthly herbal remedy most woman took in Cutters Cove to prevent pregnancy.

Morgan raked a hand over the stubble on my jaw, watching as I slid my cock through her arousal before slowly sinking into her.

A tight breath left her lips as I stretched her to the hilt, my forehead resting on hers.

"You okay?" I whispered.

"Yeah, go slow," she said between breaths.

I pumped into her slowly, letting her adjust until her hips met my movements with need. She felt exquisite, so tight around my dick and so fucking perfect.

"My fucking gods," I groaned.

I sank into her harder this time, lost in a selfish greed of my own, a possessive need to claim her as mine.

She moaned as I pulled out and slid into her again, not taking my eyes off her, wisps of hair coating her face. I pushed them away, covering her lips with mine as she fisted my hair. I couldn't get enough of her as she wildly grabbed my shoulders before sinking her hands into my ass.

I hitched her right leg over my shoulder, and a hurried breath left her in response to the new depth. Her mouth fell open in silent pleasure.

Words rushed from her. "Ohmigod... *Ty*."

"Fuuuck," I cursed as her walls clenched around me.

My thumb swept over her clit, and she held me tighter, the friction pulling me into a different world where all I could see, hear, and smell was her. Invading every sense of my being, like she was fucking my soul.

"Tell me when. Come with me," I pleaded, desperately holding on for her.

"I'm so close," she cried out, meeting my every thrust.

I slicked my thumb, and it glistened as I pressed her bud harder this time, circling it with intent.

Morgan writhed beneath me. "Oh god, I'm... *now*."

Holy. Fucking. Hell.

She milked me until we both lay crumpled in a heap together, the comedown of our sex like our own addictive drug.

I trailed my fingers over the outline of her hips, curved perfectly into her waist.

"Do you feel that?" I asked.

"Yes," she replied softly. "When you touch me, my skin comes alive."

My eyes widened. "You too?"

Still hazy from her climax, her eyes stripped me raw, peeling back every layer. "Yes. It's incredible."

She rested her head into the curve of my shoulder as I smiled into the dimly lit room.

Her fingers traced the ridges of my chest, inspecting it like one would a piece of art, and when darkness swallowed daylight, I stared at her as moonlight danced over us.

She was perfect. And she was mine.

Morgan

"Dear, how are you today?" Betty's gaze drowned with concern, moving over me as if assessing for wounds. Her normally cheerful manner was a more subdued note today, her voice kind yet cautious.

We sat on a bench seat that rested alongside the river, watching as it meandered through town, in no hurry to reach the ocean. I knew Betty's mention of a morning walk together was her way of trying to gauge how I was feeling about everything.

"I'm okay, I think..." I turned to meet her worried stare and gathered a breath of courage. "I mean, it's not every day you find out you're a witch, the lady whose house you've just moved into is your grandmother, and that your birth parents may still be alive." I let out a light laugh; you couldn't make this up if you tried.

Betty smoothed down the lavender dress she wore at the knees, shifting in her seat. "Ah yes, that is not to be expected in one's life, let alone one day. I must say, you seem to be handling it okay?"

She inspected me closely, her scrutiny rushing over my skin. My head lifted to the sky, where a flock of birds flew above the trees in V formation.

I shrugged. "I guess it's going to take some time to get used to, and to get to know you of course."

Betty nodded. "Of course, my dear. These things will all take time. I'm just truly sorry about everything, but it was your father's wishes, and as a mother, I couldn't not do everything he needed to keep you safe."

I knew she meant every word, a tension releasing from her frame as she spoke.

I veered my gaze back to hers. "What was my father like? Could you tell me about him?"

Her irises glistened at thoughts of her son, a smile wrinkling the corners of her eyes.

"Your father's name is Gerald. He was a farmer, and a mighty good one too. He liked to live off the land where possible and had a marvelous eye when hunting."

I listened with enthusiasm as Betty spoke about my father, about his kind and caring nature, her words sending a fuzzy feeling winding around my heart.

"I love hearing this; tell me more. What happened with my mother?"

Suddenly, her eyes dimmed, saddened.

Betty's hand landed on my knee. "Morgan, you have to remember, your mother wasn't well. She had... severe lapses in time where she would just sit and stare at nothing in particular. Then there were other times, when she..." Betty paused, collecting a breath. "Your mother struggled with motherhood, my dear, it's a big adjustment for anyone."

I frowned. "What did she do?"

A single tear slid down her cheek.

She drew in a harsh breath. "Your father found her one evening about to take her life. She was about to take *both* your lives, believed if she sacrificed herself and took you with her, that there was another *world* as she called it, waiting for her."

I froze, and all that filled my ears was the continuous rhythm of my heart reminding me the story did not stop there. That I was well and truly alive.

I gulped down the wad of air lodged in my throat.

Betty continued. "Your father had her committed."

Why would my father order Betty to take me away from him if my mother was locked up in a looney bin?

I clenched my hands together, knotting them between my thighs. "But..."

Betty's hands gestured into the air. "*Somehow*, Helena convinced the psychiatric hospital that she was of sound mind, and they let her go within a month. Soon after, she started asking questions about your father's lineage, and the power passed down throughout generations that could possibly come to you."

Helena. My mother's name is Helena.

"Between that, and this maddening talk of hers about this other world, he felt it was best to remove you from such an unstable situation. That is when he told me to leave and take you with me. He could not risk your safety, Morgan."

I couldn't form words. My mind was a jumbled mess of new knowledge. I pulled my hands from between my thighs to find them clammy and pale. They were quickly scooped up and cradled between Betty's own.

"You need to know that this was a tremendously difficult decision for your father. Believe me when I say it ripped his heart open to do so, but he had to. I'm *so* sorry Morgan, but it had to be."

I nodded, blinking away tears that threatened to fall.

I stared into my *grandmother's* weeping eyes.

"Where are they now?" I questioned, with unsteady breath.

Her lips pressed into a hard line. Her head dipping to our hands clutched together between us then returning to mine.

"I don't know for certain, but my guess would be back at our family homestead, which is a two-day's drive from here. I'm hoping to find someone who could check for us, as we can't risk being seen ourselves."

"Wow. This is all so hard to believe." I mused.

"Well believe it my dear, it is all *very* real." Wrinkles creased her forehead, as her expression hardened. "If your father was right, and you have been gifted obsidian magic, the threat to your life is very real, Morgan. You need to know that."

I nodded in understanding, unease churning my stomach.

Betty shifted in her seat, giving me her full attention. "When your magic comes to you, mine will also return to me. It is of utmost importance that you need to stay here, in Cutters Cove, until we can teach you everything there is to know about your gift. You are in the best place, surrounded by myself and your new group of friends to support you."

I felt the weight of the world lay heavy on my shoulders, shoveling me into the ground.

Had I suddenly become a liability to Tyler? To my friends? Was having this 'gift' as Betty mentioned putting everyone around me in danger also?

I let go of a steady breath. "I understand. Thank you for everything, Betty."

"You are most welcome, dear. I know it wasn't the most pleasant of chats, but now that we have that out of the way, I do hope things will be a lot more *enjoyable*."

She gave a final squeeze of my hand before standing.

As we went our separate ways, I had the nagging urge to find out as much as I could about witches and their history. About covens. Anything that could give me a fighting chance at fending off anything that threatened myself or my friends. I knew just the place to start.

I was determined to do some research of my own, as I tugged my jacket tighter around me, heading in the direction of the library. I knew it was on the outskirts of Cutters Cove, on one of the quieter back roads according to the town map, and I didn't mind the walk.

As it came into view, my gaze roamed over the building, a manor with walls of stone painted a regal cream.

Its surrounding grounds were immaculately landscaped, with boxed hedging and a large water fountain at its center. A striking difference against the allure of the thick forest breaching its rear. A wrought-iron balcony framed the second story above the entrance where I stood, a sign on the door reading '*Library*.'

I heaved my weight against it, moving it open, where instantly my senses became awash of aged tales buried within its walls for no doubt centuries. I loved libraries for their smell alone and inhaled its history as if it were the only thing I was to survive on.

"May I help you?" a male voice asked.

I nearly jumped a foot, my hand firmly planted on my chest, not expecting the voice that seemed to have come from nowhere.

Spinning on my heel, I found a striking set of dark eyes staring at me from behind a large desk. They had a familiarity about them I couldn't place.

"Hi. I uh…"

Shit. How did I ask where the secret supernatural department was without actually asking the question?

My gaze flew around the library's interior as I stared in wonder at the mahogany curves arching high into the ceiling. I felt the prickle of the librarian's stare as he followed me, watching as I surveyed the shelves full of books lining the walls in every direction.

It was then I noted the lack of people around. Something about that gnawed at my sides.

I cleared my throat. "I'm looking for a book on the Salem Witch Trials, please. It's for a history piece I'm doing for uni," I added quickly, as if to justify myself.

For a moment, he didn't speak. The angles cut into the stranger's jaw twitched. His expression remained impassive, his gaze passing over me through a delicate set of glasses perched on the bridge of his nose.

He finally stood, motioning to the far corner of the impressive room, his footsteps steering us away from his desk. "This way."

He slowed halfway along a wall, his finger skimming book spines until he plucked one out.

"I think this will do it. Let me help you check this out."

His stare, cold and hollow, left mine as he retreated to the large mahogany desk before completing the process. As he passed the book to me, our fingers grazed as it slid between us, a bone-chilling cold jumping from his skin to mine.

I quickly pulled my hand away, sliding it into my over-the-shoulder bag. "Thanks."

He stood again, pressing his hands into his pant pockets. "Let me know if it's not quite what you're after. There may be something else I can find."

"I appreciate it," I said, turning on my heel and heading for the door in the direction of home. A shiver ran down my spine as I looked back over my shoulder at the manor, wondering what exactly it was about the place that caused the unease inside of me to spike.

I welcomed the afternoon breeze as it purged the feeling from me.

When I got home, I sprawled on my bed, ready to learn as much as I could. The book was thick, but I was a fast reader. I would devour it in a week easily. Within the hour, I slapped the pages shut, horrid streams of images rifting through my thoughts.

Visions I couldn't come to terms with, let alone grasp the concept that this was a sickening history of my kind. I couldn't read any more, at least not now; its content had placed a foul taste in both my mood and mouth.

I placed the book on my bedside table, deciding it would be better read another time.

***

That night, the mood at Jinxed was more lowkey. Turns out I still got the job, even after my magical mishap... Perks of knowing the local supernaturals.

People mingled in groups on the old couches, some in booths. Others swayed to the song that filtered through the bar, and I found myself doing the same. I picked up another glass from the dishwasher, swiping it with a tea towel as I mindlessly hummed along to the lyrics.

I was finally getting my head around the place. Only, now I *knew* things. Things I didn't know before. The 'supernatural' as Tyler called it.

I glanced around the bar, playing my secret game of what used to be kill, marry, fuck, almost snorting at my naivety.

It had quickly changed to vamp, witch, or human. No doubt there were more, too.

If I was honest, it was harder than I thought. I mean, the witch that only last night had his lips on mine was a grease monkey.

A smile played on my lips at the thought of Tyler in a singlet and coveralls, covered in grease marks. Note to self, visit him at work one of these days.

He caught my gaze from across the bar, and I lifted my brows at him, a subtle smile in his direction. He fired a knowing look my way.

Discrete, but I didn't miss the heart-pounding moment his eyes held mine before he turned his attention to the guys again.

"You look deep in thought…" came Reid's voice from behind me, and I glanced over my shoulder at him as he walked towards me.

I shrugged. "I was just trying to figure out, you know, how you tell who is *what* around here."

"Ah," he said, leaning a hip into the bar, folding his muscular arms across his chest. "That's easy once you're in the know."

His gaze veered to the doorman at the entrance. A guy who was taller than most, his shoulders broader than Tyler's, and that was a statement alone.

Reid nodded towards him. "Werewolf. They're naturally larger than the rest of us, and most have an attitude to match. You do *not* want to piss them off," he said.

My lips pursed. "Right. Got it."

"Vamps aren't often seen in here." Reid said then, looking back at me once more. "But when they are, you may not know when you see one. Not all are pale, as the tales are false; some can walk in the sun. But be warned, as their faces are made to attract their prey, even when some are centuries old."

My brows hit the roof. "Seriously?"

He nodded.

"And because I know you're going to ask, their typical main course is human blood, but if they haven't fed in a while, their second choice is a special blend of witch blood."

Fear traced down my spine, remembering how close Jett had come to me, and it dawned on me that I was his prey that night.

If not for Tyler turning up, I may have been as good as dead.

"Witches are harder to spot. There are no broomsticks obviously," Reid said with a laugh, and I did the same. "We blend in, and that's how we prefer things. Only a sensor mage like Wes can sense if someone is a witch."

I blew out a breath. "Wow. Okay, that's a lot to take in."

He shrugged. "That's just the tip of the iceberg. You'll learn more as time goes on and once the spell is broken. You turn twenty-five on Friday, right?"

I nodded. "Yeah. Not sure if I should call it a birthday or my reckoning," I said, laughing nervously. This was all happening so fast, it was hard to take in.

Reid settled his elbows on the bar beside me, surveying the room. "I'm sure you'll be fine." He turned his attention back to me. "If anything, maybe your gift might be super sensitive for a while until you learn to control it."

I bit my lip. "What was it like for you? Learning to control yours?"

Reid stiffened slightly. "A bit like your gift, mine is rare. I'm a blood mage, meaning my blood can heal others."

My brows raised. "That *is* special."

He raised a shoulder, wrinkling his nose. "Like any gift, it has its pros and cons," he retorted.

"How can healing people have a con?"

He chuckled lightly. "You have a lot to learn around here." He patted me on the back. "Just concentrate on yourself for now."

He was right, though. Obsidian magic was apparently in my blood, and it would come for me, whether I liked it or not. My stomach flipped over on itself again, as it had been all day, unsure what would become of it.

Reid finished serving a customer, turning to me when they were out of earshot. "Have you taken any self-defense classes before? It may be worth considering."

A nervous laugh surfaced again. I didn't know Reid very well, having only worked with him once, but I got the feeling he was sincere.

"Ah, no. Protecting myself from crazies hasn't exactly been high on my list of priorities."

He eyed me sideways as he wiped a rag over the bar. "Maybe Tyler could teach you. I'm sure he wouldn't mind."

I fought the urge to narrow my eyes at him. Did he suspect something was going on between us? Admittedly, there had been the occasional public touch, and Tyler hadn't disguised his protectiveness towards me, but we'd kept to ourselves for the most part.

"Speak of the Devil!" he said, turning his attention away from me, and I spun to see Tyler approaching from the far side of the bar.

My insides warmed at the sight of him. Wearing jeans and a black jacket, he had a subtle edge about him that sent a shiver of approval through me. His gaze undid me, as if he could see right through every stitch of my clothing, exposing me bare.

Tyler conjured feelings within me, so genuine, so raw, that if I didn't have both eyes open, I wouldn't trust it to be real.

Stormy irises disguised the moment. Our secret, for now.

He rested on the bar stool across from us. "My ears are burning," he said, hinting to the fact that he'd heard his name in our conversation.

Reid nodded at him. "Ty."

Tyler lifted his chin in his direction. "Reid," he said, before turning his attention to me. "Hey." His lip quirked up into a grin.

"Hey." I smiled at him, feeling the warmth of his presence in every part of me. "Fending off the groupies, I see," I teased, nodding toward a group of girls sitting in the bar that watched his every move.

He chuckled. "Something like that. Never was a fan of the young ones."

He gave me a knowing look that warmed my insides. The good parts.

Reid leaned against the bar beside me. "I was just saying that you could help teach Morgan some self-defense moves."

Tyler's brows lifted, his eyes shifting to mine.

Reid coughed. "Being her neighbor and all."

I grabbed the edge of the bar with a scowl at how obvious he was being.

He lifted his hands in the air. "Just trying to help." He smirked.

Tyler casually leaned an arm on the bar, the roped veins in his hand flexing at the movement. "Yeah, of course. That's a great idea."

"Really, you don't need to," I insisted.

I was sure I saw a flicker of amusement behind those stormy grays, no doubt thinking about what positions that would get us into. "Guys, this is too much," I argued, my mind a disorder of thoughts and feelings.

Betty's words rang loud in my ears, her warning grating my nerves.

Right now, I wanted to snuggle up with Tyler and pretend this wasn't happening, but it seemed reality would not allow me to just *be*. Not time, not Betty, and certainly not these two, currently hell bent on convincing me to throw punches at Tyler's limbs.

Tyler lowered his voice, so the conversation stayed between the three of us. "No, it's not. If your gift is as rare as Betty says it is, you never know who or what for that matter may be after it."

I let out a long sigh. "Okay, okay," I gave in, pointing at Tyler. "*Maybe* I might let you show me some stuff."

Tyler nodded "Tomorrow it is then."

Reid's arm landed on my shoulder. "I'm going to take my break. I'll be out the back if you need me." With that, he disappeared through the kitchen doors, leaving us alone.

Tyler adjusted his jacket. "So, what time do you finish up tonight? I'll walk you home."

I couldn't help but think he came here *only* for that reason. Hiding my smile, my heart lurched at the thought.

"Oh, will you now?" I teased, wondering if this was something he did on the regular.

His tone hardened further. "I'm not letting you walk home on your own."

I leaned forward, as if to whisper to him. "Do you always walk the bar staff home at the end of the night?" I bantered, flashing him a coy smile.

Tyler smirked. "Never. Maybe I might need to make this a new thing," he lifted a brow, raising his glass to his mouth and emptying his drink. "In all seriousness though, it's not safe for anyone to be alone out there."

I tipped my head to the side in pointed agreement. "You could be a serial killer for all I know," I said, toying with him.

"Trust me when I say I'm the least of your problems out there."

I sighed at his seriousness, taking the empty glass from him. "I have an hour left. Can I get you another drink while you wait?"

"Thanks, just another beer will do," he said with a guarded smile.

Tyler straightened, scanning the room, jaw twitching. He seemed nervous, on edge even.

I arched a brow as I filled his glass. "Is everything okay?"

His knuckles whitened as he clenched his fist, worry lines settling on his forehead. "I just worry... about you."

"Well, you shouldn't. I'll be fine," I tried to assure him as I slid the drink over.

"You don't know that." He scanned the bar full of schmoozing patrons. "Anyone could be after your magic, Morgan. We can't let our guard down. Not here, not anywhere."

***

After my shift, we walked the path home, a chill winding itself around my neck. I gathered my hair closer to my skin to protect me from its harsh breath.

I laced my fingers through Tyler's. "I've never had a guy walk me home before," I said, playfully swinging our arms between us.

A half grin spread over his face, and he spiraled his free hand in front of him like royalty. "The honor is all mine," he said with a slight bow.

I looked up at him, a good foot taller than myself. The clouds had parted, and a full moon filtered the sky behind him, leaving his features shadowed. One of the street lanterns flickered down the street ahead of us, and his attention turned to it for a heartbeat, scanning the street ahead.

My spine crawled with caution. "Is someone there?" I asked.

After a long moment, he gave my hand a squeeze. "I don't think so, but stay close."

I held his hand tighter, moving into his warmth.

"Never walk home on your own, okay? If you ever need a ride, just call me," he offered.

I sighed, nodding in agreement. I really needed to get myself a car. Or a bike.

"Thank you, yeah, I get it. It's insane how fast vampires move; I could never outrun them. I find it hard to comprehend them walking around town, mingling with everyone else. It's crazy."

Tyler kept his gaze alert, continuously watching the shadows.

"It is, but that's life here," he said, his tone distracted, alert. "Friday's going to come around before we know it, so let's at least give you a fighting chance at whatever is headed our way. Reid's right; self-defense is a good idea."

We rounded the final corner, and our houses came into view. Relief spread throughout me at the sight of them.

I was sure as shit never walking home alone.

"Our way?" I said, staring up at him with a raised brow.

Tyler nodded. "Yeah, our way. We're in this together. You don't have to do this alone."

I smiled. It was a comfort to know I had Tyler in my corner. He had somehow become a strength I never knew I needed.

We climbed the steps of my creaky front porch, pausing in front of the entrance when Tyler circled his arms around my waist. He pushed a stray hair behind my ears.

"I have something I need to tell you," he stated, his voice tainted with uncertainty.

I skimmed his forearms with my hands, my head tilting with interest. "And what's that?"

His lips pressed together as he drew in a breath, releasing it sharply. "There's this event on Saturday night. As crazy as this might sound... the local wolf pack host the town of Cutters Cove for one night every year at their pack house. It's for the supernatural only, and... it's frowned upon if you don't attend."

An unease settled in my stomach. That was one supernatural being I had yet to really encounter, save for the guard at the door at the bar. And even then, I didn't see him in all his wolfy glory.

I raised a brow. "Wolf pack? As in werewolves?"

He paused before answering. "Yes, as in werewolves. They're a big part of the community. I don't like the idea of it any more than you do, putting you at risk like this, but the Alpha of the pack likes to know any new supernatural arrivals into town. It's his way of... 'keeping in the know' you could say."

Holy. Crap.

This was seriously out of my comfort zone. I felt bile rise in my throat at the thought of it, quickly swallowing before it surfaced.

"Is that really a good idea? You mentioned us not letting our guard down," I reminded him with a frown.

His head nodded to the side in agreement. "If you were to avoid it, you would be considered hiding something, untrustworthy. I know it sounds ridiculous, and it's probably the last thing we need to be worrying about the day after you get your magic, but Vampires would never step foot in the place. There's high security, and not to mention our whole group will be there as well."

"Wow, this is all so new."

"I understand if it's too much. And I'll respect your decision if you *really* don't want to go."

I paused, gripping his shoulders. "As much as I would love to come to a dance with you, this is..." I struggled to find the right words without offending him. "I mean, the spell is broken Friday. I'm just a little nervous about *everything*."

His knuckles grazed my cheek. "I know you're nervous. But if your gift is anything like mine, it will come naturally to you. If you don't feel up to it on Saturday, we don't have to go. I can have a quiet word with the Alpha, make him understand."

I stilled, knowing every word was his promise. That if I didn't want to go, there truly would be no questions asked.

"Okay," I said with a nod. "I'll think about it."

Tyler cupped my face with his hands. "I wouldn't leave your side, I promise."

"I know. I trust you." I felt it throughout me. I did trust Tyler—even with my life. My gaze dipped to his mouth. "Would you like to come in?"

"I thought you were never going to ask," he said, then kissed me as if sealing his promise.

I melted into his arms as he moved me backwards to the front door and I pulled away from his grasp, turning and fumbling with the key.

He brushed my hair off my shoulders, his breath breezing against the sweet spot at the base of my neck.

"Ty," I whispered when his lips replaced his breath, leaving a hot trail of kisses in its wake. My back arched into him, and I felt every inch of him aching to be freed.

"Feel that?" he rasped, pressing harder against me.

I moaned in response, words failing me.

"That's all you." He tugged me back against him. "You do that to me," he said, his voice low and husky.

His hand moved to the front of me, cupping me through my jeans, and I whimpered at the contact between my thighs, hearing a light chuckle behind me. Pressing his palm against the denim, Tyler teased me until I was an aching bundle of need, until his hand finally slid into the front of my jeans, dragging his fingers through my arousal.

I gasped at his touch, my palm landing on the front door. Oh. My. God. He knew what he was doing, reading my body like he could read my freaking mind.

As his fingers moved over me, sounds I didn't recognize pulled from my lips.

A smile tickled my ear. "I love the sounds you make when I touch you here," he breathed as I shamelessly rocked against his palm.

Suddenly aware we were still on my front porch, I shakily managed to slide the key into the lock until it finally clicked. His other hand caressed my bottom as the door opened, pressing on my hips behind me as he moved us into the hall.

He spun me around, his fingers never ceasing their torturous movements as our eyes connected again, then his mouth crushed mine. I swept my fingers through his hair as his tongue moved in perfect rhythm with his hand like some indecent dance of our own.

I kissed him like he was my last breath. Two souls floating on a breeze. Then we *tumbled*, scattering our mad souls. He broke me from the inside out, his touch scorching his mark on my skin, an overwhelming urge surging through me.

To touch him. To please him. His length pressed into my stomach as my back hit the wall, and I ran my hands over him through denim, earning me a lust-drenched groan.

Our foreheads connected, eyes colliding.

Tyler cupped my face, drawing a hand down one side of my cheek. "I've never felt like this before," he whispered in awe.

I swallowed at the intensity burning between us.

"I feel the same," I murmured breathlessly.

I hadn't expected this. To be consumed by one person, so entirely, it scared me to death.

He tugged at my hand, pulling us down the hall, his strides quick and short as he dragged me into the bedroom. My core ached for what was coming.

I chanced a bold tongue. "I was quite fond of the wall," I said cheekily, unable to hold back my grin.

He raised a brow, heat filling his irises as he stepped closer, taking me in his arms, my own wrapping around his neck.

"Morgan, I don't fuck. And what I have planned for you will *not* be against a wall."

My mouth practically dropped to the floor, heat rushing to my cheeks.

His irises danced like a flame before covering my mouth with his, coaxing my lips apart, his tongue caressing mine leisurely, like he had all the time in the world. I undid each button on his shirt, and he studied my hands as they released each one, pushing his shirt over his shoulders until it fell to the floor in a crumpled pile.

My hands slid up the ridges of his stomach and into his hair, as he watched me with intrigue. He pulled me in for another kiss, in no rush as he pulled my top over my head, leaving me in my barely-there black bra, his fingers slipping the straps from my shoulders.

When the clasp released, cool air circled my breasts, my nipple hardening as he rolled it between his thumb and finger. I undid his jeans, pulling him from his boxers, and a curse fell from him as I moved my hand over him, hard and heavy in my palm.

I explored the wonder of him in my hands, relishing the power I held in that moment, like an addiction I knew I could never break free from.

Tyler cupped each side of my face, landing a kiss on my mouth. "What you do to me is incredible."

His words spurred me on, and I dropped to my knees.

Steel gray storms looked down at me as I took him in my mouth, drinking in my every movement, a guttural moan forcing from him as he hit the back of my throat.

When his head rolled backwards, relinquishing all power to me, I knew I was his and his only, the small movement sent a ravaging wildfire through me. His hands gently fisted my hair, winding it around his wrist as he slowly pumped into me, and I moaned as he hit me deep.

"That's it, that's so fucking unreal," he groaned as I circled him with my tongue.

From my knees, he looked like a god as he searched a world of his own, lost behind his eyelids.

The carves of his chest lead to the subtle V of his hips where a dusting of hair gathered at the base of him. He was deliciously, utterly, so fucking beautiful. His lips parted slightly before he stared down at me.

I felt his restraint wavering before his hand pressed my shoulder.

"You need to stop. It's too much," he rasped, pulling me to my feet. He traced his thumb above my brow, his voice a whisper. "You're something else, you know that?"

I felt every word, each syllable like a beat of my own heart, thumping in time with mine.

Tyler kissed me again, devouring my mouth. He pulled us onto the bed so I was above him, discarding our clothing one piece at a time, like we had an eternity left to live and all the time in the world.

His hands slipped between my thighs again, his fingers curling against me, and I dug my hands into his shoulders as I melted under his skilled touch.

I couldn't stop the cry that tore from my lips, opening my eyes to find him watching me under heavy lids.

His voice hit a new depth, and he laced his free hand with mine. "I could watch you like this forever."

My eyes slid closed, lost in a building pleasure, his fingers still inside me as he twisted us until he was above me again. When an unfamiliar warmth wrapped around my clit, I found him between my legs, his eyes spearing mine, the darkest I'd seen.

A predatory tint of the night sky dominated his pupils as he lapped at my sex with his tongue—it was almost too much.

A rush of air left me. "Tyler, oh my God, I…"

No one had ever kissed me *there*. The sensation was so overwhelming I tried to pull away, but his arms were tucked tightly under my legs, holding down my hips.

I found it more intimate than sex, having him tasting the most sensitive parts of me, and I finally gave into his tongue.

Tyler brought me closer and closer so many times before backing off, a torture I never knew I needed until he finally undid me, the combination of both his mouth and touch arching my toes, my insides combusting around him.

I cried out, but he didn't stop. Stars burst behind my eyelids, a new heat spreading through me, lifting me like I was watching myself come apart from above.

His voice seemed to come from *everywhere,* sinking into a subconscious I didn't know I possessed. "You're so damn beautiful when you come for me."

I couldn't speak, choosing to kiss him instead. Tasting myself on him.

He slid between my thighs, hovering above me, his hand grazing my cheek. "I've only ever been with one person. I'm clean," he whispered, not breaking eye contact.

I whimpered at the thought of having him bare inside me. "Same. And I'm on birth control," I assured him.

He let out a growl of approval, then sank into me, the movement causing me to cry out in pleasure as every inch of him filled me.

A groan came from him as he thrusted into me again, and I wrapped my legs around his waist, barely able to hold on as we molded into a steady rhythm. My nails dug into his back, and he slowed his pace to match the torturously slow glide of his tongue against mine.

It was intimate and so intense, I could barely catch a breath, each and every sensation in me filled with him. His scent, his touch—he was *everywhere.*

A shudder tore from his lips and into mine as we chased our highs together until we were one, a cloud surrounding us made of licks of orange and slices of ink before it misted away again.

"Oh my..." I didn't understand what was happening. Was this magic? Did we... create this?

Tyler stared at me, wonder pouring from his wide eyes as our tangled limbs lay together.

His hand traced the line of my collar bone. "That was unreal."

"What was that?" I questioned, still catching my breath.

An expression I couldn't read embedded his face. "I think that was our magic."

I didn't answer. My body spent and lids heavy, I gave into euphoric sleep.

Tyler

I hadn't slept, too content with watching Morgan in my arms dozing peacefully. Her hair smelled of coconut and vanilla as it rested on my shoulder, a leg draped between mine as I drew lazy circles over her luscious skin.

Sex with her was unreal. Period.

She'd sent me to places so far beyond my realm of awareness, I now knew for sure she was my mate. The one person chosen for me, destined to be together.

Tied for life by a bond so strong it could only be severed in death.

I'd never believed in fate before. The whole everything happens for a reason thing? I'd called bullshit.

Until now. Now, fate had completely flipped me on my ass and given me the middle finger, my own goddess, and she was truly one of a kind.

Morgan murmured in her sleep, burying her hands under her pillow as she rolled onto her stomach. I drank in her nakedness, visible under the crisp sheet. I couldn't help thinking how lucky I was to finally get to hold her in my arms like this.

I'd had my doubts when she'd asked me about covens, that the possibility of her not being part of ours was almost a given. But would fate really pair me with someone from another coven? I hadn't heard of it before; it was something I needed to look into further.

I had a more pressing issue to sort out. Namely, how was I supposed to describe to her what a mate was? I could only imagine her face as I tried to explain it to her.

'So, I know we just met, but we're fated mates. Bonded, for life.' Yeah, good luck with that.

My mind went through the various ways I could tell her until I finally drifted off to sleep.

Hours later, I woke to silence, reaching for Morgan's side of the bed only to find it empty. Sitting up, I gave a small laugh at the mass of clothes spread on the floor from last night.

I located my boxers and jeans before pulling them on, sleepily making my way from the bedroom and into the hallway. I faltered at the mass of books blanketing the floor and what looked like a bookcase pulled from the wall.

Was that a... door? Having never noticed it before, I moved towards it, stepping between the books scattered over the floor in small piles.

Leaning on the doorframe, I watched with intrigue as Morgan sat at an easel, paintbrush in hand. Opened boxes lay on the ground, surrounded by paints, brushes, palettes, and pieces of art. I remained still, scanning the room, trying to understand why she'd hidden this until now.

I pushed a hand up my face and into my hair, drinking in the silky gown she wore that covered her to mid-thigh. A naked leg was casually tucked underneath her as she focused on the canvas before her, a rough bun piled high on her head, exposing her neck as she tilted her head to the side.

Goddamn, she was a sight.

I snuck up behind her and slid my hands around her waist, nuzzling her neck.

"Tyler!" she gasped. "You scared me."

She turned to face me, clutching her chest, and I lowered myself to my knees beside her, pulling her in for a kiss that lingered longer than intended.

Morgan laughed nervously like I'd caught her doing something she shouldn't. "You're distracting me."

I grinned. "I can see that." My head turned to the painting on the easel that looked like it should be in a gallery. "I didn't know you liked to paint."

Her eyes found mine, then dropped to the floor, her hand running the length of her necklace. Turning her attention back to the canvas, her brush delicately dabbed at it, and I watched in comfortable silence. Her brush moved like it was part of her, and still I waited.

Whatever was going on here, she needed to tell me when she was ready. On her own terms. A hallway full of books, a hidden room, pieces of art tucked away from sight. It didn't make sense.

The brush stilled in her hand before she dropped it to her side.

She inhaled in a deep breath. "I was close to both my adoptive parents. But my father and I had special bond... we both shared a love of art. He taught me to paint. It was our thing."

I let her continue.

"Ever since the accident, I couldn't bring myself to paint anymore."

"Why not?" I asked.

Silence.

A long breath.

"My connection with my parents and art was too raw; it dragged up memories I couldn't bring myself to face without falling apart."

My heart caught in my throat. It pained me to hear the words come from her. To hear the anguish in her voice.

Death speared our hearts. Ripped them open.

Left shadows of ourselves to put back together its scattered pieces.

My hand rested on the small of her back.

"You're a natural," I said, admiring her work. "Why today? After so long?"

She turned, studying me as if I were one of her paintings. Her irises a bronze against the daylight spilling through the room.

"It just felt... right." Morgan shrugged.

A knowing look moved between us. I could feel it. She could feel it. Last night, walls had come down, emotions stripped back. Raw and unguarded.

It was then I knew.

I loved Morgan.

I was *in* love with her.

I pulled her lips to mine, kissing her softly, hers responding with the same intimacy.

"I enjoy watching you paint. You go into a whole other world."

She smiled, and I couldn't get enough of her.

"Maybe I should teach you someday," she mused.

I chuckled. "Think I'll keep my hands busy with things I know best."

"And what's that?" she countered playfully.

"Cars," I said, drawing her lips to mine. "And you," I added, kissing her again.

I could have her right here, riding me on this stool in a heartbeat, but I decided against it. She was in her element, and I wanted to let her get lost in it.

I pulled away, sliding a thumb over her bottom lip. "Are we still on for a lesson in self-defense today?" I asked.

She arched a brow. "If you say so. What if I kick your ass? I could be a ninja for all you know," she teased.

I pinched her shoulder playfully, and she yelped.

"I'm serious. It's not just about defense, it's about reading your opponent and trying to gauge their next move. Besides..." I said, conjuring up a cheeky look, "I want to see you in yoga pants."

She thumped me in the arm with a grin.

I feigned hurt. "What?" I looked at her innocently, and she laughed. Who was I to turn down the chance at some compromising positions with tights like that involved?

After leaving Morgan in peace, I made us breakfast and took two fresh mugs of coffee outside, sitting on the side of the deck.

Morgan came out to join me, dressed in a long-sleeved black top and... I gulped my mouthful of coffee down faster than intended and coughed. I wanted nothing more than to take her ass in my hands at the sight of it in those tight leggings.

She gave me a funny look as she took a seat, and I composed myself, hiding a grin behind my coffee mug.

"So, how are you feeling today?" I asked carefully, avoiding the obvious.

"You mean after I found out my whole world is about to change and the fact I'm expected to be at a dance full of werewolves the day after my magic emerges? Just peachy."

I gave her a sympathetic look. "I mean after catching up with Betty."

Morgan smiled, creases appearing in the corners of her eyes. "Well... I don't really have a say in the whole thing and figure I just need to take it as it comes."

My hand cupped her knee. "I think you're handling it really well."

After finishing our coffee and breakfast, I jumped to my feet.

"Let's do this," I said, taking her hands and helping her up, a little too eagerly so she rested against me.

A half *huff,* half giggle came from her. "This isn't self-defense," she protested, pretending not to look impressed. I wrapped my arms playfully around her waist.

"First rule: Keep your friends close, but your enemies closer."

She laughed halfheartedly. "Seriously?"

"In all seriousness, yes." I released her, and she planted her hands on her hips. "Obviously, that's not always possible, or the safe option. But knowing who your enemies are, and both their strengths and weaknesses, gives you the upper hand in any situation."

She nodded. "Right."

"Now, let's go. I spoke to Colt yesterday, and he's keen to help me teach you. He's expecting us at his place in ten minutes."

"Yes, sir," she said with a mock salute.

I shook my head with a slight smile. She didn't seem to be as worried about everything as I was. Or maybe she just hid it well. For days, a tension had been building within me, my shoulders a constant ache and jaw tight as fuck.

I pulled the van out of the driveway in the direction of Colt's converted warehouse. He lived on the opposite side of the cove from Skye, the eerily calm side.

Sheltered by the decayed trees that even after death refused to bow to the pull of nature, they stood bare in the water, almost protecting the town in a way, and no one dared go beyond them. There were tales of deadly fae who lived beyond the tree line where a wall of magic supposedly kept them from entering the human realm.

I'd never encountered one, but it wouldn't surprise me if the tales were true. Nothing was out of the question where the supernatural was concerned.

"What is this place?" Morgan asked beside me as I steered the van into the driveway of Colt's warehouse.

Its iron-clad walls made it look like some sort of workshop, but I knew the disguise well.

With Reid's help, Colt had made the place his own, and for his own reasons.

"Welcome to the world of Colt." I gave her a sidelong look. "He's a private guy and likes to keep his business to himself. Just remember, he's an earth mage," I said quietly.

Curiosity quirked her lips as she scanned the building, nodding at my comment. After parking, I led her up the gravel driveway.

Pushing the door open, I let her in before me.

"Wow!" she gasped, looking to the ceiling where daylight spilled into every crack of the room from the sky above. "There's no roof!"

My hand found the small of her back. "There is... You just can't see it."

"This is insane..." she gushed in awe at the greenery *everywhere*.

I followed her train of sight as they took in every inch of the warehouse covered in plants. The foliage crawled across the walls, twisted around beams, and covered the ground in separate beds of every kind of living fauna imaginable.

"I've never seen anything like this," Morgan whispered. "I don't even know these plants... didn't know they existed." She admired a bright purple flower in bloom, tentatively reaching out to stroke its petals.

"They don't," came Colt's voice from above. "Not outside of here."

I looked up to find him descending the stairs from the loft on the second floor, where I knew his living quarters were. When he reached the ground, he walked towards us, his strides casual and unhurried.

"I grow these for Scarlet's Apothecary. She purchases them from me," he explained.

"Stunning," remarked Morgan, more to herself than anyone else.

Colt moved towards us, his blue faded jeans ripped at the knees and a white tee hugging his torso. "It's one of a kind. Flowers once every five years."

"Colton, this place is incredible." Morgan gaped in wonder at the other plants, hesitantly walking around the space.

He laughed. "Thanks. It's not for everyone. Here to train I hear," he stated.

Morgan's gaze moved between the two of us. "Apparently so."

I innocently raised my hands in the air. "Hey, if you're going to learn, you should learn from the best." I pointed at Colt. "And I learned from him."

She placed her hands on her hips with an amused grin. "Okay, so where do we begin?"

Colt moved away from us, his finger curling towards him. "This way." He led us through what I could only describe as the greenhouse into a separate room set out like a gym with an assortment of weight machines against all four walls. In the middle was vacant space.

He veered his gaze to me. "First rule...?"

Morgan beat me to it. "Keep your friends close but your enemies closer."

Colt's knuckles grazed the light stubble on his jaw, his head turning to mine with amusement in his eyes. He moved to the center of the room, motioning for us to follow again.

He was a man of few words, but over time I'd gotten used to it.

"Rule number two," he continued, "wherever you are, be aware of your surroundings. If you're inside, know where the exits are. Read the room or the situation. You can tell a lot from body language, but ultimately, your gut instincts will tell you if something is not right."

Morgan nodded, listening, but she remained silent.

It was the longest sentence I'd ever heard come from his mouth.

Colt circled us as he spoke, his presence a natural energy that I could only imagine came from an earth mage.

He was always calm and collected, had been for as long as I'd known him, and that was a long time. Having grown up in the same town, our parents were good friends. It took a lot to ruffle his feathers so to speak, and even more to piss him off.

He came closer, throwing an unexpected hook to my side that I swiftly blocked. I grinned at him, knowing he wasn't expecting my reaction, but he'd trained me well.

"Rule number three," he said, turning his attention back to Morgan, who appeared to be quite enjoying the entertainment, "think ahead. Whatever the situation, you need to be on your toes, gauging what their next move will be."

He swiftly threw his other arm up about to connect with my chest, and I fended him off again.

He nodded in approval. "Whether that be in combat or not," he added.

"I thought you were going to teach me to fight?" Morgan said, her brows creasing together, arms folding across her chest.

Colt squared his shoulders, his hands dropping to his sides. "We will. But these are the foundations of self-defense. The basics."

She dipped her head to the side in agreement.

"Ty... you know the next one," Colt said, looking at me. He took a few steps back, giving us some space.

"Rule number four," I said, moving closer to her, slowly. *Deliberately*.

I let the dominant side of me pulse through my every vein, and I knew she could sense it rippling off me, but I needed her to feel it, right down into her marrow.

It wasn't something I did often, not without intention. But I needed to show her this.

I moved closer again. "Never show weakness. Ever."

Morgan watched my every move, her doe eyes a brutal shade of earth as they studied me with interest.

"No matter what the situation. To show *your* weakness gives them the upper hand."

She stared me down, unblinking, and fuck it took all of my control to rein myself in. To remind myself we had company. That I couldn't have her screaming my name right here and now.

"Show me confidence. No weakness," I ordered, and her pupils blew out.

She liked that.

Morgan straightened, her chin tilting ever so slightly with a confidence I needed from her. I remember the last time she'd done that, backed into the wall that night in the alley, before our first kiss. The memory alone made my dick ache.

I nodded. "Good. Now, if it comes down to combat, you must be ready to move quickly. If you bend your knees slightly, this will help you balance."

She shifted, following my order. "Like this?"

"Yes, like that. Now, lift your hands up here." I lifted mine into the defense position in front of me.

She followed my instructions, and damn if she didn't look hot as hell like this.

"Now what?" she said, a slight pull on the side of her lips.

"Hit him," Colt ordered.

I could see him out of the corner of my eye slowly pacing the room.

Without warning, she flew at me with an outstretched arm, and I ducked away, grabbing it in my hand.

I didn't let go. "You're a feisty little thing when you fight," I said, not able to contain the heat in my eyes any longer. I didn't expect her to lunge at me that quickly, and it turned me the fuck on.

"I think you need to let me go, mage," Morgan said, her irises filling with a cheeky glint.

Desire crawled down my spine, lodging itself at the base of my stomach.

"Fight me," I challenged.

She took one look at Colt, then catching me off guard, jabbed me in the stomach, causing me to release her hand. Before I figured out what was going on, she flew in the air, landing a roundhouse kick to my side.

What the fuck?

I pulled myself together, grabbing her leg as it connected with me, pulling her from her feet until she landed on the ground with me on top. I hovered over her, a leg on either side of her waist, pinning her hands above her head.

She flashed a cocky smirk. "Rule number five: Keep your strengths to yourself."

"You can fight?" I said incredulously.

I threw a glance at Colt who had a huge smile on his face, holding back a laugh.

Her smirk grew to a smile as she stared up at me. "Maybe."

I shook my head. "I can't believe you let me think I needed to train you," I said, half pissed but mostly impressed.

She shrugged. "Father had me in lessons since I was young. He always said to only use self-defense if necessary."

I laughed. "And I was the 'necessary'?"

"Yeah, sorry. I was in too deep to back out once I got here."

She rocked her hips against mine, just enough so Colton didn't notice.

A moan threatened to loosen from my lips, but I knew Colt wasn't stupid, knew he could feel the vibrations pushing off me onto the earth beneath us as I held it together. I jumped up, offering her my outstretched arm and pulled her to her feet.

Colt chuckled. "Well... I think we're sorted in that department then."

"Sorry." She shot him an apologetic look. "I didn't mean to waste your time."

He pointed in my direction. "Seeing you almost put him on his ass was worth every second." He shook his head ruefully.

"Oh c'mon, she wasn't even close," I argued, nudging Morgan in the side with my elbow.

Colt raised his brows, turning away and walking back to the door toward the greenhouse. We followed him into the main area of greenery where he proceeded to inspect some vines before turning to Morgan.

"When do you catch up with Betty next? It would be helpful to know more about your history." He said.

I knew where he was coming from. If she was part of Port Fallere, her magic could be swayed by their *influence* if she were to move back there. I'd heard tales of it happening before.

Morgan ran a hand along some flowers with a shrug. "I'm meeting Betty later this week. She said she would fill me in on everything I needed to know. She just had to make a few calls, see if there was word on my parents."

My insides turned over. See what danger we were facing sounded more like it. If what Betty said was true about Morgan's mother turning into a madwoman, Betty would be trying to find out everything possible to gauge the risk. Eliminate it, even.

Colt folded his arms over his chest. "Let me know if you need any help,".

I nodded, knowing his intention.

He addressed Morgan again, "My father is part of the witch council. I could try and get you a meeting in the chambers if needed."

I shook his hand. "Thanks, man."

"I appreciate the offer," added Morgan.

We headed back to the van, and I dropped Morgan home before heading into my workshop.

Who would have thought Morgan could kick ass? It was both a turn-on and a comfort knowing that even though her magic hadn't come to her yet, at least she knew the basics of combat.

A niggling sensation, however, ate away at me. How would I explain to Morgan that she was my mate without freaking her out? I needed to think this one through. It had to be done right. There was only one place I did my most productive thinking, and that was under the hood of a car.

Morgan

The day before my birthday arrived before I knew it. Thursday. The last day of my so-called normal life. It was a strange feeling trying to mentally prepare for the unknown.

Could I handle what was to come? I wasn't sure.

What if it changed things between Tyler and me? Or ruined everything?

Salty air brushed my cheek as I sat on my front porch sipping coffee from my favorite mug, its warmth filtering its way deep inside me. It never really got warm here, like the sun had written its own obituary and already dug its own grave.

A chill swept around my ankles, and I pulled the cozy throw I'd tossed over my knees tighter around me, tugging my oatmeal beanie further over my ears.

My phone buzzed with a message from Tyler.

> Hey. I'm nearly ready. Pick you up in 10?

> Sure :)

> Dress warm. It's cold out.

>> It's always cold out…

> It's colder where we're going.

>> Right… Okay, see you soon X

Heat trickled over my skin, but this time it had nothing to do with the coffee and everything to do with *him*.

I couldn't stop thinking about him. Tyler had infected my mind and seeped his way into my subconscious as if already a part of it. I didn't understand it.

For the first time, I wished I had a close girlfriend I could divulge this information to, but the only person I was remotely close to was Skye, and talking to her about her brother was most definitely not an option.

I shook my head, gathering my blanket into my arms, my mug in my other hand, and headed inside. I was to meet Betty this morning, accompanied by Tyler and Colton. His father had connections at the witch council and had apparently pulled some strings for us, calling in a favor to help me track down my parents.

Turns out *who* you knew meant everything around Cutter Cove, and on Colton's advice, he had advised Betty and I to let other people look into the whereabouts of them for us.

We walked into a small stone church positioned in the center of town, and I grimaced as the musty smell of its interior filled my nostrils. It looked as if it had not been used in years, with dust covering the lines of pews facing the pulpit.

Colton led the way to the front of the church, with Betty ahead of me and Tyler behind me, our footsteps announcing our arrival in the unnatural silence.

"Where is everyone?" I whispered over my shoulder to Tyler.

He murmured back, "Downstairs."

I frowned, his comment not making any sense, as we were on the ground floor.

Colton led us to a door to the far right, pushing it open. A bitter cold blasted my face, and I pulled my coat tighter around me to keep warm.

Ahead, his shoulders barely fit between the walls of the stone staircase as it wound down to a lower level, and I looked behind me to see Tyler descending the steps almost sideways.

When we reached the bottom, a room with no windows or carpet greeted us.

A long stone table was centered at the front, an elderly male and female behind it, followed by another two, younger than the elders but older than us beside them. The females had their hair held out of their faces in what looked like long braids down their backs, and the men had glasses on the tips of their noses.

I felt tiny walking into what Colton had mentioned was called the chamber.

To me, it felt more like a tomb. Something I wasn't sure I would walk back out of, and I was certain other people hadn't.

It reeked of death as if the bones of its enemies were embedded in its walls or their blood smeared into the floor. I saw no such evidence that could back up my thoughts, but something about the place just *screamed* its misgivings, dissecting me like it was trying to decide my fate.

"Father," Colton addressed the elderly man. "I would like to introduce to the council Betty and her granddaughter, Morgan."

The gentleman's attention turned to Betty before sliding over me, his aged blue eyes piercing mine from behind his glasses.

Colton turned to us, his hand motioning to the elderly man.

"This is my father, Arthur, and his council." He returned his attention to the front of the room. "As you know, it's come to our attention that Morgan is new to town and has asked for your help in tracking down her birth parents."

The elderly man raised his head slightly, looking down over the tip of his nose at me through his glasses. "Welcome." His gaze fell on Betty. "The names you gave me earlier... It's not good news, I'm afraid."

Tyler's hand found mine, squeezing it tight.

Arthur continued, turning to me, "I've used all available resources. With discretion, of course. Your father has not been seen in over five years, and your mother... Well, there have been reports of her being alive, but very unstable. Her current location is unknown."

My heart *sank*.

I had asked for answers and now I had them.

"I need to clarify one thing."

My head raised to find Betty moving to where Colton was standing nearer the front of the room.

Betty continued, "When Morgan was born, it was in the territory of Port Fallere. Her mother made bad choices and like you said, wasn't in her right mind. As I understand it, she is therefore by law officially part of the Sacred Souls coven."

My jaw dropped. What the...?

So many questions needed answers, yet I couldn't sound a single one.

What did this mean? Where was Port Fallere? Did this mean I would have to move? Be forced away from Tyler and this life I'd started to build here, in a town I was actually starting to like?

A splitting headache crashed against my skull, my free hand rubbing my temples in small motions.

Tension rippled off Tyler in waves, and I snuck a sideways glance at him. His jaw was rigid, a nerve pushing from it every few seconds. If death formed a color, it had possessed his irises in the darkest form I'd ever seen, spoiling them. Then a ring of glowing amber suddenly circled his pupils.

Was that his fire element pushing to the surface?

I'd never seen it before, not like this. Was he in control right now? Or something else?

"Tyler?" I whispered.

His fingers laced through mine, his chest a controlled rhythm, rising and falling. But his eyes, they never wavered... fixed on the council ahead.

The council table stilled, heads turning to each other when Betty's voice continued.

"Morgan was birthed in Port Fallere against her will, and against her father's will. We finally managed to return her to Cutters Coven a few months later." Her hands knotted together to her front, a tale of desperation in every movement. "I know the law, and I realize being born in Port Fallere entitles her to their coven. But she has been raised, albeit by humans, and not *there*. This I know to be true."

She paused before turning to each councilor, a sudden fierceness pushing to the surface from her fragile frame.

Betty went on, "I propose she is to be legally invited to join our coven. She has great power in her, I know it. She would be of great benefit to our people."

A blanket of uncertainty wrapped itself around me.

What would happen if I wasn't accepted into Cutters Coven? Would I be asked to leave?

Tyler's grip tightened on mine. So hard I almost pulled away.

Arthur turned to the council, where they huddled closer, murmuring under their breaths. A full minute passed and still they whispered, hushed tones that I could not decipher.

"What's going on?" I whispered to Tyler, fearful of the answer.

His head dipped slightly, his stare remaining pinned to the council table. "No one from Sacred Souls has ever stepped foot in this chamber. I don't know," he said through clenched teeth.

Arthur finally cleared his throat, looking directly at me. "The council is undecided. We will reconvene in two weeks with an answer. This is not a decision we can make in a manner of minutes, based on the severity of the situation."

I didn't know how to feel, but I guess it was better than a straight-out no. I didn't want to leave Cutters Cove; this was my home. The only place I'd made friends, and Tyler...

"Please," I cried out, wrenching my hand from Tyler's grasp. I moved to the front of the room until I stood directly in front of the council. "I will be forever in your debt if you would just let me stay here."

Colton's father gave me a dismissive look, his hand waving in the air. "Two weeks."

I felt like a fraud. Worthless. Port Fallere. Where even was that?

Tyler steered me away. "Let's get out of here," he said, leading me to the stairs.

Colton rushed to my side as we walked back up the steps and outside. "I'm sorry, I'll talk to my father—try to sway his decision."

His forehead was damp, frown lines confirming his frustration.

I smiled grimly. "Thanks. I'd really appreciate that."

He nodded to Tyler. "I'll leave you guys to it; I've got somewhere I need to be."

I turned to Betty. "Thank you for what you said up there."

Her blue grey eyes warmed. "I would do it again in a heartbeat, my dear. Don't worry, we will sort this, I'm sure."

I nodded, even though I didn't share the same certainty.

"Where is Port Fallere?" I asked, looking between her and Tyler.

Tyler's hand flexed around mine, and Bettys hands found my shoulders. "Over the border, my dear."

I turned to Tyler for further explanation. "The ranges," He pointed to a line of mountain peaks, cutting into the horizon in the far distance. "It's the border between both covens."

It looked like forever away. I could never live that far from Tyler.

Betty placed her hand on my forearm. "Don't think about that for now. There's no point worrying about something that hasn't happened yet."

All I could manage was a nod.

***

Pacing to the shower, I stripped off my clothes, letting the hot water subdue my worries. Would it all boil down to this? Would I be asked to leave?

I purged the thoughts, forcing them to the back of my mind.

Whether I was ready for it or not, this new life would slam me in the face at the stroke of midnight tonight.

A nervous laugh squeezed from my lungs at the irony of it, and I rested two hands on the wall of the shower, letting the water soak every strand of my hair.

Right now, Tyler was the only thing keeping me together, stopping me from losing my mind. He'd ducked back to his place to get changed and would be back shortly, said he'd organized a birthday surprise to cheer me up.

If I was honest, I could tell he needed it too. I knew he was worried about me, tonight in particular.

Taking a deep breath, I stepped out of the shower and dried my hair, pulling on some jeans and a sweater. I hadn't celebrated my birthday since my parents died. It just didn't feel right. In some ways, Tyler taking the lead and celebrating it with me was like ripping the band aid off via distraction. It suited me just fine.

His cologne hit me before I heard him knock on my bedroom door, his spicy notes washing my senses. "Hey," I said, glancing over.

I couldn't hold back my smile at the sight of him. A heavy jacket and jeans, socks on his feet, having left his shoes at the door.

"Hey, yourself." He pulled me into his arms for a kiss, and I felt it *all*.

A desperation that hadn't been there before. He pulled away, his hands cupping my face, and a torrent of emotion drained from him.

Tyler murmured, "You need to know I won't let this happen. I won't allow you to be taken to Port Fallere. You belong here with us." He paused, his forehead resting on mine. "With me."

I nodded, emotion twisting my heart and spilling down my face, freefalling with no parachute.

My breath scattered in my throat.

He scooped me into his embrace, burying his face in my neck and I did the same.

His breath ghosted my skin, the comfort and warmth I needed. "Nothing will tear us apart. I promise. Believe me when I say I would rather stare death in the face than never have you by my side again."

I blinked away more tears.

"Say the words, Morgan," he urged. "I need to hear them."

An unsteady breath shuddered from me. "I believe you."

His hands rubbed my shoulders. "Good." Then he planted his lips on mine.

A promise in his breath.

Reassurance in his taste.

Tyler stared down at me, pulling an emotional storm from my eyes. He wiped it away with his thumbs. "Are you ready to go?" he murmured.

I nodded. "Just let me grab my jacket."

He waited as I pulled it on, slipping my feet into my shoes. Grabbing my beanie, I tugged it over my ears, splaying my hair around my neck to protect me from the cold.

"Let's go," I said, pulling the door shut behind us.

Our hands naturally gravitated together, and I eyed him sideways.

"Care to indulge me on where we're going?" I snuffled.

A low laugh came from him. "That would spoil the surprise..."

I didn't like surprises. Not *knowing* was a feeling that had never sat right with me.

"Come on, not even a hint?" I needed a distraction. Anything to stop thinking about the what ifs currently circling my mind. My magic, the coven issue, and the goddamn dance.

He lowered his head to my ear. "I will divulge the where, but not what," he whispered.

"Okay," I said with a stiff laugh. "Where is this mysterious night taking us?"

Tyler straightened again. "Cutters Cliffs."

I scrunched up my nose. "Where's *that*?"

He grinned mischievously. "You'll just have to wait and see."

I rolled my eyes with a laugh as he took us down to the exposed end of the beach, where waves battered the sides of the cliffs extending high above us.

"Tyler?" I stopped in my tracks, not understanding where we would go from here.

Ocean spray brushed my face as a gust of wind caught it, causing me to shiver. I swiped at its dewy residue.

He tugged on my hand. "Trust me."

Tyler walked us towards a cave that came into view as we got closer, leading me inside. A dampness filled my lungs as darkness swept over us. Squinting, I let Tyler lead the way, my eyes slowly adjusting to the lack of light.

"It's just up here," he said, pulling me deeper into the cave.

Wet sand squished beneath my shoes from a recently retreated tide, and my heart lurched against my ribcage, barely able to make out his silhouette in the dim light. It took every effort to focus my attention on him.

Pushing himself up onto a low ridge, Tyler extended his hand to me.

The hesitation in my tone clung to the dank walls. "Are you sure about this? If the tide comes in, we'll get stuck here." I rubbed my arms uncomfortably.

His voice came from just above me. "The tide is on its way out. It won't be back in for hours." He spoke with a confidence I needed to hear. "I've got you. Trust me."

I breathed in cool air, weighing my options. "You'd better be right," I muttered, taking his hand and letting him pull me onto the slippery rise.

We clambered over uneven rock through a gap, until moonlight spread over us again, a narrow path leading us down to an intimate beach. The sky's reflection stained the water a deep ink, and it reminded me of one of my favorite colors that I commonly used to paint the night sky. It was devastatingly striking.

In the distance, a group of people sat on some logs in a circle, a pile of smaller driftwood in the middle. Colton's large build and blond hair stood out from where we emerged, and I realized it was Tyler's group of friends who I was now starting to think of as my own, as well.

Tyler slowed, placing a hand on my arm, the other laced through my fingers. "Are you okay… with this?" he hesitantly lifted our hands between us.

A smile broke over my face as I read between the lines.

"I guess they're going to find out sooner or later."

His lips brushed my forehead, then pulled away, gleaming down at me.

I couldn't help but grin back, a giddy, stupid grin, before we continued down the beach, hand in hand.

"There's the birthday girl." I recognized Colton's voice instantly, seeing him waving at us as we walked closer.

"Hey, man." Tyler clapped him over the shoulder in greeting.

Skye approached us. "Happy birthday eve," she chimed, smiling as she pulled me in for a hug. "Why didn't you tell me?" she whispered forcefully in my ear, giving me the *look*.

I laughed nervously. "Thanks. I didn't really know how."

She pulled away, a smile on her face. Then she randomly hugged me again as if giving me a sisterly nod of approval.

"Happy birthday, Morgan," Reid said from across the circle, lifting his beer in the air in a toast.

"Thanks. It's actually tomorrow," I corrected him. "Not that I'm counting down or anything." I was certain the entire group knew my circumstances and what midnight would most likely bring. The reality was, I had no idea how I would feel after tonight, and how my magic may affect me. One last night of just being me and nothing more felt cause for celebration alone.

Wes nodded at Tyler before his gaze shifted to me, lifting his hand in a wave. "Happy birthday for tomorrow."

"Would someone get the girl a drink? It's her birthday!" cried Scarlet from where she sat perched on one of the large logs.

Colton rummaged through a cooler and, flipping the lids off two bottles, he placed them in his pocket. "Great way to see in a new year," he remarked, handing one to me and Tyler.

I took a drink. "Thanks. I didn't even know this place existed."

Colton's gaze moved behind me, focused on the mountains that surrounded the cove.

"Have you heard the story of Old Man Cutter?" he asked, his blue eyes wistful.

I recalled the comment Skye had made, something about the strange radio station.

I nodded. "Skye did mention something about him, yeah."

"There's a tale about this place, that years ago a town on these cliffs was cursed, never to be seen again. Hidden for an eternity."

My hand stilled, halfway between my lap and my mouth.

I eyed him closely. "Are you for real?" I slid my gaze to Tyler.

Tyler's hand landed on Colton's shoulder, giving him a playful shake. "Does it look like there's a town up there?"

He laughed, and Colton shook his head, lifting his shoulder in a shrug.

"Tales or truths… no one knows for sure," he mused, his gaze traveling into the distance again.

Not far from us, another wave crashed against the shore before rapidly retreating again. It was mesmerizing to watch, as it scattered its findings on the shore, only to take with it whatever it desired again.

Wesley's voice came from the other side of the circle. "So, your magic will come to you at midnight, right?"

Even in the dim light, his jade eyes gleamed.

"Something like that," I said, mindlessly picking at the sticker on my bottle. "Not sure how this whole thing works, to be honest."

Reid nodded towards the bonfire. "Well, you're about to see it for real. Light it up, Ty."

Tyler turned his attention to Colton. "Care to lend a hand?"

Colton's brow lifted, a moment passing before he nodded back.

Scarlet caught my eye. "They're so hot when they do this." She stared adoringly at the two of them from her perch on the log.

I cocked my head to the side, unsure what was about to happen, intrigue turning my attention back to where Tyler and Colton stood at the opposite sides of the circle.

A light breeze brushed my face, soon turning into a whirlwind around the pile of driftwood. Tyler stood, making fists at his sides, with Colton bending to make contact with the ground.

Power poured from them, a bright gold from Tyler and exquisite green from Colton as they tipped their heads toward the stars. It struck me as odd; I'd never seen the stars in Cutters Cove until now. But there they were, watching us watch them.

Scarlet was right. This was *so* hot seeing them like this.

A vortex appeared above us filled with licks of golden flame and vine-like spirals so bright I stared in awe of its beauty. Their hands moved in front of them, palms clawing at air before the vortex of magic shot down to the pile of driftwood, igniting the bonfire with a fury of gold.

I stared open-mouthed in awe of such a thing. Would I be capable of that after today?

A roar erupted from the group and we gravitated to the warmth of the flames, amber shadows dancing over us as bursts of orange floated high above, sprinkling the night sky like golden ash falling from the heavens. Its beauty was nothing less than stunning, and I found myself just *staring*.

Tyler settled beside me, wrapping his arm around my shoulders.

"That was incredible," I whispered, turning to face him. "You're..." I shook my head, struggling to find the words that could describe watching such a moment.

His hand fell to my knee just as a heavy gaze pulled at me, I turned my head, following the strange feeling tugging at my spine. Colton watched us closely from the other side of the fire, his expression unreadable.

I turned to Tyler again. "That was... I don't even have words. How does Colton's magic work?" I asked.

Tyler rolled his bottle between his palms. "He summons his magic from the earth, draws strength from mother nature. Sometimes he sees into people's minds when he uses it."

"He can read our minds?" I whisper-yelled.

"Not exactly. More like feels emotions. I'm not 100 percent sure of how it works."

I snuck a glance at Colton from across the fire, where he remained concentrated on us.

"What's he staring at us like that for?" I asked, chancing a look in his direction again, but this time he looked away.

Tyler shrugged. "Don't worry about him."

Hours passed, but it felt like forever, my mind constantly on the time. The clock was ticking down to midnight when my powers would emerge, and I still wasn't sure if I was ready.

A bottle of tequila came in my direction for the second time, and I took a swig from it, passing it on to Scarlet. It was nice to spend some time with her; she seemed friendly enough, another earth witch who owned the local apothecary in town. I warmed to her easily.

Music pumped from the speaker Reid had brought with him, and suddenly the night seemed wilder. A few of the group stripped off to their underwear, dipping into the water, their shrieks and splashes echoing throughout the cove.

"I'm *not* getting in that water," I said, tugging my jacket tighter around my neck. "They're mad!"

Tyler chuckled beside me. "Or drunk on tequila."

I stared dumbfounded as Colton ripped off his top while he walked towards the water, ridding himself of his bottom half entirely.

Butt naked, he strode into the depths.

"Oh. My. God"

The guy didn't bat an eyelid.

I erupted in laughter, forcing my hands over my eyes.

I looked at Tyler for an explanation, but he only shook his head with a grin. "He's one with nature, that guy. Nudity's nothing to an earth mage. Besides, the guy's got nothing to be shy about," he said, a deep laugh rumbling from him.

I peeked at Tyler from behind my hands. "I can't look."

He came closer, as if hiding behind them with me.

"Yeah, please don't," he laughed before his lips quickly brushed mine and I was pulled into his intoxicating allure once more.

Pulling away, my cheeks burned at the intimate display of affection, warmth sliding through me at his touch. Being with Tyler made me feel complete. It was such a strange feeling to have, and I welcomed it with an open heart.

As the evening went on, an uneasiness pricked my skin, growing stronger with each passing hour. Like an itch awaiting its scratch, it held me in its grasp, and I couldn't kick its unwanted presence.

Willing my fears away, I took Scarlet's hand, who had just finished hurriedly drying herself with a towel, now clothed again.

I needed to dance.

TYLER

Perched on a log surrounding the fire, I watched the girls dance, Morgan's hands raised to the sky as if summoning the stars. To the naked eye, it looked like she had not a care in the world, but I knew otherwise.

Her hips swayed freely to the music, my eyes raking over her curves as they moved, but I could tell she was holding back.

She slid her fingers over her necklace again.

Nervous.

In the back of my mind, I knew anything could happen when the clock ticked past midnight. As much as this night was a celebration, it was also for her safety. Be it good or bad, Morgan was surrounded by people who could help her, away from the prying eyes of humans. A safe place.

I hadn't wanted to bleed my magic earlier. As far as Morgan was concerned, Colt helping me out was a normal thing to do, but it couldn't be further from the truth. I didn't need his help, and he knew it. But he went along with it anyway.

With Colt's help, my magic would be at full strength again in minutes.

Fully clothed again, Colt approached, his heavy frame blocking the heat as he passed. "Why didn't you tell us she was your mate?" His tone was neutral as he sat beside me.

I nearly spat out my mouthful of beer.

"Your mate?" Wesley's voice came from behind me until he stood in view, arms folded.

"Who is whose mate?" Scarlet's hushed tone whispered from close by.

The music dimmed.

Fuck.

Waves lapped at the beach. Fire crackled as amber hues danced across the sand.

"For fuck's sake, Colt," I muttered under my breath, my head shaking. This couldn't be happening. Not this way.

Confused irises nailed me to the log, the entire group expecting a response.

"What's a mate?"

I turned towards Morgan's voice, curiosity buried beneath her lashes from where she stood not far from the water.

A deafening silence fell over the group.

Reid ran a hand through his hair.

Scarlet and Skye exchanged glances.

Colt flew an apologetic look in my direction.

Skye's voice broke the silence. "One's mate is the other half of your soul." Her tone was soft. Cautious.

A light laugh came from Morgan. "Super cute, Skye," she said, her sarcasm clear as day.

No one spoke.

"It's the truth," said Reid simply.

Scarlet bobbed her head in agreement. "When you find your mate, you're bound to them by a love so strong you feel it in your bones."

Morgan's brows raised.

"Only death can sever a mated bond," added Colt as he scratched the back of his head.

Morgan's hip darted to the side as she eyed him, waiting for a punch line. A *just kidding* remark. When it didn't come, her arms folded to her front.

"Seriously? Is this some sort of witch thing?"

Scarlet tucked her hair over one shoulder. "Supernatural in general, actually."

Morgan swerved back to look at me. "Then who are you talking about?"

Unable to deflect the conversation, I held her gaze. There was no avoiding it.

The rest of the group moved further down the beach, Morgan briefly watching their retreat.

Confusion filled her features.

Lined her forehead.

Creased her eyes.

"Tyler?" she pressed.

I sucked in a breath, moving towards her, sand inching between my toes. "Us."

She stared at me blankly, and for a moment, I wondered if she'd heard me.

"Us?" she questioned, raising her brows.

I took her hand in mine, my thumb running over a small freckle nestled on her wrist. "Yes. As in, you and I."

She didn't seem to register the words, silent syllables moving her lips. Her skin glowed a milky white, moonlight dancing over her in delicate shadows.

I repeated myself, my hand skimming her cheek.

"Mates. Soulmates—I didn't know. I only figured it out myself a few days ago."

"Mates," she repeated numbly.

A single word. A fucking breath of salt-kissed air. I wanted to catch it with my lips but cautiously, patiently, stilled in front of her.

I lifted her chin, drawing her gaze to mine, desperation tearing at my insides, against the outer calm I forced upon myself. "You may not feel it. Or maybe you do? But by the gods, you hit me hard, Morgan. Wild, like *nothing* I have ever experienced before."

Her silence grated against my calm.

A hand on each cheek, I melted in her chocolate orbs. A blink, a stray eyelash. My thumb swept over it.

I continued. "I never believed in mates, not until I met you. I felt it tugging at my soul. I have walked my entire life without you, not realizing such a love existed. Then you found me. I've never felt a love like this, Morgan. I love you... more than I thought I could love *anything*."

Her hands slid off her hips, hanging to the ground as if the earth had some powerful grip on her. A single tear fell from her eye, trailing past her cheek. Her mouth opened, then closed.

Her voice shuddered. "This can't be... I just... I don't understand." Her gaze pulled from mine to the distance.

"Morgan, look at me," I ordered, both hands on the sides of her face.

She forced her head away, grabbing at my hands.

I couldn't let this be it. The mate bond hadn't even gained its full strength, but I could feel it. Once it finally snapped into place, if she rejected me, it would ruin me. I hadn't explained that part to her yet, that the rejection of a mate had the potential to kill the other.

"Morgan," I repeated. Low, desperate. "Look at me."

She obliged, her eyes finally boring into mine, a torrential storm brewing in that beautiful gaze.

"Please don't freak out," I said, my breath so close to her lips that hers brushed my own. "I know this sounds crazy, and a little scary. But it's also exciting, intoxicating, and a little wild even," I continued, my gaze traveling south to her lips and back up again. "Tell me what you felt when you first met me."

Her hands still rested on mine, cupping her face. No longer trying to tear me away.

She sucked in an unsteady breath. "When I met you... I felt drawn to you." She stared up at me, moistening her lips. "I tried to ignore it, but it's like you were hurling towards me and I was powerless to stop it."

My fingers moved a stray hair behind her ears, trailing her jawline. "Like you had no control," I offered.

"Yes," she breathed. "When I'm around you, I can't explain it." She spoke honest truths, vulnerability in her words. "When you touch me…" She shook her head. "You're right; this is wild."

Time lapsed, fading everything outside of our connection to a blur.

"Mate." She whispered.

My heart *soared*.

Morgan raised onto her toes, moving her lips against mine with force, an inferno of relief washing through me at the contact.

My lips tempted hers to open for me, and she greedily obliged, a fierce passion pulling us under. She moaned against my mouth in a way she hadn't before, pushing her hips against mine, desperation in her kiss, her touch.

I couldn't think straight, my mind consumed by every kiss, every sigh.

At last, I pulled away, catching my breath.

Glassy irises stared back at me as she gasped for air, the reflection of the moon on the face of my watch catching my attention.

12:01 a.m.

I stilled, my breathing becoming harsh, compelled by a feeling so carnal I had to rein in my self-control.

"Mate." The word escaped me before I could stop it, a whisper coasting in the sharp breeze that licked our necks. I could feel it, *everything*.

The mate bond pummeled its way through my bones, almost knocking me to the ground. I grabbed Morgan's shoulders to keep myself upright, her hands clinging to me as I did to her. The mate bond, forced away for so long, punched its strength into us as if making up for lost time.

Morgan stared into the distance, unfocused. Like she was somewhere else, the sand lodging her in place.

I dipped my head, looking at her closer. "Morgan?"

Like a shell of the person standing before me, she stood eerily still.

My hands gripped her shoulders, harder this time. A light shake. "*Morgan*." I said louder.

My hands roamed over her face, her cheeks, her neck.

No response.

The ground thumped as another presence fell behind me.

"What is it? What's wrong?" Colt's voice registered in my mind.

A swift gasp collected in Morgan's lungs, and she regained focus momentarily.

"Tyler." She registered me for a fleeting moment.

Her body quivered, and just as suddenly, a violent shudder rocked through her, causing her to fall against me, her spine contorting as if it no longer belonged to her.

Fuck.

I collected her in my arms, looking to Colt with uncertainty. "Is this normal?"

Colt shook his head, bemused.

I didn't know. No one did.

"Holy shit," I heard Skye's voice beside me. "Get her on the ground."

Dropping to my knees, I lowered Morgan onto the sand, tipping her to the side, my hands hovering above her as we watched her convulse, helpless to stop it. I hated seeing her like this. Hated knowing I could do nothing to help.

The rest of the group ran over, a circle forming around us. Then she fell quiet. Still.

"What's going on?" said Reid, his forehead mirroring my own confusion.

I pulled my jacket off, tucking it behind her head. "It's midnight. The spell must have broken."

An almighty streak of desire charged through me, followed by an all-consuming need to protect her. Protect my mate.

My breath shuddered as it left me. "The mate bond... I was right."

Scarlet glanced worriedly around the group. "What do we do?"

"Morgan," I said, pushing the hair from her face until it lay fanned around her, like an angel in the sand, fallen straight from the sky above.

Please let her be okay.

I swung my gaze to Wes, who stood back a few paces from the rest of the group, lips pressed together.

"Wes, I need to know if this is her magic, or something else," I urged.

He rubbed his hands over his forehead, forcing them lower until his fingers pressed together beneath his chin. His gaze moved to

Morgan's fragile frame, lying between us in the sand, his emerald glare wide and unwavering.

"Wes!" I repeated.

"Yeah, okay." He stepped towards us, the group shuffling aside to let him closer.

He dropped to his knees, molding into the sand on the other side of her. Our eyes met, a fierce understanding between childhood friends. Warning bolting from me to him.

Only this time, Morgan wasn't a stranger new to the town.

She was my mate.

My everything.

Mine.

I was trusting him with my heart.

His head bobbed in a swift nod, then his arm drifted to hers.

Morgan

The thuds came in forceful pounds. Solid. Rhythmic. Becoming erratic. Voices came and went, blurred. I couldn't make out words. Muted behind the thumping. The *pounding*.

Thump. Thump. Thump.

Each became a part of me, a stamp on my soul.

I willed myself to open my eyes with everything I had. Every part of me ached as I forced them to widen, but my lids held tight, as heavy as my weighted limbs, like an anchor dropped to the ocean floor, buried in the earth.

"Let me out! Somebody, help me!" I shrieked, slamming my fists against the walls that bound me inside myself. "Can anyone hear me?" I screamed, my voice vibrating my skull. "Help!" I tried again, kicking and punching the barrier that held me at ransom.

What felt like minutes could have been hours, terror building to a point where I could fight no longer.

My breathing hollowed.

How could I be trapped inside *myself*?

Flashes of black and white pushed to the surface. Like old movies, running on a static player.

Memories.

The cave. A beach. A bonfire.

More flashes.

Tyler.

His face forced to the front of my mind, and it was then I understood the thuds. They were his. I could hear his heart, feel his fear scraping my own.

My mate.

A storm formed within me, one light, one dark. Like two worlds colliding, fighting for one universe. Then it slammed into me.

I cried out as an intense heat pummeled my spine, like flesh stripping from my bones piece by piece. My back arched against the pain, to the point where I questioned if my spine had snapped, and I locked into a curl against the force building within me.

Then came the *heat*. Firing through my veins, it raced its own path into every part of me, filling me with a searing pain so hot I couldn't breathe. I couldn't scream. Curled so tight, I couldn't move. At some point, it mellowed, eventually turning into a warm buzz, as if it were speaking to me.

A warmth. A power. A possession.

Magic.

It spoke to me in a voice I couldn't place.

To keep you safe, it had to be
A power I could not foresee
Magic will be soon unbound
She must be stopped, must be found

It no longer burned but hummed through my veins. A newfound presence that had become a part of me.

I felt alive.

Pressure lay on my arm, firm and with purpose.

Wesley's voice registered in my mind. "It's her magic," I heard him say. "It's here. Betty was right. She's a *very* powerful witch."

"Morgan," Tyler's voice tore through my senses, scalding my insides in a good way.

It tugged me from the inside, willing me to open my eyes, and my body responded, his voice my command.

Forced from my stupor, I dragged an arm onto my chest, and it was captured instantly, an immediate calm settling over me at his touch.

"It's Tyler. Can you hear me? Are you hurt?" Concern flooded his face, his steel grays darkening and seizing my world entirely. His voice was both a comfort and safety net, blanketing around me at once.

I tried to speak, but a breath of barely-there air was all I could take. "Tyler."

"There she is." He smiled down at me.

He brushed the hair from my face, his hands settling against the side of my cheek.

"You had us worried there for a minute. Are you okay?"

I glanced up at him, his features surrounded by bursts of light nestled in the ashen sky.

A part of me wouldn't believe the emotion stirring in his features, a delicate twist of fear and... love?

Muscular arms wrapped around me as he sat me up against his chest.

He whispered in my ear, "Don't do that to me again, please. I thought I'd lost you."

I didn't have the strength to move, only able to snuggle into his arms further, embracing his body heat.

His hand ran the length of my arm, sending a shiver through me, his touch intensified no doubt by this mate bond he had mentioned as it warmed every part of me.

My magic swam in my veins like it had been there the whole time, and it possibly had. But I felt it owning me, claiming me for the first time. It was both liberating and overwhelming all these new *things*.

I didn't know if it was a feeling, an emotion or a presence. It just *was*.

"I can feel my magic," I breathed into the side of his face.

A caress of his thumb skirted over my jaw. "It's always been there, Morgan; you were born with it. Now, rest."

Sinking against his chest, I succumbed to exhaustion.

Tyler

As night swallowed the cove in darkness, I'd moved Morgan to a blanket where she now lay sleeping peacefully against me, one leg curled over mine and body spent. Her breathing had eventually mellowed during the night, now light and chest barely moving.

I inhaled her scent like my drug of choice, the pull of the mate bond enhancing every touch, every feeling inside me to the extreme. It was surreal, invigorating even.

Our closeness calmed my mind, yet every touch of her skin burned a deep yearning inside me, raw desire consuming me entirely, eager to consummate our bond now at its full strength.

I pushed the thoughts away as her breath floated against my neck, sending a shiver curling over my skin.

My gaze drifted to the horizon, where streaks of bronze and gold danced across the ocean as the day woke from its slumber. My fingers grazed the small of Morgan's back between her top and pants, warmth filling my heart.

My mate, a powerful witch. I was beyond proud of her.

She stirred against me, a light hum in response to my caress.

"Happy Birthday," I whispered.

She mumbled drowsily into my chest, a hand moving over her face. "I feel like I've been hit by a bus."

I smiled, subtly shaking my head. "You just had a lifetime's worth of magic hit you in one evening. I imagine that's to be expected."

She scanned the beach, confusion settling on her face and wrinkling her nose.

"We slept here all night?"

"Yeah. You were out of it, so I thought it best you rest where you were."

She stared at me incredulously. "In the middle of winter? How are we not frozen solid?"

I chuckled. "Do I need to remind you of the fact you have your own personal heater now?"

Amusement pooled in her eyes. "Yeah, a *one bar* heater."

"I didn't mean *that*," I chuckled at her innuendo. "My body heat alone warmed us both the entire night." I placed a kiss on her forehead. "Perks of being mated to a thermo mage, princess."

Her cheeks flushed, and I wrapped my arms around her shoulders, pulling her close again.

I mustered the cheekiest look I could. "You have a filthy mind, witch."

"I do *not*!" she grumbled, playfully thumping me in the chest with her fist, her head bobbing with laughter. The sound strummed pleasurable chords within me, my dick throbbing in response.

Tugging the blanket tighter around us, I nuzzled into her neck. "How do you feel?"

Morgan leaned against my chest, staring out to the ocean, the sun having now completely melted away the night, splashing its golden glow over the cove for the first time in what seemed like weeks.

A comfortable silence sat between us as she contemplated life.

"I feel alive. I feel... free. It feels right," she admitted, turning to look at me.

The pull of the mate bond tugged deep within me again.

"Mate," she whispered.

I smiled, trying to hide my nerves. There was still so much I needed to explain.

Her hand traced my cheek, down to my jaw, the gentle caress making my dick twitch. She looked at me as if seeing me for the first time, a new intensity burning in her eyes.

"So how does this mate thing work exactly?" Morgan asked, her voice huskier now.

I sucked in a breath as she inspected me like something she could paint. "Where do I start?" I said, more to myself than to her. "Does it freak you out?"

Her head bowed a little, breaking our eye contact. "It did at first. But now..." She paused again.

I waited with bated breath, not sure if I was ready for the answer.

"Now, I get it," she finally said, a smile creasing her cheeks that now blushed a deep crimson. "I feel it," she added, as if realizing the assurance I desperately needed.

A grin spread over my face as I registered her words, knowing she was feeling the same pull inside her. The same heat at our mere touch.

I brushed my lips against hers, and the heat inside me exploded into a full-blown inferno. I needed to be inside her as my mate. I let Morgan take the lead; she had to want this, now aware of our bond and the meaning behind it.

She adjusted her body until she faced me, a palm over my heart. It beat hard, pounding in my chest. I knew she could feel it, as I could hers, a connection between mates. She climbed over me, straddling my waist, her hands crawling up my neck and into my hair. Her palm cradled my neck, a heated look consuming her chocolate orbs.

She dropped her gaze to my lips, molten with desire. "I need you. More than I've ever needed anything in my life."

Her hand dropped to fidget with my belt, eyes never wavering from mine.

"Morgan…" I wrapped my hand around her wrist, and she startled, glancing to where my hand grasped hers. "We don't have to do this. Not here. Let me take you home," I offered, but her head shook slowly as she removed my hand with her free one.

Morgan spoke lowly, "Please. I've felt nothing like this before. No one's here. It's just us."

Her words alone could've finished me—if on my feet, could've dropped me to my knees.

Her hands moved back to my belt, and this time I didn't attempt to stop her. Consumed by the mate bond, its force was an indestructible thing.

I couldn't imagine anyone or anything able to destroy such a powerful connection.

I brushed her hair from her face, tucking it behind an ear as she held my stare, sliding my belt from its buckle and undoing the zipper.

"I'm the luckiest man alive," I mused as her hands wrapped around my length.

I moved the blanket around us as her head dipped lower, taking me in her mouth.

A groan ripped from me as her warmth surrounded me, her tongue's caress sending me into a state of mind unknown. Before, everything was muted compared to this; this was something else entirely. She wound me tight as she curled her tongue around me from head to tip, all the while moving her hand over me until it fucking wrecked me.

"Fuuuck," I groaned, sliding my hand into her hair.

She took me in again, deeper this time, moaning like she couldn't get enough. I threw my head to the sky as the vibrations barreled through me, my hips falling naturally into a rhythm as her mouth slid over me repeatedly.

I let her have all of me, let her take control, the entire beach to ourselves as we hugged the hues of dawn.

I watched her in awe as she took every inch of me. "How are you real?"

Morgan took that as her invitation to glance up at me, and fuck if she couldn't be any more perfect in that moment.

I cupped her cheek, drawing my thumb over her jaw. "Come here, please."

I pulled her towards me, and we discarded our clothing until she straddled my thighs. She gathered the blanket around us before the bite of dawn left its mark, skin crawling over skin as we wrapped our hands around each other. She lowered to kiss me, a deep, all-consuming kiss that held nothing back as she lapped her tongue against mine.

Pulling away, she stared at me with those doe eyes. I was sure they could break a man, leave him begging on the ground.

"Tyler... I..." Her lids closed as she drew in a breath.

Something inside me knew what she wanted to say. The bond, like a tether to her mind.

"I love you," I whispered, my hand landing between her breasts, settling on her heart.

Her lips parted without words. Even if she wasn't ready to say them herself, I felt it.

A lone tear ran the length of her cheek, and then she kissed me again, the tang of salted tears sliding between our lips until turning into something more. A fresh hunger moved my mouth against hers, ground her hips into mine. The mate bond fueling the intensity between us until I ached with arousal.

I drew my hands between her thighs to find her already slick and ready for me, my dick aching to be inside her. Her forehead connected with mine, her intensity so raw with emotion it wracked my soul.

Morgan lowered herself ever so slowly onto me, connected as one as she moved over me in a growing, needy rhythm.

Heavy breaths and graveled whispers hushed between us as the mate bond pulled us closer. Wrapped its bond around us, securing its leash. She rode me like she was claiming me as her own, a fucking and utterly gorgeous thing to watch as she moved with me.

Lost in ourselves in nature, we took everything the other had to give, fucking under the beady eyes of wilderness, and I knew I'd never forget it.

"Take what you need, baby, come with me," I ordered as she rolled her hips over me repeatedly.

Her hands clung onto my shoulders, nails digging into flesh as she found her rhythm, grinding against me in a way I knew would hit her sweet spot. Her walls clenched around me, and I knew she was close, knew this would be quick and intense.

"I love you," Morgan breathed into the wind before crying out in waves of pleasure, and I let myself go with her.

A swarm of our magic surrounded us as we barreled over the edge together, our cries gusted away and swallowed by the stiff breeze.

Her legs remained straddling my thighs, chest heaving as she laid her head on my shoulder. I skimmed my arm around her waist, resting it in the natural curve of her hip, the other gathering the blanket around us that had slipped at some point.

Engulfed in my thermo magic, we spent the early hours of the morning wrapped in nature, exchanging kisses and swimming in the depths of the ocean, naked as the trees around us in the thick of winter.

"Tyler," came Morgan's breathless voice. She turned towards me, her attention consuming me.

"Yeah?"

"I would really like to go to this dance with you."

I smiled at the weight of her words, at what this meant for us. For Cutters Cove.

"I would really like that, too."

On the outside, I was the picture of calm as I planted a delicate kiss on her shoulder. But inside, a storm ravaged my nervous system, anxiety suddenly pitching its tent and anchoring its poles into my skin.

Morgan's magic emerging was one thing, but now it had, she was effectively public domain until she learned to control it.

I would do anything and *everything* to protect her.

I didn't let her in on the fact my nerves were spiraling into a dark abys, screaming at me that this dance was a bad idea. But the reality was, Morgan had nothing to hide, and her not attending would deem her untrustworthy to the town.

I would speak to the group, keep them on high alert.

Call in every available favor owed to me and amp up security.

Eventually, we walked along the beach towards the entrance of the cave, our shoes dangling in our hands and water splashing over our toes. Our footprints indented in the sand, quickly pooling with water like we had never been there, like this morning was our secret.

Climbing back through the cave, daylight found us again, and Morgan took off as fast as she could down the beach.

I chased her and her laughter carried in the air, a smile creasing the corners of her eyes as she peered over her shoulder at me. I didn't know if I could ever stop admiring her beauty; it was infectious.

Mate bond or not, I was addicted to everything that was her.

I didn't want to think about the what ifs, because Morgan leaving Cutters Cove was not an option. I wouldn't let it happen.

The council couldn't deny the mate bond. It *had* to stand for something.

When we got home, Morgan ducked into the shower to freshen up while I made my way to the kitchen, lowering to find the usual full-of-shit drawer every house had under the counter. Third drawer down. Bingo.

"What are you doing?" came Morgan's voice from above.

I lifted my chin to find her freshly showered, peering down at me as she leaned over the top of the counter, curiosity plunging her brows.

I pulled a plastic container out of the drawer, and standing again, lifted it into the air.

"You need to practice your magic."

She gave me a crooked smile, as if not convinced this container was worth conjuring.

"With that?" she said, waggling her finger at the container in disbelief.

"Yes, with this. I hate to remind you, but whatever you have inside you, someone else wants. Not everyone has the ability to call on both light and dark magic, Morgan. It will most likely be both a blessing and burden. So today, we practice magic, starting with this."

I gestured for her to follow me into her living room, and she did.

"Sit down here, like this," I said, dropping to the floor and placing the container in front of me.

Her head dipped to the side, but she sat down, remaining silent.

"Okay, now concentrate. Look at the container and think only about it and try to move it. Close your eyes if you have to."

She complied, her nose scrunched up as she focused.

After a long half minute, she let out a huff of frustration.

"Nothing's happening. This isn't working."

I nodded. "That's okay. When my magic first came through, it was inconsistent and would surface only when I was overwhelmed with emotion. Let's try something. Can you shut your eyes for me?" I said, and she obliged. "You have to dig deep the first time you use your power. Use any emotion you can. Anger, frustration... *desire*."

She opened one eye at the last word, and a smile spread over my face at the look she threw me. "Are you for real?" she asked.

I grinned. "I am."

Morgan looked up and sighed, worry clouding her gaze. "I'm really not sure about this. What if I hurt you?"

My hand fell to her knee. "Don't worry about me. Just concentrate on the container."

She held my gaze until her lids flicked shut again.

"Now, clear your mind and whatever emotion you choose to focus on, visualize pulling it tight, nice and close. Draw from its strength."

I heard her pull in a few long breaths, releasing them evenly again.

"I'm going to take your hands now," I warned.

Placing her hands in mine, the mate bond streaked desire between us.

"Do you feel that?" I asked, trying to keep my tone even.

Her answer stormed through me as she released it on a moan. "Yes," she breathed.

It took every effort to keep our bond in check. To not take her again right here and now. "Good. Now, look at me."

Her lids opened, and a seasoned look only made for a mate pulsed through me.

"That feeling, pull it from within." I paused, waiting, giving her time. "Now, use it," I ordered. "Push that feeling onto the container and push it away with your mind."

The atmosphere between us became magnetic. Morgan looked back to the container, and for a moment, nothing happened.

Then without warning, I was catapulted into the air, the breath squeezing from my lungs as I slammed into the wall on the other side of her living room.

"Holy crap!" she cried out, scooting across the room to where I lay in a heap. "I'm so sorry. Are you okay?"

I caught the worry in her tone but was more interested in the placement of her hand on my thigh.

"Yeah, I'm good. I think we've got that sorted now," I wheezed, trying to replace the burn in my lungs with much-needed air.

Her brows crumpled together. "Are you sure?"

"I'm fine," I promised, forcing a smile. "I think I may need crash pads and a helmet next time we try that."

She laughed out loud. "I'm *so* sorry." Her hand covered her mouth, stifling a giggle.

I shook my head, chuckling lightly. "Remind me not to misbehave anytime soon."

She gave me a playful punch, and I crossed my arms in front of my head, feigning hurt. We both laughed, and she sat beside me against the wall, a smile spread over her delicate features.

There was a shift in her. A release of self-doubt maybe, now that she knew she could use her magic. Albeit irrational magic, she had done it, and my heart warmed to see her confidence.

When my breathing finally returned to normal, we rose to our feet.

"I have a surprise for you," I said, lacing my fingers through hers.

She let out a playful groan. "You know I hate surprises..."

"This is a good surprise, I promise. Will you be okay if I duck out for a few hours?"

She nodded. "Sure. I have a few jobs I need to sort anyway."

I pulled her against me, tucking her arms behind my waist. This mate bond was firing off every nerve inside me at only her slightest touch, and when she leaned up to kiss me, I ignited again.

Reluctantly, I pulled away, slipping her hands from behind my waist. "I won't be too long, I promise," I assured her.

A devilish smile crept over her face. "Don't keep me waiting."

My finger grazed the underside of her chin, tipping it until her gaze fixed on mine. "I wouldn't dare." I kissed her once more before heading to the door.

What I needed to do was not a simple task for a guy, and I knew just who to call on to help me.

Morgan

Jet-black silk slid over my hips as if night had collected its bounty. I mean, as much as I didn't do dresses, Tyler had good taste.

The fabric shimmered as I moved, its shorter front exposing my legs strapped in gold heels. A small train fell elegantly, cutting in from the deep V that exposed what felt like my entire back.

I had to admit, I loved it. I felt... bold.

Tyler had returned with two boxes in hand, the invitation to the dance on top. He was so charming, I simply couldn't say no.

I didn't *want* to say no.

Tonight felt like an official introduction to this new life.

I didn't want to think about Port Fallere and Sacred Souls. I couldn't be a part of another coven. Not now. I refused to let myself think that all this could be temporary, a bittersweet bedtime story told to children on a stormy night.

A tremor tore through my hands, and I fisted them tightly, stretching my fingers wide again. I had reservations about attending the dance tonight, and my stomach had suddenly twisted into a knot, my nerves finally getting the better of me.

I tousled my hands through my hair as it fell freely down my back before stepping into the living area.

"Well, what do you think?" I asked nervously.

Tyler's gaze lifted at the sound of my voice, his lips parting slightly. He leaned against the door frame, hands tucked inside the pockets of his suit pants, complemented by a crisp white shirt and black tie.

My mouth went dry at the sight of him. The deliciously black tux hugged his broad shoulders, and I wanted to run my hands over it. Or peel it off him altogether. My eyes dropped to his tie, my God, he looked too good to be true.

His irises darkened as they rolled over me like molten lead. I bit my lip under the intensity of his stare. He strode over to me, closing the space between us in seconds, his suit-laden arms sliding around my waist.

"Chew that bottom lip again and we won't make it out of this house tonight."

I melted at his words, the *tone* of his artful tongue a forewarning of things to come.

The intensity of his stare prickled my skin as he pulled away, raking his heady gaze over every inch of me.

"You're dangerously beautiful. I'm not sure I want to let you out of the house looking this ravenous," Tyler chuckled, moving closer again.

His mouth found mine, and I sank into the kiss, savoring the taste of him on my tongue.

I pulled away to drink in the sight of him, the fabric of his tux soft under my fingertips. His broad frame filled out the suit jacket as if it were tailor made. The perfect fit.

He smelled intoxicating, brushed with notes of freshly pressed fabric and aftershave.

My insides hummed in appreciation.

I ran my finger down his tie, over the ridges carved into his chest, buried beneath the jacket. I laughed nervously. "I might have trouble fending the strays off you tonight."

The corner of his mouth quirked. The tips of his fingers traced the length of my arms. "There will be no strays. Only you."

I nodded, knowing he meant every word.

A knock rattled the door and Tyler straightened, smoothing the front of his suit.

"That will be our car," he explained.

I raised my brows. "Our car?"

A swift nod, then his hand fell to the small of my back again. "Alpha Aden sends a car for everyone who attends the dance."

"Right. I'll just grab my bag."

Returning to Tyler, I took his outstretched hand, a warmth spreading over my skin at his touch. It ebbed its way through *every* part of me.

A grin spread over his face and he smirked, like he knew of my arousal.

He couldn't. Could he?

"Can you...?" Oh God! I couldn't fathom the words, let alone *say* them.

His face gleamed with a mixture of amusement, his lips dipping to my ear as if in a room full of people and no one should hear him.

"I can," Tyler confirmed with a mischievous grin as a sensation of what I could only describe as fiery lust circled me.

"Can I? ... Is that? *You*?" I sputtered, certain I could feel his own.

His mouth spread into a full grin. "Cat's out of the bag."

I couldn't hide the surprise, or shock rather, that bloomed on my face. My jaw found its place neatly settled on the ground.

The tip of his finger lightly tapped the peak of my nose, then he winked. *Winked*!

"You mean you can feel when I'm.... I mean...oh my God, this is insane," I whisper-yelled at him.

A low laugh rumbled from him. "Think of it as your direct dial to room service."

I shook my head at the innuendo. "And you said I was the one with the filthy mind." I muttered.

He laughed. "You started it with all your heat and..."

I thumped him in the arm of his expensive suit before his arms wrapped around me again.

I stared up at his wicked eyes, unable to hide my smile. "I can't help it if you make me... *excited*."

Tyler dragged his mouth over mine again, pulling away just enough to speak.

His voice turned to a low husk. "Don't remind me. You're very distracting." His smile brushed my lips. "We really have to go; the car's waiting."

He reluctantly led me to the front door, and when he pulled it open, a sleek black car sat waiting for us outside, the shadows of the night reflecting off its polished exterior.

My brows nearly rose to my hairline. "Wowzers, these guys must be loaded."

"You don't know the half of it," Tyler murmured with a smirk.

The evening air lapped at my legs, goosebumps forming on my skin as I rushed towards the car. Tyler held the door open for me.

I smiled at him. "Such a gentleman, thank you."

His hand cupped my ass as if challenging my words.

Leaning closer, his lips grazed my ear, his hand giving my butt a subtle squeeze. "You might take that back when I get you alone in the back of this car looking the way you do."

"You would never," I challenged back, playfully swiping his hand away, the devilish smirk on Tyler's face disappearing as the car door closed behind me.

I'd never stepped foot in a vehicle like this before, and as Tyler settled into the seat beside me, we sank into the black leather interior, its smell engorging us. We stared at our surroundings with a matching sense of awe.

"I think I'm in the wrong profession," he joked, and I couldn't help my giggle.

I lowered my voice to a whisper so the driver couldn't hear me. "Maybe I need to upgrade my mate to an Alpha Wolf thing," I teased.

Bad idea.

"Never," Tyler growled, moving closer until he was hard against my side. He lowered his voice to a low rasp. "Don't think for a second that any of those wolves could heat your skin the way I do."

As if to prove his point, his hand slid under the front of my dress, and my thighs abandoned me, separating just enough to let him find the outside of my thong already soaked.

I squirmed under his touch, matched with the intensity of his stare that I swear could strip me bare.

"*Tyler*," I hissed, steering my gaze to the driver and back.

The car hummed as it left the curb, the driver seemingly unaware of Tyler's wandering hands.

I grabbed onto his forearm, as if to stop him. As much as I wanted his touch, I couldn't do this in here...could I?

An uncomfortable warning chewed in my mind at the outrageous idea he could touch me only feet away from someone else; but my body had other ideas, a mind of its own. Raw need clawed through me as the mate bond ached for his touch, my legs falling open wider.

Tyler palmed my sex through the sheer fabric barely covering me, his breath dusting my ear, hot and taunting. "Does my mate like to play?"

A light moan slipped from my mouth, Tyler catching it with his lips, smothering it.

I'd never been into this type of thing before, but knowing the driver possibly knew what was going on behind him surprisingly turned me on.

My arousal grew to a fever pitch, my hips seeking friction. More. I needed more.

He pulled the fabric of my thong to the side, finding me soaked, sliding his fingers through my center.

"You feel like heaven," Tyler breathed in my ear, circling my aching bundle of nerves. A low, delicious laugh came from him as he pulled his hands from me. "But not here, princess. *No one* gets to watch my mate get off except me."

He placed his hands innocently on my knee, the caress of his thumb a whole new torture.

"Damn you, mage," I whispered, my hand still fisting his pant leg in frustration.

He cupped the side of my face with his free hand, his half smile leaving me both reeling and craving his touch again. His irises danced in the most mischievous way; two pools of lead drowned with desire.

"You can thank me later when I finish what I've started," he teased, and before I could answer, his lips landed on mine as if sealing his promise.

I moaned into his mouth. "Not fair."

He tsked me, settling his hand on my thigh. "Patience, Morgan." He brushed his lips against my temple.

I loved how affectionate Tyler had become, his hand grazing repeatedly over my knee as I peered out the window at the thick forest surrounding us.

"Where exactly are we going? I mean… what do they actually *live* in?" I wondered.

His hand stilled on my knee. "Every wolf pack has its own territory and 'pack house', so to speak."

"Pack house?"

Tyler nodded. "The entire pack lives in the pack house or its surroundings."

I wrinkled my nose. "Sounds very cult like."

"I guess it does the first time you hear of it." He laughed lightly.

Our car slowed, turning into a tree lined drive so tall I couldn't see their crests. We came to a halt, large iron gates prohibiting us from entering further. The driver had a quick word to one of the two guards stationed at the entrance before the gates slowly swung open, granting us access.

"What the hell is this place?" I thought aloud as the driveway gave way to an expanse of rolling gardens leading to a large stone complex.

Proving to be something between a prison and a castle, its main building looked to be accompanied by other wings off to each side, the main entrance guarded by more security.

Our car pulled to a stop, where two identical wolf statues peered down at us. I felt Tyler's palm firmly encase mine. "Are you ready?" he asked.

I plastered a smile on my face. Was I seriously about to do this?

Butterflies had taken up residence in the pit of my stomach and were currently throwing a party. It took every ounce of control to keep from throwing up.

I let out a long breath, giving Tyler's hand a squeeze. "As ready as I'm ever going to be. I'm going to come out of this alive, right?" I said, steering my gaze back to him.

"Of course." He nodded. "I'll be by your side the entire time. I won't let you out of my sight."

My car door swung open, and an immaculately dressed male nodded in my direction, extending a gloved hand to me.

Were these guys wolves?

Pulling in a deep breath, I took the stranger's covered hand, stepping out of the car. Tyler joined me at my side, his palm landing on the small of my back.

It was then I felt his playfulness subside, the earlier tension in the chambers with the council now stiffening his demeanor once more.

I knew he was trying to hide his apprehension, that no matter how hard he tried to protect me, nothing could change the fact we were headed into a room full of people he didn't fully trust. But unlike in the chambers, the tension that now circled him was one of pure dominance, radiating off him in his every movement.

His steps were calculated and smooth, like each had a purpose, his back extending to his full height, alert. It was undeniably the protectiveness of a mate, if ever I could explain it.

Simply put, I felt safe.

We walked toward the building, and he leaned in close, as if sharing a secret. "You're a powerful witch. Remember that."

"I barely know how to use my magic," I whispered, keeping my attention ahead of me.

He subtly shook his head. "No one here knows that."

He linked his arm in mine as we started up the stairs, the solid wooden doors opening for us as we approached. Beside each door stood two more guards dressed in matching suits.

I inhaled sharply as they ushered us inside, stepping into another world.

We stood on a mezzanine floor that wrapped around a ballroom below, a grand staircase curving its way down to where a mass of dresses and tuxedos gathered at the bottom. Two bronze chandeliers hung from the ceiling, their dim glow casting shadows onto every wall, an inky presence mocking a room of glitz and glamour.

Laughter and music filtered through our ears as we watched from above, taking in the interior of the building in awe. It was the epitome of high society, dripping in wealth and luxury, and suddenly I felt very out of my depth.

What was I doing, thinking I could fit into... *this*?

These people? These *beings*?

They oozed power as they drank from their flutes. Moved through the dance floor not a step out of rhythm. Smelling like a grand scent aged to perfection, like they bathed in their own riches.

As if reading my thoughts, Tyler leaned into me. "Powerful witch, remember."

I glanced at him, a breath of air bobbing in my throat.

The expectations of the evening slammed into me with each step down the elaborate staircase, and I veered my gaze to meet Tyler's, who still had his arm linked with mine. He raised his chin, and I did the same, as if the small motion would somehow create an allure of power.

Three steps to go, two, one.

Tyler led us into the crowd that mingled on arrival, his hand suddenly tightening on my waist, pulling me flush against his side.

An astonishingly tall male approached us, towering over Tyler by at least another half foot. With wide shoulders and a square jaw framed by brown eyes that matched his hair, any woman would be blind to miss his good looks.

"Tyler, nice to see you again," greeted the stranger, shaking Tyler's hand.

He turned to me, giving me an obvious once-over.

Tyler cleared his throat beside me. "Alpha Aden, I'd like to introduce you to my mate, Morgan."

Mate.

The word struck a beat within me, and I was all for it. Tyler asserting his claim on me had my insides thrumming.

I extended my hand to the Alpha. "It's a pleasure to meet you, Alpha Aden."

I stiffened as he lifted my hands to his lips, brushing them against the top of my knuckles. "The pleasure is all mine," he nodded.

Tyler's fingers dug into my waist, and the word *mine* pinched the back of my mind.

I knew one thing about wolves in the wild, that the Alpha was the leader of the pack. I had no doubt the same rules applied here.

The Alpha's eyes moved between us, his presence one of dominance, and when he released my hand, it quickly found Tyler's strapped to my waist.

"Thank you for having us," I complimented, trying to break the unwavering tension that seemed to simmer between them. "Your pack house is exquisite."

He nodded. "Thank you, Morgan." He gestured to the crowd of people before us. "Please, go ahead. Help yourselves to a drink and enjoy your night."

Tyler dipped his head. "You too, Alpha." With that, he steered us into the crowd.

"He seemed friendly enough," I mused.

Tyler's gaze hadn't moved from the Alpha, following him as he made his way across the room. "The way he looked at you made me want to gauge his eyes from his sockets."

I side-eyed him. "Are we a little jealous?"

He didn't even try to hide his agitation, a nerve in his jaw tensing. "He should know better."

I observed the room, staring adoringly at the fabrics of all colors and textures, styles and cuts.

"Morgan!" cried the unmistakable voice of Skye through the crowd, and I turned in her direction.

I spotted her immediately, floating towards us in a midnight-blue dress that made the color of her eyes pop. Wesley stood beside her, his arm linked with hers, his dashing good looks amplified by the crisp suit hugging his lean but muscular build.

Tyler tensed beside me, and I chanced a glance at him, throwing a questionable look at Wesley.

Skye folded her arms around my shoulders, pulling away slightly. "Morgan, your dress is divine," she gushed, giving Tyler a weird look, and I got the impression she had something to do with the dress and shoes I was wearing.

Wesley stepped forward, brushing a kiss on the side of my cheek. "She's right."

Nerves rushed from me in a hurried laugh. "Thanks, Wesley. Not looking too bad yourself."

He turned to Tyler. "Skye's my plus-one for the evening. She didn't want to come alone."

Tyler remained silent, his gaze bounding between the two of them before he nodded. "Make sure she gets home safe."

Wesley straightened. "Of course."

Reid's voice came from behind us, where he wore a black suit complimented by a silver tie. "Look what the cat dragged in," he teased, and we turned to find Scarlet at his side. An emerald-green dress hugged her curves, her hair falling loose in glamorous waves over her shoulders.

The group exchanged greetings before a waiter moved between us, balancing a tray of champagne flutes. I took two, handing one to Tyler.

Colton appeared beside us, his tux pulled tight over his thick frame, motioning his hand in the air for the waiter to return. Taking a flute from the tray, he swiftly drained his glass.

Tyler frowned, and I bit my tongue. Not that I knew Colton well, but it seemed out of character for him to be drinking in that manner.

The clinking of a knife to crystal interrupted the bustle of the crowd, and Alpha Aden stepped up to the front of the room, a woman with hair whiter than a full moon at his side.

"Welcome to our annual gathering," Alpha Aden addressed the partygoers. "We wish to welcome any new arrivals to the community and, of course, bless the Moon Goddess for her offerings. Spend the evening getting to know each other, as we are all allies in the continuous war to keep our town safe from the relentless threats in *our* world." He raised his glass. "To lifelong acquaintances!"

A wave of raised glasses and a clink of crystal followed, ricocheting off the walls.

"Wow, this whole wolf pack thing is serious business," I muttered.

Reid turned, having heard my comment. "They take their pack duties very seriously. Many rogue wolves and enemy packs have tried to take over our town several times before, and sadly, it won't be the last."

I nodded in understanding, my gaze falling on the Alpha and the stunning white-haired beauty beside him. "So that's Alpha Aden's mate?"

Tyler followed my line of sight. "Yes. She is to be the future Luna of the Cutters Cove Pack, I believe."

"Luna?" I asked, turning to him.

Tyler's hand brushed my back. "Sorry, his wife. When the Alpha's mate is sworn in as his wife, she is given the title of Luna."

"And that's just a wolf thing, right?" I asked, curiosity getting the better of me. There was obviously *so* much for me still to learn.

"Just a wolf thing." His gaze speared mine, the hint of a smirk teasing his lips. "You're not still thinking of trading me in, are you?"

I held back my smile. "A girl likes to have options," I bantered with a shrug.

Heat stormed through my veins and between my thighs at the knowing look he gave me. It made me want to slide my hand into the front of his suit pants, warmth rushing to my cheeks at the thought.

Tyler laughed *that* laugh again, that devilish smile from earlier returning. "You might regret saying that." He emptied the rest of his champagne glass before placing it on a passing waiter's tray. "Care to dance?"

He held out his hand, the other behind his back, and I closed my hand over his.

"I thought you'd never ask," I teased.

Tyler led me confidently, weaving us around the dance floor until the song changed to a classic slow dance.

I eyed him curiously. "Skye said you didn't dance?"

He let out a low chuckle. "Knowing how to dance and *wanting* to dance are two very different things."

His face nuzzled into my neck. "Your perfume is intoxicating. What is it?"

Being this close to Tyler would usually have me melting in his arms, but an unease crawled the length of my spine, and I couldn't shake the strange feeling of being watched again.

"Thanks, it's new," I said with a sigh. "A name I can't pronounce"

Tyler held me close for a moment. "Well, whatever it is, I love it." He pulled back, his fingers lifting my chin. His brow furrowed. "Something's wrong. What is it? ... You don't feel safe here?"

"No. Yes. Gosh, I don't know." I shook my head, trying to clear my anxious thoughts. "It's everything, I guess. I just don't feel like I fit in here."

He pulled me closer, his fingers sinking into my hair. "You're safe here. I spoke to security before we arrived. Also, wolves have a unique sense of awareness. They would know if there was someone here who shouldn't be."

I let out a breath, exhaling a sense of relief. "Thank you... for everything, and for being so understanding."

His hands massaged my shoulders in lazy circles. "If you don't feel comfortable, we can leave; it's no problem. That was always the deal, and it still stands. Just say the word."

I knew he meant it, and that alone warmed my insides.

I pushed my arms over his shoulders, moving over the nape of his neck. "No, it's okay. I'm fine, just a few jitters I guess."

His strong arms held me close, pulling back to look at me as he spoke. "It's okay to feel this way. It's a big thing attending something like this for the first time. But you need to tell me these things. Be real with me, and in turn I'll do the same."

Tyler pressed his lips against mine, his kiss searing its way through every part of me and turning my unease into a new sense of calm.

His lips brushed my ear. "Did I mention you look absolutely ravishing tonight?"

His hand floated over my hip, knuckles grazing my sizes.

The temperature in the room seemed to soar when Tyler reduced the space between us.

"I don't know how much longer I can keep my hands off you..." he murmured, a finger skimming the length of my spine.

I arched against him, his touch sending flares sparking over my bare skin.

"Then don't," I challenged.

I slid my hand discreetly between us, running it over his hardness, and a deep groan filled my ears, his breath hot on my neck.

Knowing how ready he was for me destroyed me, the temptation in the room rising to a fever pitch. When his lips claimed mine, need rushed through me, my insides melting.

Tonight, there was no delicate tasting. No teasing.

Tyler took what he wanted, what he needed.

I was suddenly acutely aware of the company we were in, the attention we were attracting. But the mate bond screamed at us for mercy, pulling me under its spell until I ached for more of him.

Tyler's lips left mine, turning to the front of the room to where Alpha Aden stared back at us. The Alpha's irises flared, like a storm rolling in on a clap of thunder before finally turning his back on us.

A streak of satisfaction laced Tyler's molten gaze as he cupped my face in his hands, until I could look nowhere but up at him.

"You're *my* mate, Morgan. *My* beautiful witch. And I know you could bring any man to his knees in a heartbeat, but gods help anyone who looks at you that way again."

My heart slammed into my chest, as if it were fleeing from danger, arousal settling between my thighs as he undressed me with his wicked eyes, right in the middle of the glitzy pack house.

I needed him so badly, the ache of my sex a silent yet exquisite plea.

He sensed my undoing, my control slowly waning. The decency I clung onto by a single thread.

"Follow me," he whispered into my ear, closing his hand around mine.

Tyler weaved us through the room of couples pushed together, drunk on a mixture of champagne and their own lust.

We exited the grand ballroom into a dimly lit hall, our feet mere whispers on the carpeted hallway. He moved to the side, pulling me into a library where books towered above us from floor to ceiling, their history lingering in my nostrils.

"Should we be in here?" I whispered.

Two fingers touched my lips, hushing me with a grin as he tugged me into an aisle.

"You are so bad," I mused, letting him lead the way.

Stopping, he walked me backwards, air collecting in my chest in a rush as my back hit a set of bookshelves.

"Tyler…"

The look in his eyes was one of pure lust as his hands skimmed the length of my arms, stopping to lace his fingers through mine.

"These," he said, motioning to each of my hands, and he lifted them so I held onto the shelf either side of me, "stay right here."

I didn't dare move my hands, fully on board with whatever he had in mind.

I followed his every move. I'd never seen him like this, so in control. And I liked it. *A lot.*

He placed his hands above me on the shelf, his lust-drenched eyes roaming the length of me as if admiring artwork. I almost laughed at the irony. In reality *he* was the piece of art, a perfectly sculpted masterpiece, but he had no idea. So humble.

I dared a bold tongue, sex drenching my tone. "I thought you didn't like it against the wall."

He pressed his body against mine, his hard cock pushing against me. Those same eyes held a devilish spark in them now. "Someone changed my mind."

Greediness flooded my insides, and I rocked my hips, yearning for his touch. A needy moan pulled from deep within me, and he quickly stifled it with his lips, dragging an urgency from me as his tongue devoured mine.

His hands lifted the front of my dress, slipped beneath the lace of my thong, sliding into my arousal waiting for him. He cursed. "So damn soft."

His fingers circled the most sensitive part of me, my hands clawing the shelves at my sides at his expert touch. When he pushed inside me, I drew in a swift breath, my head leaning against his as he drew them out and back in again, devastatingly slow.

Noises I didn't recognize purged from me until a lone finger landed on my lips, silencing my pleasure as he watched me with ravenous intent.

"Come for me. Right here. Right now," he ordered.

His filthy whispers breathed heat throughout me, his hands seeming to get hotter every second. What the hell was happening to me?

I didn't understand the intense heat igniting the flesh between my thighs, until it dawned on me.

Was he using his magic on his hands?

...On me?

"Ty... your hands," I gasped, struggling to put words together. "Oh God, is that...?"

His lips brushed mine, an unmistakable smile teasing my mouth. "You're mated to a thermo mage, princess. You like that?"

Oh. My. God!

I cried out as his hands heated against me. Inside me. Every part of my sex on fire, bordering on the point of pleasure and pain.

"Tell me if it's too much," he insisted.

I shook my head against the euphoria spreading within me. "Yes."

"Morgan?" He started to pull away.

The words rushed from me. "No. Please." My fingernails scraped the shelves they desperately clung to. "Don't stop."

"That's my girl." His voice was low and husky in my ear. "Give these books a show."

Another world captured me as my insides combusted into a thousand embers around his sinful hands. I cried out, unable to contain myself. His lips crashed into mine again, a desperation in his kiss matching the curling of his fingers.

Suddenly, I was in the air, Tyler backing me against the shelf, and I instinctively wrapped my legs around his waist as he adjusted his hold on me.

Books slid from their shelves followed by a drum of dull thuds, then the unmistakable rip of a zipper. Moments later, Tyler buried his length in me, stilling as he filled me with every inch of him, the stretch of him a delicious pain I would never stop craving.

His eyes turned predatory, a darker layer to them, and I was sure I was *sinking* as I stared into the graphite depths of him.

"You're *my mate*, Morgan. Say the words for me, my beautiful witch."

Still reeling from the feeling of him inside me, my voice came out unsteady. "I'm yours."

He remained still, and I rocked my hips against him in frustration, earning me a low, graveled laugh.

"I'm your what?" he pressed.

Those eyes. His words. He undid me in ways he would never know.

Every word struck a beat within me. I rocked against him again, but he pinned his body hard against me this time; I couldn't move an inch.

A greedy whisper tore from me. "I'm *your* mate. *Your* beautiful witch."

As soon as the words left my lips, he withdrew slightly, only to slam back into me again. He took me over and over, his nails digging into me as he held me in his arms.

I released my hands from the shelves, one holding his neck, the other sliding down his front. His suit had come undone, and I skimmed my hands over the angles carved into his chest beneath his crisp shirt, grabbing a fist full.

Clawing my way underneath, my palms finally sank into his flesh, holding onto him as he muffled my cries with his mouth.

I kissed him with frantic need as he buried himself in me repeatedly, a madness of sorts claiming us. Our magic wrapped itself around us, the mate bond an all-consuming and utterly beautiful thing as we came together cursing the gods for creating such a connection.

The mate bond held me at ransom, with my heart in its delicate hand, and my soul on its sleeve. I'd never felt anything like it before.

When Tyler released his hold on me, I slid down his front until my feet found firm ground. Tucking himself back into his suit pants, his hands found the sides of my face, holding me delicately.

Our breaths came in short bursts, our chests rising and falling simultaneously.

Our heads pressed together. "The mate bond," he rasped, shaking his head in disbelief. "I could feel it before. But you're under my skin, in my head... I can *feel* you. It's so fucking intense."

I couldn't find words as his hands weaved their way through my hair, his mouth closing tenderly over mine. I loved him so much I could barely breathe.

It filled my heart with so much joy I couldn't help my giddy smile as he stared down at me.

"Bit of light reading, I see."

We turned to the unexpected voice, horror rushing through me at the sight of Wesley. He sat in an aged leather armchair in a far corner of the library, a smirk on his face.

Tyler glared at him. "What the fuck are you doing here?" he demanded, his hands ensuring my dress covered me.

Wesley dragged in a breath from a cigar, motioning lazily to Tyler. "Alpha Aden is looking for you."

Tyler ignored his comment. "What did you see?"

Wesley didn't answer, playing the same game.

Heat moved to my cheeks, the gleam in Wesley's eyes telling me he'd seen more than I liked if not everything.

Tyler smoothed over his shirt, straightening his tie. "For fuck's sake, you get off on the weirdest shit." He shook his head like he was used to Wes watching people fuck, before shifting his attention back to me. "I need to speak with Alpha Aden. I shouldn't be long."

Wesley stood from the chair, moving towards us. "I can accompany Morgan back while you go ahead."

Tyler turned his attention back to me, uncertainty filling his features.

I nodded. "Sure. You go."

Tyler pecked a kiss on my forehead. "I'll see you shortly for another dance." He turned to Wesley. "Don't let her out of your sight."

Wesley nodded, leaning against the opposite shelf of books. His arms were folded across his front, the cigar balanced precariously between his fingers, curling its smokey essence around him.

I narrowed my eyes at him. "How long had you been sitting there for?"

His looked briefly at the books scattered on the floor. "Long enough."

If the ground could just open up and...

"Your magic is powerful," he said too quietly, interrupting my thoughts.

Gone was Wesley's usual banter, the angles of his jaw now rigid and fused with tension.

"I'm not sure I follow." An uncomfortable chill settled on the base of my neck.

A fleck of something indifferent passed over his gaze, a vivid bright green slashing his emerald irises.

I scrunched my brows. Something didn't feel right.

An icy shiver streaked through me, and my heart started to pound against my rib cage, a deep thump that matched the pace of Wesley's dress shoes as they moved towards me.

He inched closer, until he was only an arm's length away.

Extending his hand to me, he offered me the cigar. "Want a drag?"

I swallowed, a deep sinking feeling making my stomach churn. "No, I'm okay, thanks."

His voice left him as a whisper, but it roared in my ears. "I'm sorry."

Seconds later, his hand covered my mouth.

Then darkness.

Tyler

Adjusting my tie, I entered the ballroom, torn between not wanting to leave Morgan and respecting Alpha Aden's wishes to speak with me.

Scanning the room, I wound my way through people mingling in groups, numb to the scandalous eyes of a blonde woman whose gaze traveled the length of me as I passed. My focus was like tunnel vision; my goal to speak with Alpha Aden and get back to Morgan as quickly as possible, but he was nowhere in sight.

I spotted Colt leaning against the back wall, his tie uneven and the side of his shirt untucked like he'd either just gotten laid or just didn't give fuck, like he had better places to be.

I'd never seen him like this before, and if I was honest, I didn't believe either of those scenarios as it just wasn't Colt. He downed the rest of his drink like he was hell-bent on burying whatever had created the troubled lines now creasing his forehead.

I noted the empty glass in his hand, another perched beside him on the mantle by yet another statue of a wolf.

He lifted his chin upon noticing my approach.

"Alpha Aden requested I speak with him. Have you seen him?" I asked.

Colt set down the empty glass on the mantle. "Not since we arrived. Try over at the elders' table." He nodded toward the other side of the room, and I followed his line of sight.

I nodded before moving through the crowd, veering towards the far wall where the Alpha came into view. He was speaking with an elderly woman as I approached, and resting my hand on her shoulder, the bones of her aged years jutted into my palm.

"Excuse me." I politely smiled at her. "My apologies, Alpha Aden has a requested a word with me."

The Alpha rose to his feet, smoothing the front of his suit jacket. "Tyler, sorry but I'm not following."

I frowned. "Wes said you needed a word."

The Alpha's expression remained blank, my wary gut turning over.

He slid his hands into the pockets of his suit pants. "I haven't spoken to Wesley since he arrived. Is everything okay?"

All the blood drained from my face, the color I was sure dissolving rapidly at an alarming rate. What the fuck was going on?

I turned on my heel, pacing back through the crowd, no polite excuses as I pushed my way back to the library.

The second I landed beneath the doorframe, I scanned the room. To the books still scattered on the floor, but I heard and saw no one.

"Morgan?" I yelled, storming inside, my chest heaving beneath my tux.

A silence lingered among the shelves, and I traced Morgan's lingering scent, heightened from the mate bond back to where I'd left her.

Confusion rolled off me in heavy waves, tumbling me into its uncontrollable riptide.

The Alpha entered the library behind me, his two Betas at his side.

"Is there a problem? Do I need to alert security?" his voice commanded.

Reid entered the library next, hurriedly making his way to my side, his usually relaxed nature depleted and on edge. "Ty, what's going on?" he said, concern rippling his forehead.

I knew it in my bones. Felt fear rush into me, claiming its new owner.

I directed my attention at the Alpha. "Alert every fucking pack member you have. Someone's taken my mate."

Reid's hand clamped onto my shoulder. "Let's not jump to any conclusions. Can you feel her through your bond?"

I threw my attention to him. "There's nothing."

I had begun to sense her through the bond, had been starting to pick up on her emotions. Where there used to be a comforting presence was now an empty void, and the loss of such a feeling was fucking devastating. Like I'd been stripped of her entirely.

Pacing the room, I threw a book across the wall where it landed with a *thud*. Knotting my hands into fists, they burned with rage.

How could I let this happen? It had to be a coincidence they were both missing.

"What about through mind link?" suggested the Alpha.

I threw my hands into the air. "What the fuck is mind link?" I seethed.

The Alpha's stare sliced through me. Cold and brutal. Extending to his full height, his presence dominated the room, but there was no way in hell I'd back down to this wolf.

He didn't own me. And I was not one of *them*.

I knew of his distaste for me. He had strongly disapproved of my relationship with Ava, and ever since, we had found ourselves in a mutual agreement. Acquaintances and nothing more.

Reid extended a hand between us. "Alpha, Ty has only yesterday felt the mate bond at its full strength. They're still coming to grips with its workings."

He veered his gaze back to mine. "You don't feel Morgan at all?"

I shook my head. "There's nothing. If anyone hurts her..." My voice trailed off, unable to finish the sentence. I meant every word. No one would lay a hand on Morgan and walk away alive.

Alpha Aden cleared his throat. "Let's not get ahead of ourselves here. She's possibly gone for a walk."

A blanket of rage smothered me. "She hasn't gone for a walk!" I roared, venom slicing my tone. "I left her with Wes. He was to accompany her back to the ballroom to wait for me. Tell me how something so simple could go so wrong?"

Reid gripped my shoulders. "Wes has no reason to take her. I know it looks bad, but you know him. He wouldn't do this."

I wanted to believe it with every fiber of my being. But something snagged my insides, my intuition telling me there was more going on here.

"What about her magic?" I grimaced, not wanting to consider it.

Reid shook me this time. "Betty said her magic was rare. That it would be sought after. Anyone could have her, have them both even."

I didn't speak, afraid words once aired couldn't be taken back.

The room stilled.

My heart beat furiously in my chest.

"Find. My. Mate." I gritted out.

Alpha Aden addressed his Betas, his authority commanding the room. "Get your teams to run the perimeter. I want every part of this complex searched and secured. We need to know if Morgan's still on the grounds. Understood?"

"Yes, Alpha." They nodded and left the room.

As we waited to hear word from security, Skye walked into the library, surveying the room. "What's going on?"

Reid quickly filled her in on the details.

"Wes wouldn't do that." Her voice was immediately charged with conviction.

"How sure are you of that?" I sniped, already regretting my tone at her.

"Really fucking sure, Ty." Her irises flashed a florescent shade as her own fire element surfaced. "How can you think for even a second he has anything to do with this?"

Her wide eyes tore at my heart as she stared at me with absolute assurance.

My own element simmered under my skin, my blood growing hotter with each passing moment. "As much as I want to believe that, why would he lie to me then conveniently disappear at the same time as Morgan does?"

Skye's lips set into a thin line as she fidgeted with the ring on her thumb. "I still don't believe it, and neither should you."

Rising to my feet, I strode over to the far wall, my gaze following the security team gathered outside.

Alpha Aden's voice came from behind me. "I can confirm Morgan's not on the premises."

Rage speared through every inch of me.

"Fuck!" I overturned a bookshelf, its contents spilling to the ground. "Where would he take her? How do I find her?" I seethed. "If he lets anyone touch her, anyone hurt her..." I stabbed the air with a finger. "I'll rip his throat out."

"I think we need to talk to Betty," Skye said quietly.

Reid nodded. "I agree. She needs to know what's going on."

This couldn't be happening. Morgan had come so far; she didn't deserve this. *We* didn't deserve this.

The room slipped into a thick haze, a blanket of fear threatening to suffocate me. A cold, dark place I had been once before in the midst of grief and would not return to again.

Alpha Aden stepped forward. "There's a car out front. The driver will take you wherever you need," he offered, his eyes glazing over as if his thoughts were somewhere else.

I nodded at him. "Thank you."

Charging down the front steps of the pack house, Colt rushed to my side, lines striking his forehead.

"Alpha Aden filled me in. We'll get her back, Ty," he said with a nod before sliding into the car beside the driver.

I held a door open for Skye. "Get in," I ordered, and she shimmied into the back seat, myself and Reid following on either side of her.

Scarlet came running down the stairs next. "Wait... let me in!"

She opened the car door, staring at the already packed car, Reid closest to her.

"God's help me," he muttered. "Jump in." He took her hand, helping her through the door until she perched precariously on his lap.

The sharp bite of leather forced through my nostrils as the car veered back into town, a midnight sky glooming over us as we rounded the streets of Cutters Cove. How could this be happening?

I'd only just found her. One minute, she was jump-starting my heart, then just as suddenly, she was gone like she was never there.

A tense silence filled the air, mixed with an uncertainty no one wanted to address. The elephant in the room, an uncomfortable beast. I sank into the leather, my fist finding my lips before connecting with the car door.

Wes had *never* given me cause to believe he could be after Morgan. I mean, what the fuck? To think he'd screwed me over sent thoughts of all kinds of sick revenge charging through my mind.

Skye fired me a look that said 'get your shit together' before peering through the gap to the front once more.

I lashed out again, my fist burning in protest until Skye's arm wrapped around my wrist. "Get a grip and pull yourself out of whatever the hell this is. Morgan needs you, but not like this."

From the front seat came Colt's voice. "She's right."

I desperately forced back the fury threatening to unload from my palms deep within me.

I glared at him, something I rarely did. "Easy for you to say," I said through clenched teeth. "It's not your mate that's *missing*, and we don't know if she's hurt or how to find her."

Everyone shut their mouths at my comment.

Reid pointed down the street to a house with a flowerbed below the mailbox. "It's that one."

A small cottage wrapped in white weatherboards came in to view. Its curtains were drawn, Betty would most likely be asleep.

The driver pulled the car to a stop, and we stepped outside, moonlight casting its glow over us. Looming behind us, our silhouettes stalked us as if in chase, and I willed myself to wake up from the sick reality I'd set foot in, a nightmare I wanted to rid myself of.

Skye rapped on Betty's window, its echo slicing into the brittle evening. "Betty, open up, it's Skye," she whisper-yelled.

Fuck this.

My knuckles hit the front door. *Hard*.

"Morgan's missing!" I yelled, rapping at the solid timber.

A curtain fluttered before the door creaked open. Betty stared at us blankly, as if we'd woken her from a deep sleep. A purple nightgown hung to her knees, and she instinctively wrapped her arms around herself as the cold air pressed against her.

A pained expression embedded the usually soft lines of her face. "Morgan's missing?"

I nodded. "We need your help to find her."

Hell, I'd get on my knees if I had to.

Betty motioned us inside. "Of course, dear. Come in, tell me everything."

Skye filled her in on the evening events, and Betty's irises widened at the mention of Wes.

"And you're certain he's not gallivanting about with some woman?" she asked.

"He's not out with a woman and he didn't do this," Skye said firmly. "He would *never* do something like this. He's known Ty his entire life!"

The room tensed at her outburst.

Reid's fingers thrummed his bicep as he stared awkwardly at the both of them. "We don't *know* it was Wes," he cautioned. "He just happened to be there, and now both him and Morgan are missing. At this stage, who took Morgan is … unclear."

Betty's voice cut the silence. "When was the last time you all used your magic?" she asked, leading us into her living room.

Skye shrugged. "I'm at full strength."

Reid and Scarlet agreed.

I gripped the base of my neck with my hands. "Colt and I used ours last night, but we should be at full strength by now."

Betty nodded. "Tyler dear, can you please fetch the candles in the spare room? Skye, the matches are in the second drawer down." She motioned across the room to a dresser standing against the wall.

I located the candles, handing them to Betty, where she placed them in a circle on the living room floor.

"Please sit," she beckoned, and we dropped to the faded rug that covered the floorboards. "Tyler, you need to prepare yourself for anything, or anyone. There are many people who would sacrifice Morgan to claim her magic as their own as you know."

I nodded.

Dread had a taste, and it had settled in my mouth. A heavy weight of lead lodged in my throat. I gulped and it sank deep within me, a dark, dreaded thing that clung to my heart.

Betty instructed us to hold hands, then turned her attention to me. "You're about to learn how far your magic can take you. You need to call on your mate bond and its connection to her. It will lead you to her if you let it."

I nodded once more.

Betty hummed in approval. "I need everyone to channel your magic. Open it up to me. Let me use your strength."

Our circle joined as one, with Betty speaking syllables I didn't understand. It was clear she knew the real craft, a bit like Scarlet. She started to chant a verse, the same verse over and over, and the group joined her, our whispers turning louder with each anxious second.

Energy whipped around me as I forced my eyelids shut, pulling deep within myself. Magic scalded my sides as it entered me, its current an unimaginable force of every element in the room.

I felt them all. The warmth of Skye's fire element swept against me in a subtle wave. Colts earth element climbed my limbs, its strength an incredible presence I had underestimated, mirrored by Scarlet's, only gentler.

Betty's air element ghosted through me, and I almost threw up at the raw slash from Reid, the taste of blood filling my senses as his gift muddled with mine, sliding through my veins.

I shut off my mind, letting them in, Morgan my only focus.

I'm coming for you, my love.

Morgan

Darkness haunted me from beneath my eyelids, cold palming my cheek as damp air crept over my skin. A shiver curled my legs to my chest, the pads of my fingers scraping against a grainy surface.

My lips stuttered as I drew in a breath.

Why was I so cold?

I ran my tongue over my lips, coating them with what felt like heaven. A light flickered. My thick lashes struggled to open as if rising from a deep slumber, but when the fog clouding my sight finally cleared, confusion startled me, pinning me in place.

Stone walls surrounded me on three sides. The fourth, a wall of steel bars, my only chance of freedom if ever I was granted it. My dress lay splayed around me, its silk now creased and edged with smudges, and I slid my legs underneath me, wincing as my bare feet dragged over uneven ground.

Where was I?

My head felt heavy, like sleep could take me at any moment, and I rubbed at my temples as if it could ease the pain tearing through my skull.

Climbing to my feet, grit crunched between my toes as I stumbled over to the bars, my palms closing around them to steady myself. I slammed my eyes shut as the room began to blur, clinging to the bars as if they could keep me conscious. I blinked, then blinked again, until my vision slowly cleared.

I forced a wad of air down my throat as my eyes adjusted to my dim surroundings, dread sinking to the pit of my stomach. A chamber of cells lined the opposite wall, the same as the one currently holding me captive.

I looked like I was in a basement. Or even worse, a dungeon...

"Hello? Is anyone there?" I cried out into a rigid silence. "Somebody, help me!" I shrieked, pushing and pulling against the bars, my desperate attempts to move them useless.

My magic.

I wrapped my fingers around the bars with purpose this time.

Focused.

I pulled on the light I knew would help me, while the dark I'd felt, the first time I used it tipped its head in laughter.

Forcing my magic into my hands, I let it consume me. I pictured Tyler, the focus and strength I needed, just like we had practiced. I forced the magic from me, but it remained stagnant, rebounding against my skin.

What the hell?

I pushed again, but nothing happened.

The dark side of my magic mocked me. Baited me to use it, but it seemed if I wanted to, it would be pointless.

Why could I not use my magic?

A scuffing drew my attention from somewhere nearby.

"Is someone there?" I yelled.

More shuffling, followed by a moan.

The air stilled in my lungs.

"Who's there? Hello? Where are we?"

An eerie silence hung in the air. The kind that spiked the hairs on the back of your neck and slithered down your spine.

A voice came from somewhere, stiffening the already raised hairs on my bare arms.

"There's no way out. Don't bother," it rasped.

Male.

"Who are you? Why are we here?" I asked. "How *long* have you been here?" The questions barreled out of me in a lone breath.

"Many years."

The voice lacked energy. Void of hope.

My back scraped down the wall until I hit the floor, my knees pulling to my chest.

"You must have something she wants," he said.

"*She?*" I pressed.

Another pause.

"Someone you must never give in to. A witch."

"But what does she want?" I wrapped my hands around my legs in an attempt to keep warm.

"Magic. If it runs through your veins, you must protect it."

I let my head fall against the wall. Of course. Shit. Shit. Shit.

"Did she take yours?"

There was a brief pause. Then, "Yes."

The despair in his voice itched my skin. I needed to get out of here. Had to find a way.

My looked beyond the bars to the window beyond reach, my only escape route being the large door that led to who knew where.

"Why does she want other people's magic?" I asked the stranger.

"As she gains more power, she gets stronger."

"But for what reason?"

"She wants to open the portal to the Underworld. Believes that light and dark can live as one."

I'd heard of portals in movies, but hell, it didn't surprise me they were a thing, too. I didn't want to think about what existed in this Underworld he spoke of. His words clung to the damp air that lay dormant in the room.

Although I couldn't see this man, I felt his dismay choking the life from his soul.

It scared me to think it could claim mine, too.

"How did she take your magic?" I said quietly.

A long silence followed.

"There are very few people who can take one's magic and force it on another. No one in their right mind would do it, but given the right circumstances, anything is possible."

His words chilled my insides.

This was some sick and twisted reality that apparently, I was to be a part of.

My head lifted as a heavy *clunk* vibrated off the walls, the large lock on the wooden door sliding across.

In walked a woman with sleek hair held back by a tight low knot, her cheek bones hollowed and skin ghastly pale. I stilled, an icy chill coating my skin as realization hit me. The woman from my nightmares. Her manicured fingertips of black whipped in the air as she spoke to someone behind her.

"Bring her to me," she ordered.

Her voice scraped my spine like sandpaper on my skin, causing a shudder to move over me.

She stepped to the side, revealing a figure behind her. I could tell by the fit of the jeans, the way they balanced on narrow hips, that the figure was male. There was a vague familiarity about the stranger, even as a black hoodie covered his face.

When his head angled up to look at me, my gaze locked onto a set of green eyes I placed instantly.

Everything became clearer, the last few moments in the library returning to me.

"Wesley?" I whispered.

He barely looked at me. Remained silent.

Why was he in different clothes? How long had I been here?

The woman passed Wesley a large key, and I watched as he took it. His head dipped low.

"Wesley? I don't understand..." I trailed off, unable to make sense of what was happening.

He didn't lift his eyes from the ground as he walked to the door, sliding the solid key into the lock of my cell. He pushed the door open, and it groaned as it swung wide.

"Don't make this any harder than it needs to be," he said, his tone flat.

"Wes!" I said with urgency this time. "What the hell is going on?"

He moved towards me, but I couldn't decipher the look on his face. Was that desperation?

I didn't understand his reason for being part of this. How could he do this? To me? To Tyler? He'd known Tyler since they were kids. None of it made any sense.

His hand gripped my upper arm, and I tried to shove him off, pushing and pulling against his grasp, but his grip held tight. I tried every move known to me, my fists pounding into his chest repeatedly, but it was no use. His strength overwhelmed me.

I lowered my voice so only he could hear me. "Don't do this, whatever this is. Whatever is going on, we can fix this. Ty would do anything for you, you know that."

Wes faltered, an almost pained expression tormenting his face before it disappeared just as quickly, before manhandling me from the cell. It was then I got to see the face of the stranger I'd been speaking to between solid walls.

His beard concealed his mouth and long hair tangled over his ears. The eyes that sank into his frail form were fierce, slashing imaginary scars into the woman's sides.

"Let her go, don't do this," he said, stumbling to his feet, his milk-white knuckles wrapped around the bars.

She ignored him as if he was never there. "It's time," she said with a twirl of her finger. Wesley stiffened beside me. "Come along."

He nudged me forward and I tried to escape from his grip again, but he held firm. I turned back to look at him, forced my face closer until my breath muddled with his, staring daggers at him, imagined piercing his bright green eyes with my nails until they bled.

"Tyler will kill you if anything happens to me," I hissed.

His voice dipped low. "Just do as she asks. *Please*."

"What the fuck?" I side-eyed him, my head spinning in confusion.

He edged me onwards, my bare feet inching forward as he maneuvered us into a large room that resembled a church.

The building was a fortress of stone, layers upon more layers of gray, like depression had embedded itself in its block walls. But the *unused* smell hit me first and foremost. Musty. I could almost feel the dust rising through my nostrils.

My head turned to the front of the room, where the brown-haired woman sat on a throne-like bench, one knee crossed over the other.

Who was she?

I wrestled against Wesley's grip to no avail, my efforts swiftly rewarded by his arms wrapping around my front, holding me in place.

"Behave," Wes hissed against my ear.

I threw him another death glare over my shoulder. "Fuck you!" I spat, trying to shove my elbow into his side.

I turned my attention back to the woman, who watched me with intrigue.

I wouldn't let her see my fear and stood tall, straightening my shoulders, chin raised.

"What do you want from me?" I demanded.

She surveyed her nails, flicking between each one. "That's not the way to address your mother, dear."

My what? No fucking way.

Only then did her resemblance to the image I looked at in the mirror become clear.

It couldn't be. *Helena.*

"You will never be my mother. A *real* mother wouldn't do this to her own child," I seethed, wrestling against Wesley again.

She let out a frivolous laugh. "Wesley mentioned you were a feisty one."

I ignored the comment.

"Morgan, my darling, you were taken from me so many years ago, and I believe you and I are one in the same."

"Like hell we are!" I exclaimed.

To think after all these years, I'd longed to know who my mother was, had imagined one day we would be reunited in a story I would one day tell my children.

What a joke. I'd wasted pockets of my time, not to mention sleep on something that was clearly never going to happen. Until I moved to Cutters Cove, love had abandoned me, my birth parents having been nonexistent and my adoptive ones now dead.

I thought of Tyler and the connection we shared. How much I loved him. In that moment, I swore nothing would tear us apart. *Nothing.*

Helena continued, her head tilting to the side, "Morgan, you possess magic that can do great things. *We* could do great things... if you would let me guide you."

Rage consumed every part of me. Scarred my heart. Buried itself in my bones.

I remembered what the stranger in the cells had told me. His words of warning.

'You must have something she wants.'

Her eyes pierced mine. Like calls to like. Was that how the saying went? Well, I would prove whoever made up the stupid saying wrong.

If she was darkness, then I was the light. I was everything she was not.

I steadied my voice. "I would never hurt anyone or use my magic for anything other than good."

Helena's hands white-knuckled the throne-like thing she sat on.

"With all due respect, Morgan, you haven't truly become one with your magic."

I wrestled against Wesley's hold again, spitting my words at her. "I have the rest of my life to learn, and it won't be with your help."

"Very well then." She nodded to Wesley over my shoulder. "You know what to do."

Horror tore through my veins, filling my insides with dread. I glanced back at Wesley, where his lips pressed grimly into a thin line.

I forced myself to look back to Helena as she rose to her feet, each footstep towards me its own countdown to whatever came next. Her demeanor changed. Eyes disgusted and uninterested, she looked at me as if I was nothing but an inconvenience in whatever her sick and twisted plan was.

She glared at me menacingly, folding her hands in front of herself. "If you won't use your magic the way it's meant to be used, then it is to be mine."

I lowered my voice, spite filling my tone. "I would rather die than let you have my magic, you sick bitch."

Helena dismissed the comment, her wrist flicking through the air again.

"You know, it took a long time for me to track down this sensor mage to help me find you. To think you were living under his very nose..."

Anger rippled through me at Wesley's betrayal, my fury boring into him. He dropped his gaze to his feet.

"Once he syphons your power from you, it will be all mine, and I can finally do what I've wanted all these years."

I stiffened at the word *syphon*. Could Wesley really do that?

"And what exactly do you plan to do with my magic?" I sneered. If I was to survive whatever was about to go down, I needed to know what her intentions were. Was the stranger in the basement correct? He had mentioned something about opening the portal to the Underworld...

"There are places you could only dream of, Morgan, ones that exist right under our very feet. Only a power like your own could produce enough magic to take us there."

"I hate to burst your bubble, Helena,"—I refused to use the term *mother*—"but there is no *us*."

She curled a finger around a loose strand of her hair. "Very well then. I hope your magic is more useful than your father's."

Ice-cold realization slid through me.

I motioned toward the cells. "*That's* my father you have locked up in there?"

She ignored the question. "Do it," she ordered.

Wesley tensed behind me, his body turning rigid against my back.

Helena stepped closer. "Wesley, do I need to remind you…"

"On it," he replied through clenched teeth.

Wesley's hand clamped down on my shoulder, and I flung around to face him, anger funneling through me as we clashed in a standoff.

"On your knees," he ordered, his grip on me trying to force me to the ground, but I refused to yield.

"Why are you doing this? You're better than this, Wes, and you know it."

"Now." His voice came louder this time, as if he was trying to convince us both.

His irises had turned a murky shade of green, so dark they bordered on black, but my feet remained rooted to the ground. I would not bow down to him, to either of them.

I pulled myself straighter, lifting my chin and staring him down.

As if my defiance demanded punishment, an unseen force drove me to the ground and I was at its mercy, succumbing to it immediately. My knees crunched as they hit the floorboards, aching at the forced landing.

His wide eyes darted to Helena with a confusion that I was sure mirrored my own.

The force hadn't come from him.

"You're welcome," Helena said matter-of-factly, looking back at him with boredom. "You know what needs to be done."

Fear bobbed in my throat, my limbs numb, having completely abandoned me at this point, frozen in place in some haunting stupor.

I slammed my eyes closed, willing my magic to come forward once more, focused on Tyler. His scent, his touch, the bond. *Anything*. It produced nothing but a stabbing ache in my head, and I cried out.

Frustration poured from me, expelling in the only form it could.

"You bitch! How could you do this?"

Helena's heels clicked closer. "Your magic won't work, Morgan. Simple really, once you know how."

I'd never used the word hate in my life.

It had always revolted me.

But now I knew its true nature and it was standing right in front of me in the form of my apparent *mother*. It clung to my every word, causing my voice to lower, my syllables slick with it as it wrenched at my heart.

"I'm glad my father sent me away. You could never raise a child. You're nothing but sick and twisted. Tyler will kill you if anything happens to me." I hissed.

She tutted, "Careful now, Morgan. Dare I remind you that snarky little mouth of yours can be easily sealed shut? It's sad, really. This all could have worked out so much differently."

I stilled at her last comment even when every fiber of me wanted to scream at her, tear her eyes out with my nails until blood spilled down her death-like cheek bones and stained the floor.

I forced myself to look at Wesley in one last-ditch effort to stop whatever happened next. "You don't have to do this. Whatever's going on, we can fix it. She's gone mad, and you know it."

Wesley's knuckles popped against the silence, ricocheting off the stone walls. One. Two. Three. Four. Five.

He stared down at me, sinking any hope I had of changing his mind into a pit of hopelessness.

Helena's footsteps faded into the distance as I pleaded with him. Every soul-drenching piece of me a silent plea as I stared up at him until he lowered in front of me, his gaze meeting mine momentarily.

The cracking of his knuckles again tore through the stifling silence between us, his breathing becoming heavier.

Was he stalling?

Through clenched teeth, I whispered, "Whatever you are about to do, please don't," I leveled with him. "You don't have to do this."

We were at the same height, the Wes I once knew now tainted with a darker version of him or was that... desperation?

Just as quietly, his voice hit my ears. "Don't fight me. You need to let me in, or I could kill you."

I shook my head. "You can stop this; you know you can."

Wes grimaced. "I can't. Now let me in."

His eyes slid shut, head rolling from one side to the other as his hands sank into my scalp. I held my breath, knowing what was coming next, a giant breath bobbing in my throat as I stared into the blackest form of the night sky embedded in his skull.

Oh, hell no, not this again.

"No!" I gasped.

I'd succumbed to Wesley's power before, the last time willingly letting him in, and he had done so gently, but not this time.

The pads of his fingers gouged into my scalp, fighting for access, and I pushed back, mentally shielding him from entry. I willed my subconscious to stand firm, but he was too powerful, his essence first blotting as it seeped through my mental shields before spreading like spilled ink as it scrawled over my subconscious.

Intense pain fired through my limbs. White-hot, like shards of glass slicing through every vein.

"*Stop!*" I yelled, clawing my scalp in agony.

I would never let him in. Not this time. No one would take my magic from me.

I withdrew into a slice of myself he hadn't found yet, hiding from him in the depths of my mind. I pictured my deepest love, the warmth Tyler brought to my soul, the desire that rocked me in his mere presence.

Something snapped inside me, and I let out a piercing cry, internally praying Tyler could hear me.

Help me! I screamed as a wave of sobs shuddered my chest, wracking my body.

I couldn't hold on any longer, the fortress I'd wielded internally being torn down piece by piece, Wesley's power unfathomably strong.

Hold on, princess.

My breath caught in my lungs, breaking my concentration at the sound of Tyler's voice in my head. His voice flooded through me, and I wondered if I was imagining it.

A beat.

A breath.

A distraction.

I felt him then. Clawing. Wesley's power flooding my subconscious, taking what was *mine*.

My magic slipping from me as if it were never there.

The one thing gifted to me at birth, my magic, my soul, was being ripped from me through this tether Wesley held over me, and there was not a damn thing I could do to stop it.

Blood-curling screams filled the room. *My* screams. Spine-curling, earth-shattering like he was tearing my soul into a million tiny pieces and discarding them among the stars.

My head throbbed as if it had its own beat, tears spilling down my cheeks. My heart squeezed so tight it burned, like the devil had lashed it, claiming it as his own, and I knew this was the end.

Glass shattered somewhere as I fought back against Wesley, my scream tearing at my eardrums as I felt the last of my magic leave me.

The clawing in my mind faltered for a split second.

A quiet spread over me.

I felt weightless.

Without warning, air forced into my lungs in a quick breath as my magic shunted *hard* back into me. So hard I flew backwards.

Then darkness.

I had never seen such a thing. There were no warps or shades to its devastating beauty. A treasure kept from the night sky and the darkest of storms reserved only for this moment. I sank into its pit of nothingness. It was a welcoming and addictive place.

Deeper and deeper.

Until I could sink no further.

Tyler

A force shoved me forward, the room distorting as I slammed my hands in front of me to break my fall, but it never came. Plucked into the air as if weightless, my eyes opened to find myself spinning wildly, a vortex twisting me into its fury.

Excruciating pain sliced through my back, my vision blurring completely as the shards of pain roused like a beast spreading its newborn wrath. A roar ripped from me as it molded to my bones, wracking my soul as it contorted me. Taunted me at its peril.

Son of a bitch, it *burned*.

I clenched my jaw, trying to block it out as the ground rushed towards me faster than the air heaving into my lungs.

The earth thumped beneath my feet as I landed, one hand barely steadying me.

Where the fuck was I?

Quickly I stepped back, shrinking into the shadows of the forest that surrounded me, thankful for the momentary cover. My gaze swept over my immediate surroundings, my sight insanely sharp. Magnified.

The haunting tale of a raven's cry forced me back to reality. Turning my gaze to the canopy above, its curious eyes looked down at me, a single blink before flying away.

Whispers of rodents scratched the forest floor, inching me forward, as if speaking to my mind. A shadow bounced off a nearby tree and I spun on my heel, searching for movement. It appeared again to my side, and I pivoted, my muscles tense.

Holy fuck.

The shadow was mine.

Blood rushed through my veins, faster with each passing second as I stared at the shadow protruding from my back.

Wings.

What the fuck?

I whipped my hand behind me, and feathers laced through my fingers.

"Ah fuck." I winced, pulling away at the pain.

I hadn't noticed my top barely clinging to my chest, torn to shreds at the back from the wings that had slashed my skin, emerging fully spanned at my back. Coarse and black as a moonless night, rimmed with a golden glow around the edges.

They resembled what I would imagine a phoenix to look like, and something gnawed at me about my family history that I was sure Skye had mentioned before. A passing comment about a half mage, half shifter somewhere back in a previous generation.

A cry tore through the forest, my attention turning towards it somewhere up ahead.

It stripped me of pain, a chill scaling my bones.

Morgan.

I knew that voice as if it were my own. My mate's cry hurtled me forward, charging onwards so fast, I lifted into the air with the grace of a fucking newborn giraffe through a gap in the canopy.

My arms circled for balance, eventually finding their natural place as I soared above the ground until a church emerged ahead of me. My back burned with each dip as my wings brought me closer to the ground, but I pushed through, my only concern being Morgan. I had to find her.

Flying didn't come easy to me as I maneuvered through the air, easing myself to the ground gradually, at one stage almost flipping on my back.

As my feet found firm ground again, I stuck to the shadows of the forest, my ears alert, eyes scanning the tree line. With a full moon illuminating it from behind, the church stood within an overgrown graveyard about fifty feet away.

Limbs of deceased vines crawled its walls, almost camouflaged with the forest behind if it wasn't for the turret extending from its pitched roof.

I stalked forward, my footsteps muffled by moss clinging to the ground, my gaze scanning the tree line once more before focusing on the church.

A solid timber door looked to be the main point of entry from my vantage point, the only windows high above. I inched closer, my fingers wrapping around the edge of the door that stood ajar. It slid open silently, and I ducked inside, keeping close to the wall.

Stone formed its interior shell, rows of pews blocking my way to the front. It smelled like it had be shut up for years. Like ass.

Movement to my right stole my attention. *Wes.*

Our eyes connected from opposite sides of the room, confirming my worst nightmare and I froze, betrayal gripping me tight.

He stared back at me, and I couldn't gauge the look on his face. The face I had grown up with for the first ten years of my life. My blood ran hot, searing through every part of me, my palms itching for release as if forcing me to accept the deceit.

My strides pushed forward in his direction.

Wes held his hands in front of him. "Ty, I had no choice."

Rage twisted inside me. "You always have a choice!" I growled through clenched teeth. "*Always!*"

"I swear, if it wasn't for..."

"Wasn't for what!" I roared, unable to fathom any explanation he had. "What reason could possibly convince you to capture my mate? Because I can't think of a single fucking one!" I stabbed a finger at the air between us.

As I closed in on him, Wesley's steps angled backwards toward a side door I hadn't noticed before.

His head shook in defeat.

Coward.

Suddenly he bolted toward the exit and instinctively, my palms spread wide, my magic coming forward like a hit of euphoria as I let a fireball loose in his direction before his form disappeared.

Then I saw her, splayed on the ground at the front near the pulpit.

"Morgan!" my voice boomed off the walls.

I charged towards her, swallowing the lump lodged in my throat and sinking to my knees when I noticed her eyes closed and skin depleted of color. Her dress was crumpled, and grit stuck to it like she'd been sitting on the ground, her arms splayed out at her sides in awkward angles, the same as her bare legs.

"Morgan, wake up," I urged, my thumb skimming a dampness on her forehead, the other palming the pearl of her ghostly white cheek.

When she didn't respond, I pressed two fingers under her jaw, my cheek resting against hers.

I stilled, silently pleading for the faint beat to hit my fingers.

"Baby, it's me. You need to wake up," I pleaded, caressing her hair.

When the lull of her heartbeat never came, I heaved my hands against her chest. Pushed a breath into her mouth.

She would come back. She *had* to come back to me.

Heaving. Breathing. Heaving. I became a rollercoaster of life support, riding my adrenaline to the edge of its limit.

"This can't be it. We don't end like this... Breathe, Morgan!" I choked, filling her lungs with air again.

Her body remained limp, skin pale, clammy.

I don't remember how long I tried to breathe life into her, to jumpstart her heart. But it felt like a lifetime, her body refusing my efforts.

Pain sliced through me, so fierce I arched against the white-hot heat tearing at my insides. I pulled her body flush against mine as the pain engulfed me, nearing blackout myself.

I wouldn't accept it. This life was meant for us. Fate had decided it. They *knew* we were meant to be together.

I cradled into her neck, the mist of my breath circling around us as if protecting our moment from the outside world. I would rather have never met her than for it to end like this. To know such a love existed, then have it be taken so unfairly.

"Morgan, come back to me. *Please*," I whispered in anguish, trailing my fingers over her lips. "It's not supposed to end this way. I only just found you."

I pushed onto my hands, the terror in my heart exploding into every part of me. Droplets glistened on her cheeks, fresh from my eyes, and I swiped them away with my thumb.

Then it dawned on me.

Why had I not thought of it before?

I needed to get her out of here and back to Reid. His healing gift could help in some way. I didn't even know if it was possible, and I would never force such a thing on him, but I had to at least try.

Scooping her into my arms, I started for the door, only to find both exits blocked by an inferno of flames. Fire I'd created after hurling my magic at Wes.

I cursed at myself for not noticing earlier, when it was small enough for my magic to extinguish it. Now it was too far gone, even for me to stop.

An agonizing sound left me. I didn't recognize it. Smoke chocked my lungs, bringing me to my knees once more.

The pain became unbearable, bright stars blurring my vision, and I slammed them shut at the incredible force shredding my heart to pieces. In that moment, I believed the tales from my elders, that a mate bond being severed could kill both partners.

I engulfed her body desperately with mine, my legs intertwined with hers, heart to heart. One beating. One still.

My voice cracked. "If this is it, I need to tell you something," I whispered against her ear, taking in every scent of her, committing it to memory. "I should have said it when I got the chance, because I knew you were meant for me the minute we danced in the doorway. Your heart stole a part of mine, and I will be forever grateful to have found you, even for only the smallest fraction of my life."

Tears fell freely as I took in every fine detail of her. Her lashes, thick like her hair, framing her head angelically. The small freckle under her eye that crinkled when she smiled. Her lips, oh god she was everything I was not.

She was delicate, a treasure of sorts that glistened brightly. I placed my lips on her forehead, then nose, caressed her cheeks, her hair.

I cupped her face. "I love you, Morgan. I will *always* love you."

I breathed one final breath into her lungs, not ready to say goodbye, my lips lingering on hers.

I'd never felt a love so pure. So right. A love that could steal your breath, make your heart skip a beat.

My heart stammered in my chest as warm air found my lips. Faint, but it was there, dusting them ever so slightly.

"Morgan?" I said incredulously.

The faint rise and fall of her chest left air rushing from me. I cradled my arms underneath her, holding her tenderly to my chest, not believing it to be real.

Color returned to her cheeks ever so faintly, and my pain seemed to dull.

I grasped her hand as if I was her tether to this life.

"Breathe for me, that's it."

Her breath against my neck was the single most incredible sensation I'd ever felt. A gift.

"Tyler," she whispered.

I held her face in the palms of my hands. "Who did this to you? I saw Wes… did he?"

I couldn't bring myself to speak the words. Betrayal, a bitter taste I couldn't swallow.

She nodded while murmuring something I could barely make out. It sounded like the word Helena.

Brutal realization ripped through me at knowing Wes had something to do with this. The deceit was next level. *Devastating*.

My hands fanned through her hair. "I thought I'd lost you. I've never felt so…" Lost for words, I soaked in her doe eyes. *My* doe eyes.

I brushed my lips against hers, an agony of emotions charging from me into the kiss. It pulled me into an emotional state I wasn't ready for.

Tears drenched my cheeks. "I love you so much. You're *everything* to me."

A faint smile curved her mouth, her breath barely there. "I love you, too."

I held her in my arms until our mate bond helped her regain strength, just as Betty mentioned it would.

"We really need to leave," I said, motioning toward the licks of flames spreading fast.

Fear possessed her features when she saw the inferno I'd created.

I choked on a breath. "Can you walk?"

She hesitantly nodded. "I think so."

I helped pull her to her feet, questions burning her gaze as she stared at me.

"You've got *wings*?" she breathed. She moved behind me, studying the new extension from my back. Her eyes filled with awe. "They're like a phoenix."

She ran a finger along a feather, and a delicious shiver grazed my spine, my mind veering on the edge of the gutter.

I straightened. "So it seems, but right now, we have to get out of here." I coughed as another wad of smoke filled my lungs.

A mixture of magic and adrenaline charged through my veins, my vision so clear I could see the tiniest of grains magnified.

Movement caught my eye and my head spun towards it. A woman, crouched behind a large structure at the front of the building.

Morgan's grip on my arm tightened. "That's my mother. You need to stop her," she wheezed.

"Your mother?" Did I hear her correctly?

Morgan nodded in desperation. "She suppressed my magic, then tried to steal it. She wants to open the portal to the Underworld."

"She tried to steal it?" I said incredulously.

Morgan heaved in a breath. "It was Wesley, he tried to syphon it to her."

Wesley could syphon magic? What the fuck?

She doubled over, releasing smoke filled air from her lungs. "It left me, I felt it leave me, Ty. Then for some reason it crashed back into me again." Her tired eyes pleaded with mine. "You need to stop her. *Please.*"

I frowned. "Are you sure you want me to do this? I could…"

Words failed me, unable to finish the sentence. Morgan knew how powerful my gift was. She didn't need to hear how easily using it could end her mother's life.

Morgan's mother looked directly at me, a desolate hatred weaving through her irises. No doubt at my interruption to whatever shitshow I'd walked in on. She looked like death on a stick, her scrawny frame and hollowed out cheek bones a sickening sight.

Her steps echoed off the stone floor as she came closer, her head tilting to the side.

Inspecting me.

Sizing me up like prey.

"And who might you be?" She came closer still, zeroing in on me. "Who dares to interrupt me, and set a blaze to this church?"

"You tried to kill my mate," I said, my tone even.

She sashayed her hand in the air. "I did no such thing to your *mate*." Her frivolous laugh echoed through the church. "You're a very brave man, aren't you?" she mused, her neck craning. "Do you have any idea who you're talking to? What I could do to you in a mere heartbeat?"

I clenched my fists, caught in the indecision of using my magic for fear of killing Morgan's mother.

I deadpanned her. "I don't give a fuck who or what you are. Now, fuck off before I incinerate you," I seethed.

Fire pummeled through my veins, a continuous, vicious heat burning to be freed again at my will. I had no doubt this woman was powerful; the way she held herself and looked at me like nothing more than a piece of shit on her shoe told me that alone.

I put my body between her and Morgan.

"No one hurts my mate and gets away with it."

She folded her arms across her body, her painted fingertips fluttering on her arm. "Your pathetic little mate could have done incredible things. Instead, she cowers behind you."

I remained still, my vision focused on her every movement.

Her footsteps became cautious as she moved closer again, a mere thirty feet away now.

A cunning glimmer spoiled her irises. "Should we play a little game of cat and mouse, do you think? I do like to chase," she taunted.

I lowered my voice, venom dripping off every syllable. "Touch her and I'll rip your throat out."

She glowered, like I'd just dangled the bait right in front of her.

The woman's arms rose up beside her, shocking swirls of magic crawling from her fingertips and misting into the air above her. The shadows stretched like tendrils, their deathly presence a ghastly thing lunging toward us.

Morgan screamed behind me, her cry penetrating the walls of the church and vibrating throughout me. "Tyler!"

I forced my magic through my veins and into my palms once more. It was pure euphoria, like a riptide pulling it from me as I expelled my magic and aimed for the woman. Two fireballs tore across the room, colliding between us with her shadow magic in spirals of gold and ink. I commanded my fire element to form a wall of flame, forcing it against her magic, but she was incredibly strong, her shadows pushing hard against my fiery barrier.

I cursed, and an almighty roar left me. Blood rushed through my veins under the immense pressure of it all, pushing to the surface and cording my forearms like a braided river.

What the fuck was this woman? I'd seen shadow magic before, but this? This was next level insane.

Our magic dueled between us, pushing and pulling against the other until perspiration coated my neck, my forehead.

Helena was relentless. A powerful witch.

Locking my jaw, I twisted my arms as if it would release some new energy into my element, every muscle inside me tensed to the point of exhaustion.

I wouldn't let her overwhelm me.

Morgan, my only priority to keep safe.

Smoke filled the air around us, teasing our magic and making my eyes water. I became aware of Morgan's presence at my side.

"Morgan, you have to try, I can't hold her off much longer!"

I turned my head to find her staring down at her splayed-out hands like they weren't her own. As if pleading with them.

"I don't know if this is going to work!" She cried out, before black orbs collected in her palms, glistening. They floated ever so slightly above her skin, her mouth falling open.

"You can do it," I urged, as Helena's magic pushed even closer. I felt the tendons in my neck popping from the immeasurable pressure. "Now!"

Beside me, Morgan raised her arms to the side, palms facing her mother. With one sudden movement she threw them in front of her with an almighty scream, her element expelling to join mine.

Helena's shadows retreated, but not by much. I felt her magic waver ever so slowly as our wall of magic enveloped her, surrounding her.

Morgan sank to her knees inhaling a chest full of thick air. I feared she would lose concentration, stall her magic.

"Stay with me!" I grunted, stealing a glance at her before turning back to Helena. What I saw, nearly popped my eyes from my sockets.

Surrounding her was Betty and our friends. *No*, an apparition of the group, in a tight circle, holding hands just as I had left them.

What the fuck?

Eyes closed and lips moving, the licking of flames suffocated their voices.

A chant. A spell?

Immediately I felt their elements join ours, the light brush of air, the metallic taste of blood.

Our magic tightened around her, swirling, until an almighty wave of magic shunned into her, rendering her immobile and dropping her to her knees. She let out a bone chilling cry that vibrated off the walls and up my spine, before collapsing to the ground, deathly still.

Cautiously commanding my magic to retreat, I stood frozen in disbelief of what had just happened. I couldn't explain it, but knew I'd find out more if we made it out of here alive.

I turned to Morgan, where she remained motionless, her lips moving in soundless syllables.

I stared at her in awe. My powerful mate.

"We need to get out of here." I said, wrapping my arm around her waist.

"Wait, my father... we need to get him out!"

My brows pitched. "Your father?"

Morgan didn't respond as she motioned toward a large door. She started towards it, and I followed her close behind as she ran towards it.

Blinking furiously, my eyes slowly adjusted to the dim light spread over what appeared to be some sort of tomb-turned-dungeon.

"Father!" Morgan ran towards a cell block near the back of the room, glancing back at me. "Please help him."

I rushed beside her, staring at an older man with a full beard and frail frame, frantically scrambling to his feet inside the cell block. He stilled, registering Morgan's words.

Clutching the bars in his hands, confusion stapled to his forehead. "Morgan? Is it really you?" he exclaimed.

Tears soaked her cheeks. "Yes, Father, it's me."

Bars between them, they wrapped their arms around each other, emotion shuddering their bodies.

She took his face in her hands. "Stand back. We need to get you out of here."

He vigorously shook his head. "No. You go. Save yourselves."

She pushed him away, giving me the nod. "I'm not leaving you," she snapped, standing her ground. "Now, stay back."

I took the bars in my hands, my fingers curling around them, willing our mate bond to replenish my magic in record time. I knew it was limited, aware I would need magic to get us out of here.

My thermo powers melted the bars faster than expected, and I tore them apart enough to pull her father out. He fell into Morgan's embrace, but we were on borrowed time.

"We need to go. *Now*," I urged, and they split apart.

We ran back through the door into the main building, where flames now towered above us.

"There's no way out!" cried Morgan beside me, wildly searching the room.

"This way!" I said, pointing to a part of the ceiling that had collapsed, the night sky teasing us from beyond licking flames as they ravaged what was left of the ceiling beams.

Morgan stared at me as if I'd gone insane. "What?" Without warning, she collapsed into a coughing fit as smoke filled her lungs.

I hurled her back to her feet, my arm gripped around her waist.

"Hold onto me," I ordered her father, and he did as instructed without question. "Tight. I'm still getting used to this."

We clung to each other, and a rush of air gusted through my wings as I fanned them out, my jaw clenched from the returning pain.

"Hold on!" I ordered.

Tensing every muscle, I pushed off from the ground until air filled its place, roaring in agony. Morgan's scream tore through my ears as

I took us higher until we coasted through the gap in the ceiling and into the sky, pure grit and determination fending off the burn slicing through my back.

I recited the locator spell we'd been chanting at Betty's house, repeating it over and over, blocking everything out until its verse was all I heard, its rhyme on repeat, synching with the thundering of my heart.

Suddenly, we landed with a *thump,* the air forced from my lungs at its brutality.

I groaned, untangling my limbs to find Reid looking down at me from where he stood in the middle of the lounge.

"Well, fuck me," he muttered, surveying my ripped top, the blood, the new appendage hanging from my back.

Skye rushed over, falling to her knees beside Morgan, concern clouding her features. "My god, Morgan! Are you okay?"

I rolled to the side to find Morgan sitting upright, Skye engulfing her in a hug.

"I'm fine," she assured, giving a small wave to the group.

She gave me a lazy smile over Skye's shoulder, and I felt the tug of her mate bond once more. The warmth of her soul colliding with mine again.

Morgan's father spoke behind me. "Bruised bones, but we're in one piece."

"Gerald?" mouthed Betty, her words barely above a whisper.

His attention darted to Betty. "Mother?"

"Son!" she gasped.

Her hands flew to her mouth as she flung herself into his arms as if a lifetime had separated them.

"I thought I'd never see you again," she cried in disbelief, tears falling over her cheeks. "What happened to you? We tried to find you but..." Bettys questions came on a quick breath, astonishment in every word. Every syllable.

Gerald held his mother's shoulders. "It's a long story. She poisoned me. Held me prisoner."

Fucking hell.

"Can someone explain what the hell just happened? Because I felt like I was somewhere else, but I wasn't" Said Scarlet, her brows furrowed.

"I could ask you the same question? How did you guys..." I didn't know how to put it in words.

Colt cleared his throat. "When I used my magic I felt your fear. I knew you needed our help."

Ah. That creepy, looking to the future shit he kept to himself.

"Impeccable timing. Thanks." I grunted, rubbing at my side.

Betty smiled, pulling her nightgown tighter. "Scarlet, that was a *very* old spell, one I will teach you another time. I'm just thankful everyone is ok."

Skye rushed into the room holding a glass of water and Gerald eagerly drank it in one go.

He smiled. "Thank you." Swinging his gaze between Betty and Morgan, he rubbed at his overgrown beard. "Morgan, the best decision I ever made was to keep you safe. I do hope you will one day forgive me."

Morgan nodded, silent tears streaming down her face. I watched as the three of them hugged, holding onto each other as if afraid to let go, before finally she was back at my side again, her hand reaching for mine.

I slid my arm around her shoulders, nuzzling her neck. "I'm so sorry I left you alone. It was stupid of me."

She turned to face me, her hand grazing my cheek. "Don't say that. No one could have known this would happen."

I clasped my hands behind my neck. "I don't get it. Why he did it, I mean."

Skye threw her hands in the air. "Can someone tell me what's going on here? Where is Wes?"

The group waited expectantly for an answer. Tension carving a slick silence through the room.

I folded my arms to my chest.

"Wes is a traitor. He won't lay a foot back in this town."

The group remained silent, soaking up my words. Accepting my truth.

I didn't want to believe them myself, but the truth had been laid on a silver platter for me, clear as day.

Skye's irises seemed to flicker and die, and I cringed. They'd spent the first ten years of their lives tied at the hip.

"I think we all need a stiff drink," murmured Betty, heading for the liquor cabinet.

Colt arched a brow. "It's 4 a.m."

She turned to him with that damn glint in her eye. "It must be 5 p.m. somewhere in the world!"

Gerald grunted. "Some things don't change," he murmured, a light laugh escaping from him.

"Fine," huffed Betty. "Coffee it is then... but I'm still lacing it with a dash of the good stuff." She smirked.

A knowing smile bounded around the room at Betty's comment.

Morgan snuggled into my front, stifling a yawn.

"If everyone's okay, we might head home. It's been a long day," I said.

Colt nodded. "Yeah, I'm beat. Let's debrief tomorrow."

Reid went to slap me on the back, but I fended him off. "Easy, open wounds need to heal."

He laughed, shaking my hand instead. "Sorry, forgot."

"Any advice on how I change back to my human form?" I joked, half serious. I moved sideways to avoid my wings hitting the antique chandelier hanging low from the ceiling.

Skye shifted awkwardly, her voice unusually soft. "Ring Father. His great-grandfather was a phoenix shifter. I believe decades ago, there was a half-blood somewhere in our family. He will know more about it."

I nodded in thanks.

Scarlet moved closer, giving Morgan a hug, her hand resting on my arm. "I'll bring around a herbal tonic I've been working on to help with your recovery. I'm glad you're both okay."

I smiled at her. "Thanks. I appreciate that." I turned to Morgan's father. "Gerald, I have a spare bed at my house if you need somewhere to crash?"

Betty stepped forward before he had time to speak. "No, it's okay, dear. Gerald can stay in the spare room here; it's no trouble. Besides, we have a lot of catching up to do."

Gerald nodded his head in my direction. "I appreciate the offer, but I'll stay here for now. But thank you... for everything." He shook my hand. Turning to Morgan, his hand gingerly grazed her arm. "Maybe I could come and visit sometime?"

She smiled. "That sounds like a great idea." Their arms folded around each other, holding tight for a long moment before breaking apart.

As we said our goodbyes, joy and relief spread over Morgan's face as we made our way down the footpath, toward the dirt trail that would lead us home. The forest was waking from its slumber, a dawn chorus following us as we walked hand in hand.

"You know, I was thinking... we don't have to walk," I said, raising my brows suggestively. "No one would see us."

Her head dipped to the side. "What exactly are you implying?"

A deep laugh came from me as I gripped her waist, now certain the mate bond was replenishing my magic instantly.

"Hold on, princess." I pushed off from the ground and we lifted into the air.

Morgan clung to my front, her legs wrapped around my waist as I took us high above the houses, until we soared among the clouds to where a blanket of stars shone down on us.

"Ty, this is breathtaking," she gasped. "Look!" She pointed to a collection of stars. "That's Sirius, to the left of Orion's Belt. That's the brightest star in the sky."

I pulled back to watch her eyes light up with wonder. The very same eyes that had captured my heart so suddenly I had feared it.

I tilted her jaw to meet my gaze, a storm rushing my insides at the intensity of us.

"He's a beauty for sure," I agreed.

She giggled. "I wish we could do this all the time."

"I knew you'd say that. Might have to check the rules for shifters on that one," I chuckled.

I kissed her amongst the watchful stars, an all-consuming kiss that spoke of a thousand words uttered in only a breath.

As they faded to scattered bursts of light in the distance, our houses came back into view. I lowered us slowly to the ground until we landed in a forest clearing nearby, away from human eyes. She unwrapped herself from me, her doe eyes staring up at me like she was seeing me for the first time.

"I could never have guessed my life could be like this. I've found my father. I have magic." Her hand fell over my heart. "And I found *you*."

Wesley had completely blindsided me, kidnapped Morgan, and then disappeared off the face of the earth. I didn't understand any of it. Didn't want to think about it. I needed to be around Morgan right now and wanted nothing more than to curl up in bed and wrap her in my arms.

I pulled her close, nuzzling her neck.

"I thought I'd lost you, I've never been so scared in my life. I love you so much. You need to know that."

My lips moved against hers, and I savored every second.

Her kiss was a promise of hope.

A future I could never see until now.

Her hot breath slid between my lips. "I love you too, Tyler. More than anything in this world."

Morgan

I tensed as my neck craned to see the four council members enter the chamber, filing into the room one by one in a line, the last swinging the door shut behind her as they made their way to the front.

I'd never been this nervous in my life, my entire world riding on the decision Colton's father was about to make about my future. If I were to stay in Cutters Cove or not.

Tyler stood beside me, his grip on my hand reminding me of the last time we were here, trying to find the whereabouts of my parents. Well, I found them alright.

I stared at my father, my *birth* father, who stood in front of me with Betty. Now cleanly shaven and with his hair cropped, he looked handsome, and it warmed my heart to see them standing side by side. It seemed like a lifetime ago since the dance, since the nightmare Wesley and Helena had weaved upon us.

None of us understood why Wesley had done it, especially Tyler. He hadn't talked about it much, preferring to change the subject whenever it was brought up, but I knew when he was ready, he would.

The scraping of a chair on concrete brought me back to the council members now seated at the front of the chamber.

Arthur pushed his glasses further up his nose, then adjusted his robes.

He cleared his throat before speaking. "In light of recent events, I've conversed with the council at Port Fallere. This is not something I do often, if ever, but I felt under these circumstances, and after speaking with both Betty and Gerald, it was necessary."

My chest tightened, the insides of my stomach curling with anxiety.

I gripped Tyler's hand tighter.

"Cutters Coven and Sacred Souls have come to an agreement that Morgan was taken from her coven against both her and her father's will. In light of this... it has been decided that Morgan is to stay in Cutters Cove with her mate Tyler, under the council of Cutters Coven."

A torrent of relief left me in a rushed breath, Tyler's hands wrapping around me at the same time as his lips found my temple.

I stood motionless as if in a daydream, not believing it to be real.

That my life had fallen into place in the space of one sentence.

My hands clenched together in front of me. "Thank you," I said, pitching my voice over the murmurs of relief expressed by Betty and Gerald. They turned to me with smiles lighting their faces.

Arthur nodded in my direction. "I will sort the paperwork in the next week."

Tyler grabbed my shoulders, we had no words, pure shock reducing everything we needed to say into a mere look exchanged between us.

"Congrats, Morgan." I turned to find Colton beside us, a smile on his normally serious face. "You're officially one of us now."

Tyler pulled me into his side, looking between us with a grin. "Indeed, she is."

My hand rested on Colton's forearm. "Thank you. Whatever you said to your father, I'm truly grateful for it."

"You're welcome," he replied earnestly.

We exchanged hugs from Betty and my father, the five of us on a high I felt I could never come down from.

"We need to celebrate," said Betty from behind me as we made our way out of the church.

I laughed, looking back at her. "Betty, you don't need to do that. Really, it's okay."

She waved me off. "Nonsense! I will be in touch, I'm thinking my house, sometime in the next few weeks."

Tyler side-eyed me, and we shared a knowing look. Smiling, he shook his head, and I knew I had no choice in the matter.

I held my hands in the air with laughter. "A celebration at Betty's it is."

We walked outside and into daylight again, but it felt different this time. Like somewhere I belonged.

After our goodbyes, Tyler pulled me against him, his warm breath buried into my neck. "I still can't believe it. You get to stay."

I couldn't help the smile warming my cheeks as we pulled apart. The raw emotion of the day had been so intense and I hadn't realized how much it had dragged me down until now. I felt like a weight had lifted, free.

"I know. It's still so surreal; I don't think I've yet grasped the fact this is my home now."

Tyler brought his lips to mine, a kiss that held nothing back as he pulled me flush against him. Cutters Cove misted into nothing as he kissed me with everything he had, lifting me off my feet and into the air.

A cheeky glint enlarged his pupils. "Let's go and have our own celebration."

I didn't argue.

***

Two weeks later, I watched, smiling from Betty's kitchen counter as the people I loved so dearly mingled together in celebration.

Betty sat in her lounge chair with my father to her side, a cup of coffee laced with only she knew what on her lap. They had quickly become close, having caught up on many years apart, and I couldn't wait to spend more time with my father after giving them their own time to rekindle.

My attention moved to Reid and Scarlet, who stood with Skye, talking to Jade quietly in the corner. I hadn't seen a lot of Jade, as she mostly kept to herself, but she seemed to fit into the group somehow, and I was sure I would soon figure it out.

Leaning against the kitchen counter, my heart felt full as I stirred the pot of spiced port I'd offered to make. I lifted the spoon to my mouth, and its spicy tang enriched my taste buds. Oh, this was a good batch.

My ears pricked at a conversation behind me, registering Colton's deep voice.

"Have you heard from Wes?"

"No," came Tyler's voice from close by.

I moved to the side, subtly watching them from the corner of my eye.

Colton shook his head, grazing his knuckles together. "I don't get it. None of it makes any sense."

Tyler caught my eye as he spoke. "You and me both."

I turned back to my task at hand, not wanting to eavesdrop any further when heavy arms wrapped around my waist.

"I love this little number on you," Tyler said quietly from behind me.

I smiled as his breath tickled my ear. I turned to face him, attempting an innocent look. "Oh, this old thing?" I joked, knowing full well he'd been eyeballing the little apron over top of my pants all evening.

A laugh rushed from him, and he cupped my butt in his hands, landing a peck on my cheek.

I giggled, swatting his hands away, looking into the gray coals that had become home to me.

"I love seeing you this happy," he murmured.

Running my hand over his chest, they stopped on his waist. "I've never been this happy before. I feel like life has suddenly come together for me. For both of us," I corrected.

Tyler's eyes danced as my words crashed into his heart. "I feel the same." He grabbed my hand, pushing his own into his pocket, then turned open my palm.

A long bronze key dropped into my hand. My brows furrowed. "What's this?"

"It's the key to your own art studio."

My free hand clutched my chest. "What?!"

He took my chin in his hands, tilting it up. "I know you love painting and want you to have a studio that's yours, where people can enjoy your work as much as I do."

Completely and utterly gob smacked, I had no words.

"I don't know what to say… Thank you!" I stammered.

I wrapped my hands around his neck, giving him a huge hug, staring down at the key in my hand with disbelief.

He grazed my cheek with his thumb, looking down at me with what I could only describe as admiration. "I'm so wildly in love with you, my beautiful mate."

"I love you, too," I said, rising onto my toes and pressing my lips to his.

For the first time in my life, I felt settled and content. I was so proud of us and how far we had come, and what our love had defied.

Over the last few weeks, I'd continued to practice using my gift. It had not come easy to me, learning each element and how to wield them individually. I knew it would take time to master, but with

Tyler by my side, and the support of my newfound friends and family, I was eager to learn and felt safe to do so.

There was a dark side I could call on, but I knew my boundaries and had made the conscious decision to never be like my birth mother. She was all the reasoning I needed not to use it.

Over the past few weeks, Tyler had managed to trace his families lineage back to a half blood in which he had inherited the same phoenix genes. Turns out, a little magic of the mind was all it took for Tyler to disguise the wings I had grown fond of. They were just another piece of him I loved dearly.

Happiness caressed my heart. I had found real love, the undeniable kind. I had found my father. My grandmother.

My mate. My world.

Dear reader

Firstly, I need to thank *YOU*. You put your trust in me, a debut author, and that means the absolute world to me. I fell in love with every one of these characters in their own way, and each one has a story in my head waiting patiently for their turn. I know what you're thinking... Rachel, why Wes? The hot, cheeky, lovable sensor mage? Well I'll let you in on a little secret – from the moment he opened his damn mouth I knew EXACTLY what his story would be, and trust me when I say, you're going to love it.

If you enjoyed reading Untraced Magic, please consider leaving a review, even if only a few words. I would be forever grateful.

Rachel x

Acknowledgments

Ashley, thank you for all your guidance through the editing process. You will never understand how amazing your support, and gentle advice, molded my writing into something I could be proud of.

Sarah, how you take a few ideas and create such a masterpiece is beyond me. You are a very talented woman and cover designer.

Elliott Rose, thank you for answering all my publishing questions. I'm learning from the queen of fantasy & paranormal romance!

Gem, my book buddy, and cheerleader. I look forward to our many more teasers and GIFs. *One day* I will finally watch Supernatural, but you will never convince me Jensen is hotter than Damon.

Grandma, for showing me the fairy toothbrush in the periwinkle. May you rest in peace.

Thank you. x

About the Author

Rachel Scotte is a New Zealand author living in the stunning Marlborough Sounds. Between running a full time accommodation business, and juggling family life with her two daughters, she is forever pushing her limits (with the help of caffeine) to write in every free moment she gets.

Get her newsletter updates straight to your inbox:
https://rachelscotte.com/pages/newsletter

Join her Facebook reader group:
www.facebook.com/groups/rachelscottereadergroup/

Socials on Facebook/Instagram/Tiktok/Pinterest
@rachelscotteauthor

Milton Keynes UK
Ingram Content Group UK Ltd.
UKHW022209040824
446478UK00004B/227